The
Missing Link

by Katharine Farrer

Introduction by
Tom & Enid Schantz

Rue Morgue Press
Lyons Boulder

Introduction

Meet Katharine Farrer

Since, as a critic once remarked, all dons read detective stories, it's not surprising that many mystery novels have been set in the English university town of Oxford. From Dorothy L. Sayers to Colin Dexter, fictional detectives, amateur and professional, have prowled its streets, its pubs, and even the halls of its many colleges. Academics have often been featured as detectives, most notably in the works of Edmund Crispin featuring Gervase Fen. While they might well have enjoyed many of these books, only a handful of Oxford dons actually wrote detective novels set at their colleges. J.C. Masterman, a fellow of Christ College, is a prime example of a don who excelled, however briefly, at the form. His *An Oxford Tragedy* (1933) not only provides an accurate portrayal of Oxford but also is an entertaining and well-constructed classical detective novel. But where Masterman's novel is at its best when he sticks to college life, Katharine Farrer, the wife of an Oxford don, moves with assured ease from the college halls to the private homes of that ancient city, especially in her marvelously titled first novel, *The Missing Link*, which involves the kidnapping of a don's baby.

While it might have seemed natural to make her detective a don, given her background, Farrer chose to use a professional policeman as her protagonist. In many respects, the Oxford-educated Richard Ringwood resembles other gentleman coppers in the genre, including Michael Innes' Inspector John Appleby and Ngaio Marsh's Roderick Alleyn, though his casual disregard for such legal amenities as search warrants might cause either of those gentlemen to frown. Ringwood was, in many ways, inspired by Katharine's husband, Austin Farrer, who was described by Rowan Williams, the Archbishop of Canterbury, as "possibly the greatest Anglican mind of the twentieth century." Ringwood is 33 years old when *The Missing Link*, the first book in the trilogy, opens, newly engaged to Claire Liddicote, a 22-year-old recent Oxford graduate who is staying on at the university for another semester to enjoy learning for its own sake. Their courtship mirrors that of the Farrers, who married in 1937 when Austin was 33, already well-established in

5

his profession, and Katharine 26. But while there are some other minor superficial similarities, it is in their attitude and outlook on life and to each other that Richard and Clare most resemble the Farrers.

Chief among these attitudes is the sense that their marriage is to be a partnership. Richard may be older and more experienced than Clare, but he respects her intellect and her abilities, even to the point of soliciting her help in carrying out his current investigation. He is more interested in gaining her approval than the appreciation of either his fellows or superiors. He is never happier than when he can discuss a point in a case or in a book or in a play with Clare. They are the two halves that make a whole. As Clare remarks, after Richard quotes from *The Wind in the Willows*, "Have you noticed how we have all the same favorite books?"

All evidence points to the fact that Austin and Katharine Farrer shared a similar relationship, even though he enjoyed a far more celebrated public life. His work as a theologian is so revered, even today, that in 2004, on the centenary of his birth, major celebratory workshops on his teachings and writings were held in Oxford and Baton Rouge, Louisiana. He was Chaplain and a Fellow of Trinity College, Oxford, from 1935 until 1960, and Warden of Keble College, Oxford, from 1960 to his death in 1968. Most of his scholarly writings on theology remain in print. But he was more than a scholar. His fellows also described him as perhaps the finest pulpit preacher of his era, a minister who knew how to reach his congregation, primarily students at his college.

It was probably only natural that Katharine was attracted to a theologian, since her own father, F.H.J. Newton, was a noted minister. She was born in 1911 in Wiltshire but brought up along with her brother in two successive parsonages in Herfordshire. She attended St. Helen's School in Northwood, and at 18 went up to St. Anne's, Oxford, where she read Classical Mods and Greats. While still a student, she published her first short stories under a pseudonym. Education was an important aspect of her family life. On her father's side, she was related to Miss Frances Mary Buss, a pioneer in higher education for women in England in the nineteenth century. Miss Buss, as she was known, opened the North London Collegiate School for Girls in 1850 at the age of 23 and later worked with Emily Davies in opening exams for women at Cambridge in 1865. On her mother's side, she was related to the Des Anges family who were involved in the Port Royal movement in France during the reign of Louis XIV. The movement was started by Cornelius Jansen, who taught that people are saved by God's grace, not by their

Cast of Characters

Richard Ringwood. A 33-year-old Oxford-educated Scotland Yard Inspector. He's newly engaged.

Clare Liddicote. Ringwood's 22-year-old fiancée, a recent Oxford graduate who's staying on for the fun of it.

Sam Plummer. An Oxford policeman with bloodhound eyes and a drooping mustache. He responds well to regular meals.

John & Perpetua Link. Two thoroughly modern parents. He's a don at Oxford and she was his first female student.

Perdita Link. Their two-month old baby, the "missing Link."

The Lukes. Kindly neighbors to the Links. He's a don, she's a good mother. **Widdy** and **Pippa** are their children.

Gladys Turner. The Lukes' conscientious nanny. Sister to **Ivy,** who isn't quite so conscientious, and to **Syd**, who is just plain bad.

Mrs. Harman. Gladys and Ivy's loquacious landlady.

Mrs. Buckland. An imposing gypsy woman with the gift.

Dr. Victor Field. Reader in Post-Embryonic Psychology.

Edna. Servant to Dr. Field. She's a nice girl with an I.Q. of 67.

Old Costard. A Fellow at the college with a taste for vintage port.

Bevan. A cousin to an ex-cabinet member, he lives near the Links.

Max Birkham. A naturalized German, he's anxious to make friends.

Dr. Robin Shawyer. At Richard's request, he sported his oak for the first time since coming to teach pathology at Oxford.

Andrew Thorne. Richard's friend, listed as missing in action during the war.

Leslie Gray. A nasty piece of work, he has plans for Ivy.

Mary Reed. A child psychologist. Pity the child.

Books by Katharine Farrer

The Inspector Ringwood Trilogy

The Missing Link (1952)
The Cretan Counterfeit (1954)
Gownsman's Gallows (1957)

At Odds with Morning (1960)

Being & Having by Gabriel Marcel (1949)
(Translator)

own will power, a theological position that fits in quite well with the teachings of Katharine's husband.

At Oxford, the Farrers naturally gravitated to like-minded Christians. Austin—and presumably Katharine—belonged to the Inklings, a group of scholars dedicated to the destruction of scientific materialism, whose other members included founder J.R.R. Tolkien, author of *The Lord of the Rings*, Charles Williams, the metaphysical poet and novelist, Dorothy L. Sayers, the creator of Lord Peter mystery series, and C.S. Lewis, the Christian apologist who was the author of science fiction and children's fantasy literature. Lewis, in particular, held the Farrers in high esteem, dedicating one of his books jointly to them. Austin ministered to Lewis and both he and Katharine took care of him while he was dying. The gravesite of the Farrers (Katharine died four years after Austin in 1972) is one of the stops on the C.S. Lewis walking tour of Oxford. Although there are plenty of inside jokes about Oxford life and personalities in *The Missing Link.*, C.S. Lewis isn't mentioned. However, one of the other Inklings is referred to when Clare admonishes Richard to stop talking like a character in a Charles Williams novel.

Other elements in *The Missing Link* reflect aspects of the Farrers' life together. Living in a place like Oxford, they were exposed to all kinds of ideas on the rearing of children. Katharine certainly shows where her own sympathies lie. One of the highlights of the novel is the contrasting theories on how to raise a baby, the loving attentive one displayed by one don and his wife and the thoroughly modern creed of benign neglect practiced by the, as Jacques Barzun so accurately describes them, "terrifyingly intellectual" Links, an approach that today might well earn them a visit from Social Services. But there are even more personal touches from the Farrers' home life. The affectionate portrait of Dr. Field's developmentally disabled—"deficient," as her employer describes her—serving girl no doubt is drawn from their experiences in dealing with their own daughter. Katharine's own work as a novelist and a scholar took a back seat for many years while she cared for their daughter at home.

When she returned to work, Katharine's own scholarly endeavors complemented those of her husband's. In 1949, she translated Gabriel Marcel's major 1935 work, *Etre et Avoir,* into English as *Being & Having: An Existentialist Diary*. It's worth noting here that Franco-American scholar Jacques Barzun was very critical of Farrer's French in her third and last Ringwood novel, *Gownsman's Gallows*, published in 1957.

Of course, translating French into English requires different skills than doing the opposite, the chief requirement being a full understanding of what the author you are translating actually means to convey to his audience. That's why fellow mystery writer Anthony Boucher's translations of Georges Simenon's Inspector Maigret novels are so much better than those done by ordinary translators, however good their French might be. In this case, Farrer obviously knew her Christian existentialism.

Farrer's only mainstream novel, *At Odds With Morning* (1960), reflects her interest in theology, featuring, as it does, a satire of a self-appointed saint. But even her three Ringwood novels, *The Missing Link* (1952), *The Cretan Counterfeit* (1954) and *Gownsman's Gallows* (1957), occasionally hint at the theology she shared with her husband. A policeman's lot is a pretty thankless one, as Clare comes to find out. The reward is not in being praised by those you help but in just doing your job—and doing it well—because that's how people ought to live their lives. Being good and being good at what you do should be reward enough. A good Christian doesn't get into heaven by doing good deeds. He or she gets into heaven because God is good. But for all her interest in theology, God isn't mentioned much in *The Missing Link*, although there are obviously touches of the supernatural, especially in the prophecies made by the old gypsy woman. A literalist might say if you believe in God and if God is good, why doesn't He just tell Ringwood outright where the baby is hidden. The answer to that question lies in one of Austin Farrer's writings when he comments that when Jesus was confronted by a bent nail in his days as a carpenter, he didn't resort to invoking the spirit of the Holy Ghost to straighten it. He got out a hammer and anvil.

But you don't need to know theology to appreciate the mystery novels of Katharine Farrer. She well knew that the first role of the mystery writer is to entertain. *The Missing Link*, whose clever title you will come to appreciate more fully once you finish the book, is a sly, witty book that meanders its way, often comically, to one of the more exiting—and terrifying—climaxes to be found in any traditional mystery.

Tom & Enid Schantz
Lyons, Colorado
October 2004

PROLOGUE

ON AN evening just after the end of the summer term at Oxford, Detective-Inspector Ringwood of Scotland Yard and Miss Clare Liddicote
were sitting on after their dinner in a window of the Mitre Hotel. What
had just passed between them was of no interest, perhaps, to anyone
else, but it was all the world to them. They sat there quite oblivious of
their surroundings.

By degrees they became aware of a waiter standing by them and
coughing in a marked manner. He had, to judge by his expression, been
coughing for some time. They loosed hands.

"Mr. Ringwood, sir? Telephone call for you, sir."

"But I'm—I'm engaged." He suddenly blushed, and spoke peremp-
torily to cover it. "Ask them to ring me back later, will you?" He returned to the object of his contemplation.

"It's the pleece, sir," said the waiter with a kind of stern sympathy.
"They said it was urgent."

"Well, look…Tell them to hold on a minute, will you. I'll come presently." He turned again to Clare. "Anyhow, darling, if it's a case *now*, I
won't take it on. Rather than that, I'll leave the Force."

"Yes, do. Or, no, let me be a policeman too. I'll spoor them as
gently as any sucking dove…Besides, I'm frightfully good at worming
confidences out of women."

"Shame on you, you ought to be panting to hear all my confidences.
Still, I'll have to take the call, I suppose." He sprang to his feet. "Come
and help me telephone. I still have to see you to believe in you."

She rose to her feet, her fair head not quite level with his shoulder,
and he shepherded her out of the room with a hand under her elbow.

"Love's young dream, eh?" said the fat Birmingham tourist at the
table by the door.

"I wouldn't know," sniffed his iron-faced wife. "Not having enjoyed your opportunities."

"Hallo! Sorry to have kept you waiting. Richard Ringwood here… Yes, Detective-Inspector Ringwood, but I'm on leave…*What?*…Come round to the station?…I'm sorry, but you know I'm on leave. I've got…I mean I am engaged this evening…Sorry! Could you say that again?… No, I can't possibly. Won't tomorrow do?…Strictly speaking, I'm on leave, you know. What is it, anyhow? That's very unusual, isn't it?… Whose baby is it? *John Link's,* did you say?…What college?…Good God! How awful!…Yes, I know him. Actually, he was up with me. I say, would you hold the line for a second and I'll see what I can manage?…Sure you don't mind?…I'll ring you back if you'd rather… Very good of you."

He put his hand over the receiver and spoke rapidly to Clare.

"Look, darling, this is rather serious. A baby's been kidnapped. The father's a man I know, not that that ought to make any difference, still…He's a Fellow now. It's a frightfully young baby, and it may die if we don't get it back to its mother quickly."

"Oh, dear, how awful! But why can't *they* get it back?"

Richard laughed ruefully.

"Apparently all the local detectives have gone to Coventry to recover bicycles pinched from the citizens, and all the local bobbies are busy pinching the citizens' bicycles for being left about in the road. It's their perennial problem, you know. They called in the Yard, and the Yard—blast them—told them to apply to me, knowing the place and being on the spot."

"On it and in it," she said sadly. "Oh, dear! Poor us."

"I know, darling. But poor John Link. And I do feel specially anxious not to let down the human race just now. One wants to deserve you."

"Richard, dear, it's quite the other way round. But of course you're right. Look, couldn't you get them to come round here and see you? Even not letting down the human race," she added, "one must keep some sense of proportion, mustn't one?"

Richard accordingly proposed that arrangement; it seemed to be unwelcome, judging by the flood of argument that ensued, but he won his point.

"You see," said Clare when he had finished, "perhaps we could coax them into letting me come round with you a bit, don't you think?

And cooperating when you're investigating things."

"You're the only thing I want to investigate just now. Investigate? A very vile phrase. No, contemplate!"

No time Richard could have gained would have seemed much use for his purpose, but he had no sense of any time having passed at all when he was overtaken by the arrival of the police. They had ascertained the bare facts of the case. The missing baby was a girl of six weeks old. Its mother, Mrs. Link, had last seen her child quietly asleep in a perambulator in the front garden of their house at 50 Merton Street, at ten minutes to five, when she had peeped out to make sure all was well before going to a room at the back of the house on the first floor, where she entertained a woman friend to tea. There were no servants, and the father, John Link, was away at a conference in London.

Mrs. Link had been twice interrupted at teatime—by a stranger who came into the house without ringing, and by a gypsy who had knocked at the back door. Mrs. Link had not accompanied either of these strangers past the perambulator and off the premises. The bedclothes in the perambulator had not been stolen.

When Richard asked whether any of the regular criminals on the books were in Oxford at present, he was told that none had been reported, except one bogus company director who did not appear to be promoting any companies.

"Well," he said. "It looks as if I'd better go along now. I don't need any help tonight. Can you let me have a spare man and a car first thing tomorrow?"

They promised to do what they could and went away with suitable expressions of gratitude and relief. Richard turned to Clare.

"It's nine o'clock. I'm going down to 50 Merton Street straight away. There's no time to be lost if we're going to get this baby back alive. Are you coming?"

"Certainly," she said. "Thanks to helping Daddy with his county history, I can take shorthand notes and read them afterwards. I bet you can only take shorthand notes."

Thursday

CHAPTER ONE

TWELVE HOURS before, about nine o'clock on that same Thursday, John and Perpetua Link were sitting at breakfast. She was in her late twenties, he in his early thirties; she dark, pale, and pretty in an earnest and bony style; he a fading blond Adonis, with a look of anxious amiability. He was an Oxford philosophy don and she had been his first woman pupil. They had been married for nearly five years.

Their baby, Perdita, was wailing with piteous determination from her perambulator in the front garden, and they both kept glancing out of the window nervously.

"Do you think she's all right?" asked John, handing his wife a cereal packet. "Don't forget your Bemax, you know you need a lot of Vitamin B."

She carefully measured it out in a tablespoon as she replied

"I looked at her just before we sat down. She's quite dry and she had a good feed, and there are no signs of wind. I'm simply longing to pick her up, of course, but you know what Mary Reed said. She's got to be taught at once to deal with things herself, or she'll run the risk of nervous fears later. Oh, dear, I do wish it was time to feed her again."

"You think it's some emotional trouble that's making her cry like that?"

"Well, it can't be physical, can it? If she's dry and—"

"She couldn't be sickening for something?"

"No, John, I don't think so. I took her temperature and it was ninety-eight point two, and she had a good feed at six. Should I take it again at ten, do you think?"

"No. I'm sure that's conclusive. It must be emotional. All the same she does sound pathetic. Don't you think just this once—?"

The wailing suddenly stopped and both parents looked much relieved.

"There!" said Perpetua. "Are you ready for your tea, dear? She did something so clever this morning. I must tell you. When I was giving her her six o'clock feed, she knew when she'd finished one side. And, do you know, she practically asked to be moved over to the other. (In her own way, of course.) I do think that's a sign of intelligence, don't you?"

"Well, she *ought* to be intelligent, oughtn't she?" John said reasonably. "I mean, you're the most intelligent woman I know, and I—well, I've not made much of a mark yet, I know, but still—"

"Don't be silly, dear. You can't be an Oxford don without being intelligent. And look at the reviews of your book. As for me, you know perfectly well that I owe my First to you."

"Darling!" he said fondly but vaguely across the table. "Could you put another slice in the toaster? But look, what I was going to say was: If Perdita shows signs of being very intelligent—and I think she does, don't you?"

"I should say so!" she replied emphatically. "Why, look how she screamed that day the bath water was too hot."

"Yes," he replied doubtfully. "Well, as I was going to say, if so, we ought to put her down for some good schools straight away, oughtn't we? She'd repay good teaching. Look out, that toast's burning. We haven't discussed about girls' schools, have we? We were so sure she was going to be a boy."

"Well, you know, I said Dartington Hall or Bedales. That would have done for either. But you said a traditional public school, because that puts a boy on the map for later on, didn't you?"

"Oh, yes," said John, "for a boy. But a girl. I don't know, of course. A progressive school'd be much better from the psychological point of view, wouldn't it?" He hesitated. "Though, I must say, I've had very good pupils from Wycombe Abbey and St. Paul's. I do think they work harder, you know."

"But, John," said Perpetua, dropping her spoon and clasping her bony little hands, "don't you think the psychological angle is more important? You should hear some of the stories Mary's told me about girls from the traditional schools. She says they've masses of repressions, and often power-complexes as well. We do want Perdita to be really normal, don't we? I can't see that the social pull matters, compared with that."

"In the abstract, and ideally considered," said John, crunching toast and speaking rather indistinctly, "I agree, my dear. The old type of public school is a pure anachronism. But one has to get somewhere before one can do anything. We can't work towards a better state of things unless we get the right people into key positions, and that may still be true even when Perdita's growing up. So we ought to give her a good start—qualify her for a key position. I mean, look at me, I'm really progressive, aren't I? But I have to play along with the old men who aren't, don't I? Or I wouldn't get anywhere."

"Of course, darling," she said earnestly. "I do realize that. Otherwise, I'd almost—well, not mind, of course, because I don't want to be possessive..."

"No, of course not!"

"...not mind, but feel a bit worried about your seeing so much of Costard and all those old Tory bachelors."

"Well, actually, of course," he said as one making confession, "I do like them rather, you know. Old Costard can be very charming over a glass of that special port of his. He makes one feel no end of a chap. He's so easy to talk to and yet so impressive, somehow."

"I don't think you need feel too badly about that, John. After all, it's quite a help that you do like him. He's quite an important man, really. I do see that."

"It's wonderful how you see every side of a question," said John gratefully. "Is there still some more tea in the pot? Have you had your halibut oil capsule? But I feel rather badly about that speech I made in Congregation, in a way. You know, he really put me up to it."

"Why? It was a marvelous speech," she said, swallowing her pill with the ease born of much practice. "Everyone talked about it."

The speech had been directed against a proposal to set up an experimental department in psychology for which undergraduates in certain schools were to be the guinea pigs. The proposal had been made by a progressive whose eccentricity was too notorious for John to feel quite happy in supporting him; and he had easily been persuaded by Costard, over a glass of his special port, to speak against it. He was not proof against the older man's urbanity and flattery, and also not unmoved by his veiled hints of the probable reward that awaited him in the form of prestige and reciprocal support. And he had spoken very well indeed and carried the house with him. But it had seemed to many people that the speech represented an unexpected change of front in John Link himself; though his enemies maintained that John Link had no front. "Just," they said, "a mass of careful feelers." In any case, after the triumph of the speech, the defeated progressives had cut John with a thoroughness observed even by their colleagues.

"I enjoyed the success, I don't mind admitting that," said John, looking a little bolder. "But I wish I hadn't come down quite so heavily against the Planner. After all, he is one of us, in a way."

"But he's a vote-loser," said Perpetua consolingly. "He'll never put his stuff across."

"No, perhaps he isn't much good, really, not from our angle," agreed her husband. "Anyhow, it's no use worrying now. But we might try to conciliate him a bit later. You never know. Is there any tea left?"

She tilted the pot and a cold inky dreg came out.

"It's very bad for you," she said, smiling. "Still, we don't choose schools for Perdita every day, do we?"

"So I'll get pickled in tannic acid to celebrate. Oh, Pettie," he said rapturously, "isn't it wonderful how everything's coming out just as we planned it? You got your First—"

"You did, darling. It was all due to you."

"And then you had that year at the Board of Trade learning how to apply what I've taught you…"

"And then we got married and got this house straight way…"

"Yes, and then we got the car. Do you remember, we thought it'd take three years and we only took two and a half to save up the money…"

"Yes, and then just as we needed a change there was that sabbatical year in America…"

"Perhaps we'll go again when Perdita's at school," suggested John tentatively.

"M'm. And then we thought it was time to have a child. And, really, we couldn't have worked it out better. She might have been made to order."

"Well, she was, in a way. We took the best advice, didn't we? And, Pettie dear," he added affectionately, "you're the best person I've ever met at carrying out instructions. Whatever you do, it's always so thorough. I think you're wonderful."

She stretched out her hand across the table. "I get cooperation," she said warmly. "Honestly, John dear, I can't understand people who just muddle on like Mummy did, can you? They're bound to slip up if they won't make a plan and stick to it. There's no such thing as luck."

"Well, we might have had twins," said John, though agreeing in principle.

"It wasn't much of a risk," she replied. "There were none in the family on either side. It would have been awful, wouldn't it?"

"We couldn't possibly have given them a good education," said John. "Though I sometimes wonder if Perdita will mind being an only child?"

"Well, we can take advice. I'm sure a lot depends on handling. And who knows? Perhaps your book will be a best-seller. Then we can have another baby in about two years, if I'm fit."

"Why, darling?" he said anxiously. "Is your back hurting you again?" He came round the table and kissed her. "Yes, I can see it is. Look, I don't have to be in college till tea. You go and lie down and I'll do the breakfast things. No, honestly, I've got lots of time. Go on. There's no future in standing about when you're not well. Up you go."

He watched her lovingly up the narrow staircase, and then began to clear away and wash up in the methodical and hygienic way that his wife had taught him. It was soon done, and the little dining room was as bare and tidy as an office, which indeed it much resembled.

John Link ran upstairs to say goodbye to his wife, snatched up a sheaf of papers, and set off cheerfully for his meeting in college, resisting the temptation to peep into the perambulator at his newborn daughter, although he thought she looked particularly charming asleep.

Halfway down the street he was somewhat discomposed to see a colleague of his approaching from an intersection. But he remembered what he and his wife had been saying about not offending progressives, so he waited for him to come up and wished him good morning.

"Eh?" said Dr. Field, peering through his thick bifocal glasses. "Who is it? I can't see with, the sun in my eyes."

"John Link." Dr. Field sniffed and began to walk on. John Link kept close at his side and did not stop talking. "I'm so glad to meet you. I've been wanting to talk to you for ages, only you know what the end of term is. I was so afraid you'd think I'd gone over to the wrong side, after that business the week before last."

Dr. Field stumbled over a loose paving stone and John caught his elbow and steadied it. Field shook off the hand and said nothing.

"You don't mind my speaking frankly, do you?" John went on. "I sincerely believe in the ultimate value of your measure, and of course I admire your own work immensely, as you know. But I don't think the time is ripe yet for that particular measure. It would raise a storm of protest outside Oxford. Quite frankly, and between ourselves, I'd like to see it brought up later in a much more ambitious form, and I believe that given the right occasion, we could carry through without any trouble. It's just a question of the right time. N-no hard feelings, I hope?"

He smiled uncertainly as Dr. Field stopped dead in his tracks and peered into his face. Then the doctor spoke, his north-country accent a little stronger than usual.

"I don't waste time on analyzing my emotional reactions, Mr. Link. And I advise you not to waste your time trying to stimulate them. Soft soap doesn't cut much ice in the modern world. Verifiable facts are all we care for. And it's a fact that you opposed a forward-looking measure although you knew it was right."

"Ultimately right, yes. But it wouldn't have succeeded now, so I thought it would be better to wait and make sure of it later. You didn't think I was against the principle, surely?"

Field stood blinking and rubbing his chilblains. Then he smiled woodenly.

"Well, Mr. Link, you may have a chance of showing your principles at once." He pronounced them *channse* and *wonnce.* "We're going to discuss the kitchen and cellar accounts after the meeting this morning. Strike a blow against all this snobbish luxury and waste of good money, and I shall know what side you're on. Not that I care, mind you. A reactionary is his own worst enemy. He'll just wake up one day and find himself redundant. I wonder how you'd like that?"

They were now entering the college lodge, and an older Fellow who was turning over a pile of letters looked, up, then strolled over and laid his hand on John Link's shoulder.

"John, my dear feller, you're the very man I wanted to see! How do you contrive to look so healthy at this time in the morning? Doesn't he, Field? I'd say it was a good conscience, wouldn't you?" Under his bushy eyebrows he darted a look at Field equally compounded of humor and malice.

"It depends what you mean by that term," said Field in a perfectly colorless voice. "I don't suppose you'd use it in the same sense I do. To me, a man's conscience is his public conscience. In that sense of the term, I certainly hope you're right. I hope so, Mr. Costard." He spoke the last words with considerable emphasis.

Costard stared back with the calm intense intelligence of a cat at a mousehole.

"Ah, well, hope springs eternal, doesn't it? I'm glad to see you in such good spirits. No more attacks from your patients, I trust? Good, good. My dear John, we seem to be early for our meeting. Shall we take a turn in the sun? I want to ask your advice."

The spindly figure with the leonine head moved out into the quadrangle, and John, as though pulled by an invisible leash, followed him. Field brought up the rear. He desired John's support, and was prepared to fight though not to truckle for it. Costard had begun to talk rapidly in a low voice, looking up every now and then with his famous smile to appeal for confirmation to his younger companion. Field could only catch a word here and there.

"A very good vintage...should be ready to drink in 1961. Keep a couple of dozen for you, if you like...too good to waste it all on the common room at large...Perhaps you'll have taught your younger colleagues to appreciate it as *you* do...I'll be dead by then, of course, though by no means fully matured...relying on you for the future."

John was listening with an embarrassed smile, dreadfully conscious of Field just behind them, but half-captive to the charm of the man at his side, which was balm after Field's bluntness. When Costard stopped, he made a polite noncommittal sound.

"Well?" said Field's voice harshly behind him.

"Ah, Field," said Costard, turning instantly with an air of immense surprise. "Come and join us. We won't bite, I promise you. I was just telling John about our wine prospects this year. He's one of our experts, you know. We all go by his opinion."

"Well, what is it? Eh?"

"Really, I don't know what to say," John replied. "Er—I suppose good wine is always an investment, isn't it?"

"My dear John, you're not suggesting we should sell such an acquisition?" cried Costard.

"We're squandering quite enough on luxury articles as it," mumbled Field.

Poor John was put out of countenance, but tried again. "One has to consider the college prestige, doesn't one? I mean, we have to keep up certain standards for distinguished guests."

"Most of them drink whisky," murmured Costard sadly.

"He drinks more in a term than the guests drink in two years," shouted Field, trembling with righteous indignation and pulling his red fingers till the knuckles cracked loudly. "The time is past when people should expect to live in idle luxury just because they can teach outdated subjects. Plain living and high thinking, that's my motto."

"Now I," purred Costard with deadly affability, "know by long experience that high living leads to plain thinking. Plain thinking and no nonsense, my dear doctor. That's what we all want, isn't it? Though not, of course, at this hour in the morning, when my brain is by no means at its best. Is that the Provost going in? Perhaps we should follow him."

Walking, like Faustus, between his contradictory angels, John passed into the paneled room where the Fellows were waiting to transact their college's business.

CHAPTER TWO

THE COLLEGE meeting was over, not a minute too soon for John Link, who was on thorns throughout, and he had only time to pack a bag before he caught the midday train to attend a weekend conference in London. In spite of a pang at leaving his wife and baby, he was not at all sorry to be away from Merton Street for a few days. He feared awkward encounters.

Yet it was a lonely street out of term. By the late afternoon of the same day it was to all appearances deserted. And no wonder, for the sun was beating down and shimmering in waves of heat over its brown cobblestones, and hardly a breath of wind was stirring. The man who lurked in a corner behind a stone buttress near the Links' house was in the full glare of the sunshine, and he did not appear to be enjoying it. He kept shifting softly from one foot to the other, as though his elaborate shoes were too tight for him, and pushing the hair off his forehead. But his eyes hardly wandered for a moment from the house he was watching, though there was no living creature in sight except the baby crying in its perambulator by the Links' front door.

Presently, however, one of the upstairs windows was thrown open. The man shrank back farther into his corner, and a spasm of hatred and alarm distorted his fair, rather epicene features. But nothing else happened, and soon his face was once more a petty, sullen mask—the mask of a man not much over twenty.

He took a pink comb from the pocket of his tight mauve jacket and slicked back his long golden hair, squeezing in the wave with two fingers. He looked at the result in a pocket mirror, and it seemed to please him. Then he took out a packet of cigarettes, but he put it away again untouched. Perhaps the smoke, in this still bright air, would have given away his hiding place. So he pulled out a nail file and did some work on his already natty nails, shifting uncomfortably from one swollen foot to the other. Slowly, deeply, in round vibrating notes, the tower above him chimed a quarter-hour from its fretted stone, golden against the cloudless blue. Then he spoke to himself in a whisper.

"God!" he said disgustedly. "It's quiet!"

As if in answer to this objection, the baby in the perambulator set up a fresh wail.

"God! They'll come and start snooping if that damned kid don't shut up," he continued.

The fact was, he was nervous. This place was too still. The sound of the bells lingered on the air, separate and distinct from the baby's voice; here everything was individual, and there were no crowds or traffic to cover what shunned inspection. In London, flashy as he was, he melted into the scene as a peacock (presumably) melts into the Indian jungle.

The baby stopped crying, and he relaxed. But then he heard soft footsteps padding along the other side of the road, and shrank back again. Was something going to go wrong with his plan after all?

Max Birkham was wandering over the hot irregular cobbles of the deserted street, feeling discouraged. This was, indeed, his usual condition, but his mind picked at it still as his fingers picked at the never-healed pimple on his chin. Now, yesterday evening, at the sherry party in Magdalen, he had escaped his familiar devil and been a success. He was naturalized, not? He was a member of the University, not? An Exhibitioner of Hertford College? Already in philology a not undistinguished student. Not? Naturalized. *Naturalisierung, Natülichkeit.* Good! Let us, then, be natural. Let us make friends, enjoy life, assimilate to national customs.

"What are you drinking?" the blond young god in white flannels had asked, passing with a bottle. How happy and sure of himself he looked!

National customs. Quick as a flash he had the solution.

"Mine's," he replied, "a gin and Votrix." He bowed slightly from the waist, proud of his quick ear and ready memory.

The tall young god had paused with a delighted smile.

"Say that again!" Surely there was a quickening interest?

He repeated his phrase, taking more trouble with the accent.

"*Schnell!*" said the god, and, darting off, returned with two full glasses.

"Sorry," he said, "only gin and orange left. I do hope that's all right. I say, my name's Bevan. What's yours? But, of course, yours is a gin and Votrix, isn't it? Sorry, I forgot." He laughed uncontrollably.

"Max Birkham," said Max formally, joining in the laughter, though he did not quite see the joke—a pun, no doubt—"Exhibitioner of Hertford College. And you, Bevan. Like the ex-Cabinet Minister, not?"

"Just like the ex-Cabinet Minister, old man. Don't you notice the likeness? Some people say that they can't tell me and Cousin Aspirin apart. But I tell them they're wrong. He's softer, much softer. Too soft, in fact. Now me, I'm a man of iron. From now on, a man of iron. I say, shall I tell you all about my life, or will you tell me all about your life? Same story, no doubt, but somehow sweeter on the lips of another. Or don't you think so?"

He bent suddenly at the knees like a Cossack dancer.

"Sit down," said Max, responding to the occasion magnificently. "Sit down, and tell me, as you propose, about your life. I am naturalized and you may speak to me securitably." He patted Bevan's shoulder reassuringly.

"Securitably," said Bevan, collapsing. "That's what I need. No one to trust. Bite the hand that feeds 'em. You've put the matter in a bombshell."

Automatically noting this idiom, Max patted him again.

"Tell me," he said, in his beautiful fruity voice.

So the god told him how his girl had deserted him for another, and how his father would not pay any more of his bills, and so on. He came to a gradual stop as sobriety began to return, and, with it the sense that this chap was really a bit of a bore.

Max, for his part, was not bored. He was proud and excited, but the danger signal in his blood was still in working order, the psychic security police of the refugee. It even warned him to make the first move of departure. People who go first are not remembered as bores.

"Now I buzz off," he said, rising regretfully. "Cheery-bye! I must go to other parties. When shall I see you again? To meet you has been for me an experience."

He gazed at Bevan like a hungry dog.

"Oh," said Bevan evasively. "Well, I'm always about. Come up and see me some time."

"O.K.," said Max, very tough and Anglo-Saxon. "Where?"

"Merton Street," said Bevan. "Well, good-bye. See you soon. Lord, I must fly!" He rushed away with a last dazzling smile, and by the time Max had said goodbye to his host, the theophany was over.

That had been yesterday, and the afterglow of hope remained; hope of so influential a friend, so charming a milieu, such powerful contacts (for was he not the cousin of a Cabinet Minister?), but hope was already beginning to give way to doubts about his own behavior. Had not Max made some false steps? Should he have patted his new friend quite so often? Had he not assented always too readily? Should he not rather have insisted on telling his own story, and forcing sympathy, admiration, and support? Should not he, too, have been wearing white flannels? Surely he had made a slip somewhere, or why had Bevan not left him a card, which was he understood the English upper-class practice?

Softness. That was the trouble. Saying too much. Bevan was by his own description a man of iron. That was what the English admired. The Iron Duke. "The silver shuts, the iron opes amain." Today, Max must show more *Hochmut.*

"I mosst be togh," he murmured. "Togh like leather. Togh like leather. If I should be more togh, I should have become more accurate informations."

He continued down the street, softly trying the doors. So far, he had not found any unlatched. Despite his heroic resolutions, he did not feel quite tough enough to ring any bells.

He came to the end of the street, to the door of Number 50, the house with the perambulator outside it. He paused and looked into the perambulator for a moment and then turned away and softly tried the door. It was not locked, and the discovery sent him down the steps in an involuntary nervous recoil. But he recovered almost at once. If he failed now, there might be no more chances; now was the time to show himself a man of iron. After all, Bevan had been very indiscreet.

"Mosst be togh," he told himself, and walked into the house.

After a short time he came out again. There were beads of sweat on his forehead, and the whites of his eyes were enormous. He shut the door with exaggerated softness. A little whimper from the baby caught his attention, and he paused by the perambulator, rocking it until there was silence. Then, his arms hugged across his chest as though he carried a secret burden, he started back up the other side of the street. He passed directly in front of the buttress. A young man was standing behind it, as if he had paused there to light a cigarette. His face betrayed no interest. But Max, seeing him, felt all too much interest. There had been men of just that type lounging on street corners in Berlin, and Max remembered how his father had always hurried past them without explanation.

"Why, dear child? Always you ask why! At school, yes, you should ask why. That is education. I pay for that, and good value it is. But do not ask your stupid old father why. It is better to ask him…this!" And the good man would hold up a bright coin between his thumb and finger, smiling with his head on one side, luring the dear child to decide between a kite and a chocolate eclair. And the sinister blond young idlers would be forgotten, till the time came when he no longer needed to ask why. And he was hurried, a bony anxious child of sixteen, out of danger and away to a foreign land where there were no Gauleiters and no treats. He heard later that both his parents had disappeared.

So Max crossed the road away from the man, hugging his arms over his chest, and made as quickly as he could for the safety of the crowded main streets. In his mind, and in the mind of the lurker by the buttress (who still did not dare to leave), was one and the same thought.

I have been seen! What now?

Dr. Field came into the dining room of his house off Merton Street as the clock struck half past four. At the same moment Edna opened the kitchen door and brought in a brown pot of newly made tea, which she placed triumphantly before him.

"You said: 'Bring it in when the clock strikes half past four,'" she said, with a bright smile.

"Good girl!" said the doctor kindly. "Run and have your tea now."

Punctual for once, he thought. Well, that's something. It can be done, with hard work and patience and the right methods. He gulped down a cup of strong, sweet tea, and began plastering shrimp paste liberally on the thick bread-and-butter. His scholarship to Queen's had broken him of the high tea habit in early manhood, but some of the Wakefield tastes lingered. He still craved something strong and salty in the late afternoon. And he still saved his newspaper till then, though, unlike his father, he had plenty of time to read it at breakfast; so it was a virgin copy of the *Manchester Guardian* which he spread out on the dark varnished table. But his mind was neither on his meal nor his newspaper. He read and ate hastily and abstractedly, and drank a great deal of strong tea. With his fourth cup he took two digestive pills. Then he scraped his chair back with a jerk and rose to go to his study. At the door he paused irresolutely, and then called:

"Edna!"

"Y-yes?" she replied in a muffled voice, coming to the opposite door. Her mouth was full.

"I've finished. You can clear. And, Edna…" He twisted his bony hands till the joints cracked.

"Yes?" She stood patiently, waiting for the oracle.

"I—I…Will you…? It doesn't matter. I'll be going out for a bit. I'll see you later on, when I come back to pack and go for my train."

Still she stood.

"Run along then, can't you? What are you waiting for?"

"Will you come back soon?" she said uneasily.

The doctor twisted out a smile.

"Yes, me dear. I'll see you in about half an hour. Then I must go for my train, but I'll be back late tonight, when you're in bed, and I'll see you at breakfast tomorrow. You get on with your work like a good girl."

He turned and fumbled for the handle of the study door, opened it, and slammed it behind him. He bumped his knee as he pulled his chair in to the desk, but he was used to that. To a short-sighted man, the world is full of attacks from the hard or sharp objects strewn about his path. He peered through his thick glasses over the desktop till he found a pile of manuscript and a fountain pen. He settled to it with a sigh, reading it through and making a correction here and there in a neat characterless hand. It was a lecture headed *Some Psychological Aspects of the Individualistic Viewpoint in Politics,* and he was to deliver it in London that evening. It was finished except for a peroration, the part which always came hardest to him. He pulled out a small drawer labeled '4,' placed it on the desk before him, and began to look through its contents, which consisted of aphorisms on slips of paper, meticulously collected and preserved to help him in such moments of rhetorical need. "*We need hard work, no soft soap, from those who claim to be progressives.*" No, perhaps that was a bit blunt. Not much soft soap about King's College, London, anyhow, thank goodness. You know where you are with those chaps. What's this, now? "*So-called humanists have sneered at what they call standardization. But their famous Aristotle could tell them if they read him, that human excellence is conformity with the norm, vice a deviation from it.*" No, too long. And, anyhow, some of them may have read Aristotle, and I'm not sure I've got it right. Ah, what about this? "*The traditionalist is always bolstering up other people's egos. Why? So that they will do the same for his. Against the clean straight appeal of science and reason, this tortuous approach is his only weapon. But any psychologist is aware of the inherent weakness it betrays. Mutual back-scratching only appeals to the man who has a deep-seated misgiving about his own personal validity.*"

That'll do. That's the idea. A really powerful, really clever man has no need to be 'different.' It's only the flashy, gormless chaps who have to do everything in a special lah-di-dah way so as to make an effect. A real man gets on with his work; he doesn't bother about making an impression.

Compressing his lips, he gathered up the papers and fastened them with a paper clip. Then he looked at his watch. A little time yet before the final stage of his experiment was due to take place. He drew out a small black notebook and opened it with avidity. It was his diary, which he always kept fully and faithfully. It recorded the outline of his experiments, his committees, and other memorable aspects of his daily life, and served him as hobby and confidant at once. Now he looked through it to remind himself of the progress of the experiment he was about to complete. A passage caught his eye and he cracked his finger joints again as he read it through.

"*M,*" he read, "*full of vague literary social aspirations...v. talkative.*" There's a good scholarship wasted! And that's bad early environmental factors, mind you. There was material there for a really useful economist. But no! The social racket won. And why? Because that stuck-up mother was working behind my back. Church of England, of course, that was it. All religion's an escape, but bar the Romans the Church is worst. Mum and Dad were ignorant enough, goodness knows, but they did respect hard work. And they kept themselves to themselves. The front blind was always half down, and they didn't open their doors to all and sundry, clean though the house was. But that woman—she was always traipsing about here and there, and asking people in. And she didn't keep her best clothes for Sundays, either. Stands to reason if her children don't settle to anything. She brought them up vain and silly.

Now I didn't waste my scholarship. Nine hours a day I did, wet or fine, for three years. No social racket for me. Of, course I talked to the other men in the lab. Maybe I'd have got to know some of them, only it's a handicap if you can't see their faces clearly. And they all seemed to talk alike. Of course, I didn't need contacts. The contact I wanted was a good First Class, and I got it—I got it. The important people were all anxious to know me then—yes, and send me to Vienna, and create a special Readership for me here. And very soon the playboys who waste their time impressing people with their secondhand humor —they'll find where they get off. Yes, they'll find out. Rhetoric isn't going to be much of a help in the new order of things. They'll see how ineffective they are. "Frankly ineffective!" he said aloud. "Living on the capital of a prestige which has—has ceased to pay dividend."

He breathed loudly through his nose, seized a pad, and made a note of this aphorism for Drawer 4. Then he read over the last entry in his diary, and adorned it with two large ticks and the word EXCELSIOR in neat block capitals.

He looked at his watch again. It was time to go. Putting his head out of the door, he shouted:

"Goodbye, Edna, dear. Be a good girl, now!"

Then he returned to his study, gathered up a pair of stout gloves, a bottle, and a bag containing a banana and a small pineapple, and set off down Kybald Street into Merton Street with a jerky, determined gait.

He did not see the man behind the buttress, for he was shortsighted and intent on his own thoughts. He did, however, stoop and peer into the perambulator for a while. Then, with a curious smile on his face, he straightened up and stumbled on his way.

CHAPTER THREE

IT WAS just before nine o'clock that evening when Richard Ringwood and Clare Liddicote came briskly down Merton Street in the gathering twilight to interview the bereaved mother and her neighbors. They found that the Links lived in quite a pleasant little modern house, which stood in the elbow of Merton Street adjoining another, larger, modern house. Last time Richard had seen the site, one of the noblest chestnut trees in England had towered and flowered there, but it had been destroyed in the great tree-hating period between the wars. Both the houses had small front gardens enclosed by low stone walls, and separate alleys at the sides led to the two back doors and back gardens.

"We'd better try the next-door house first,'" said Richard, "before we go to the Links. It's better to get the shorter interview over first, and I see there's a light in that window. This is just routine, darling, so I think, if you don't mind, it would be best if you sort of merged into the background. They'll think it's more usual, and I'll be very quick."

Clare obediently slipped into the back alley, and Richard rang the door bell of Number 51. The porch light was presently switched on, and a small fat man in his middle forties opened the door. He was beaky and spectacled, with rough hair beginning to turn gray, and he held a book in his hand with his finger still marking the place. Richard descried with difficulty that it was a large annotated volume of Burnt Njäl in the original tongue. The natural benevolence of the man's features was at present overlaid by a look of defensive impatience; he stood there like an owl disturbed in daylight, blinking, confused, but prepared to dispute possession of his retreat.

A language scholar, thought Richard. Well, he'll be a clear witness, anyhow, but he doesn't look as if he'd have much to witness about.

"I'm so sorry to disturb you, sir," he said, "but I'm a police officer from Scotland Yard."

"Where's your badge?" asked the owl-like man unexpectedly, fixing him with a piercing eye.

"We don't have badges. That's in America. But here's my warrant-card. No, it isn't; wait a minute, though. Yes, here it is."

The man peered at it with interest,

"Pity they don't use better paper. Well, what can I do for you? Shall I wait while you get out your notebook?"

He spread himself across the doorway and seemed determined not to let Richard in.

"I don't need a notebook, thanks," replied Richard a little stiffly. "I can remember simple facts. I'm collecting evidence about a—a circumstance which took place outside Number 50 some time between a quarter to five and a quarter to six this afternoon. Was there anyone in your house at that time, and if so, did they notice any—er—suspicious characters in the street?"

"Well," said the man, also with a touch of austerity, "I see that you are observing official discretion. Whatever this *thing*—as I prefer to call it—was that *happened* at that time, I wasn't there to see it. I had an alibi—or, as I should put it, was somewhere else. My wife and I were at the Vice-Chancellor's garden party, and we went straight on to a sherry party with old friends in North Oxford afterwards. We were persuaded"— he sighed —"to stay on to dinner. My wife's still at it, in fact, but I came away. I'm very behindhand with my work, you see."

And tired to death as well, thought Richard. Social life, or work, or what?

"Our nurse was in the house, minding the children," the man continued, "but of course I sent her home when I came in. My wife asked me to. When? Oh, I don't know…not long ago. I haven't got half a page written yet…No, the nurse doesn't live here. She comes by the day, and was kind enough to stay on later this evening, I suppose…My wife would know; she arranges that sort of thing. Still, I think she would have told me if any *suspect,* or shall I say *fishy* people had been making a nuisance of themselves next door. That is, if she noticed anything, but very likely she didn't. She's a good girl, you see, and minds her work."

Then, remembering his manners, or perhaps repenting of his emen-
dations of the police jargon, he suddenly gave a very sweet smile and
added:

"But, I say, won't you come in and have some beer or something?"

"That's very good of you, sir," said Richard, and indeed the invita-
tion had evidently been a moral effort, "but I've got to collect some
more evidence—I mean, ask other people some questions. You weren't
there, you say, so that's that. But I'd like to have the times and places of
the two parties you went to. You were right. I shall need my notebook
after all."

He made his notes and the householder watched his quick neat
jottings with pleased surprise.

"I say," he said with new respect, "have you always been a policeman?"

"Ever since I went down," said Richard. "Now, about the nurse.
Where does she live? H'm, a good way off. I may have to leave her till
tomorrow. Could I call again then? She'd be here tomorrow, won't she?"

"Sure to be. We shall took forward to seeing you," said the other,
present relief written large on his innocent features. "And now, if you
don't mind, I'll get back to my work. Good night."

With another quick delightful smile, he popped in and shut the door,
like a jack-in-the-box in reverse. Clare, who had been eavesdropping
from the alley, rejoined Richard laughing as he came out of the front
garden.

"Poor Mr. Luke! I had no idea that was where he lived. What an
ordeal for him! He's the most fanatical hermit in Oxford, didn't you
know?"

"Darling, how invaluable you are! Go on, go on."

"Well, they say his wife stops anyone from getting at him on condition that he takes her to two parties each term. I don't know if that's
true, but certainly no one ever does get let in to him."

"How do you know all this?"

"Oh, just English school gossip. You know how one hears things."

"But why this hatred of his kind? I thought he looked rather ami-
able."

"He's an absolute poppet. But he just lives for his work, you see.
Nothing after the Dark Ages is quite real to him. He's only edited two
short texts in his life, you know—that proves what a good scholar he is.
And the notes are so learned that I just couldn't read them at all."

"Obviously an outstanding chap," said Richard dryly.

"Oh, he is," said Clare, not perceiving the irony. "They say he dozed off in Bodley one hot afternoon, and started talking Old Norse in his sleep, and then one of the librarians tried to wake him up, and he changed over to Erse."

"Very unlikely story," said Richard. "He wouldn't mix up two languagae groups even in his sleep, if he's as good as you say he is. Well, now I suppose I'll have to go and see Mrs. Link. Anyhow, you can come with me this time. We'll need all the notes we can get."

Perpetua Link let them into the house, explaining as she did so that her husband had not yet been able to get back from London. Richard had always found interviews with bereaved relatives a harrowing business, but this was worse than usual—her perplexity and astonished resentment seemed to remove her from the reach of ordinary consolation. He spoke to her kindly, telling her that he was a friend of her husband's (which was perhaps an exaggeration) and that her own evidence could be of great help to him. The second point really cheered her a little. Clare he introduced without explanation, and Mrs. Link greeted her as a minor official, rather absentmindedly. She took them into the little dining room and sat down on a hard chair, facing Richard across the table and twisting her hands together as she poured out her answers with nervous volubility. Richard prompted her to tell him the story of the whole day, and as it unfolded, Clare wrote busily.

Since Perdita Link was being brought up according to the latest rational methods, she had never in her short life shared her mother's bed or been danced on her mother's knee. No one sang to her, or kissed her, or tickled her, or asked her if she wasn't a clever, clever girl. She seemed to spend most of her day in her perambulator in the back garden during the morning and in the front garden in the afternoons, according to the sun. The Luke children next door were full of pity for her, and often asked their nanny if they might take her with them on their afternoon walks. Occasionally, they had gained their request. They had been particularly anxious to be allowed to take her today, as they were to visit the Bestiarick Gardens and they thought that the monkeys in the new ape house would be interested to see such a very small human being. So there, at three o'clock that afternoon, the two children had stood on their neighbor's doorstep with their strapping young nurse, waiting to ask Mrs. Link for the loan of her baby. The cobbled street, warm in the sunshine, stretched away behind them towards the Canterbury Gate of Christ Church.

Mrs. Link came to the door. Her pink, creased hands showed that she had been disturbed at the washtub, but she had as usual whipped off her apron before answering the bell. She was most conscientious in trying at all times to do her husband credit.

"Please," said the six-year-old Pippa, before anyone had time to speak, "do you think we could take your baby for a walk with us? We want to show her to—"

"We want to show her the monkeys, Pippa says," interrupted Nanny quellingly. "We'd be ever so careful of her, Mrs. Link. We're just going to go quietly round the Bestiarick Gardens, being as it's so hot today. There's a nice bit of shade there in the afternoons."

"Well, that's very kind of you," said Perpetua Link in a noncommittal voice, her brow creased with the always painful process of practical thought. Then, brightening: "As a matter of fact, I've just remembered there's some shopping I ought to do. So it would be a great help if you could really be responsible for Perdita. I never take her to the shops, there's such a lot of infection about, isn't there?'

"That's right, Mrs. Link...Mind your dolly, Widdy, you're dropping her."

"But you will keep her very quiet, won't you, Nanny? You do realize that over-stimulation in infancy may completely vitiate the whole nervous system?"

Nanny gazed into the pram and said nothing. This was a bit out of her depth.

"Absolute noninterference, complete psychological independence are what we are aiming at," continued the mother. "Though of course one can turn her over quickly and quietly if she seems to be having wind. But do avoid artificially stimulated thought processes, won't you? Let her deal with her problems herself in her own way."

The child seemed to be dealing with its own saliva in a rather wasteful and incompetent way, but Nanny replied stolidly that we'd take great care of baby—wouldn't we, dears?—and expertly maneuvered the perambulator out of the narrow gate, sticking out her behind as all decent nannies do. They set off sedately towards the High. The baby, meanwhile, tore with tiny clawlike fingers at its own hair, a black mop extraordinary in so young a child, almost hiding its mournful little brown eyes.

The Bestiarick Gardens are a small zoo presented to the university in the seventeenth century. They lie between the High and the river, hidden behind a great wall and entered by a noble gateway which, like most of the city's better buildings, just missed being designed by Sir

Christopher Wren. The compass of the place is too small for large and obvious zoo animals; but there is a charming collection of tiny deer and curious marsupials, of humming birds and fantastic tropical fish. There is a pillared aviary like a hall of state, and a serpentarium (slightly later) in a mirrored grotto; the vistas are planned with meticulous care; and the whole original design seems to put architecture first and zoology a long way second.

But the nineteen-thirties have rectified the balance. A simple-hearted manufacturer of vacuum cleaners, anxious to get into the House of Lords, was advised to pay his obol to Culture, and he found an object in the endowment of a new building for the Bestiarick Gardens. "I haven't got much use for highbrows," he was reported to have said, "but I've always been fond of animals ever since I was a kiddy. Any animals. They can have whatever they like, tell them, always providing they keep to the estimate and no extras." A battle royal ensued between the various academic parties. The powerful and vocal Faculty of Politics, Psychology, and Sociology (commonly known as the P.P.S.) had got in first with a request for an ape-house to further the study of man's relationship with the higher mammals. And although the forestry department had (almost inaudibly) desiderated beavers, while the most amusing and malicious old man in Oxford had loudly asked why not Blatant Beasts, you could get those *free,* and had suggested many sources of supply, the Spirit of the Age was not to be withstood; the apes had won the day. A fine new building, combining the salient features of German Baroque and Aztec Imperial in a manner never before achieved, was erected outside the original walls, effectively spoiling the strip of greensward by the river, and in it were housed all the varieties of primate and a few monkeys for good measure. Learned men, too, with private keys, were often to be found there, communing with the future of the race.

During the war and its aftermath, lack of staff and a decline in the manners of visitors had led to the Gardens being closed to the general public. Now they had just been reopened, to the great joy of the Luke children. Pippa and her four-year-old sister Widdy (whose baptismal name was Fridenwide) had been allowed several visits already and were eager to introduce their friends.

Perdita was duly shown to the apes, who were disappointingly unimpressed, but Pippa hoped that they would discuss the experience after closing time. Widdy, on the other hand, was alarmed by animal loquacity. She greeted a parrot with "Hallo, old bird," and the parrot returned the salutation with perceptible irony. Widdy knew that animals in Beatrix Potter talked English, but it seemed a portentous and terrible thing to happen in real life and without warning. She burst into tears, and the party all went out into the garden to sit on a seat in the shade and collect their spirits.

They were still sitting there and beginning to feel cheerful and composed when a middle-aged man came up behind them from the back entrance of the ape house. After peering at them for a moment, he shambled up and laid a red knuckly hand on Widdy's head from behind, rumpling her smooth pale hair.

"Penny if you guess who it is," he cried with jerky joviality.

This had happened to Widdy before, as he was a colleague of her father's and lived near them, but it still made her jump.

"Dr. Field," she said in a small sad voice and buried her face in her nurse's sleeve.

"Quite right, quite right," he said, feeling in his pockets.

He pulled out two half-crowns and a sixpence, peered at them, and stowed them away at once. "Ask me for a penny next time I've got one," he muttered awkwardly.

"We've been showing the monkeys our baby," said Pippa, changing the subject quickly. She was a tactful child for her age, and social intercourse already came easily to her.

"What, another little sister already?" said the doctor, reverting to his Children's Hour role. "Well, aren't you a lucky girl? Or is it a brother this time?"

"This is baby Link, sir," said Nanny. "We took her with us this afternoon."

The man's face twitched, and then he leaned forward and gazed into the perambulator, perhaps to cover his *gaffe*.

"I don't read the announcements of births. Waste of time," he said, apologizing in the north-country manner. "Boy or girl? Funny-looking child, I must say. How old?"

"She's a little girl, sir," from Nanny.

"Two. Two months, I mean," from Pippa.

"Really? Well, never waste a specimen, that's my motto. Mind if I take some measurements?" he said, whipping a tape measure out of his pocket and looking suddenly cheerful and at ease.

"I'm sorry, sir," said Nanny, "I can't allow it. Mrs. Link told me most particular. Baby mustn't be disturbed, and not being my own, I couldn't take the responsibility, you see." And she interposed her solid young person between him and the perambulator.

Dr. Field went red in the face, seemed about to speak, restrained himself, nodded woodenly and walked away, muttering under his breath and stubbing his toes against loose stones.

"I don't think I like Dr. Field, Nanny," said Pippa in a surprised way, for dislike was not a common experience with her. "I wouldn't like him to make me better when I had a temperature."

"Bless you!" said Nanny. "Why should he do that? Don't you worry, dear, he's not the sort of doctor that looks after ill people. He's the sort that talks on the Third Programme. Doctor of Science, or something."

"Don't those sort of doctors *ever* make you better, Nanny?"

"Now come along, do, and don't ask so many questions. There's watercress for tea."

They went back to Merton Street and returned the baby to Mrs. Link, and Pippa was not to be restrained from giving a full account of their walk.

The baby then remained in the perambulator in the front garden, crying from time to time, but more in anger than in sorrow. Mrs. Link meanwhile was entertaining a friend to tea in the little back drawing room on the first floor. From there she could hear her child but not see her. The friend was Mary Reed, the child psychologist whose words were Perpetua Link's gospel, so the conversation was absorbing to them both.

They had just finished tea when a heavy step on the landing outside startled them. Perpetua Link went out to see who it was. A square-headed young man in horn-rimmed spectacles confronted her, untidily dressed and wearing a turtle-necked sweater where his collar should have been.

"Where is Mr. Bevan?" he asked in a strong foreign accent.

"Mr. Bevan?" repeated Perpetua in perplexity.

"He lives here, not? Where is his room, please?"

"No," she said apologetically. "As a matter of fact, I live here. Oh, I see what you mean. You thought these were lodgings and he had rooms here."

"Well, that's what he told me at Magdalen," said he severely. "There is perhaps a mistake. Excuse." He glared at her and stumped off down the stairs. She heard the front door close as he left the house.

"I think it would be wise," said her friend when she returned and related the incident, "if you made a habit of locking the front door.

Because if you were feeding Perdita and someone burst in like that, it might alarm her very much. You know she is not ready for the danger element in her life till some months later than her present age."

"I know," said Perpetua with some feeling, "and also it would alarm me very much if it happened often. But you can't lock an Oxford front door and keep having to answer it, you really can't. John's always in and out, and he never remembers to take his key."

"Would it really alarm you, my dear, if a stranger came in when you were alone? Because if so, I think we ought to get this sorted out at once in Perdita's interests…"

Perpetua looked at the clock and saw that it was half past five. She need not feed Perdita till six, so she sat down and prepared conscientiously to be sorted out.

But the inquisition had only lasted a little while when they heard a loud rapping on the back door. Perpetua went downstairs to answer it, leaving Mary Reed to light a fresh cigarette and wait for her return. It seemed to her that the time was passing rather slowly, and presently she looked out of the window to see what was happening at the back door, but it was out of sight round the corner, and she could only hear voices indistinctly. One voice was deep, resonant, and rather husky. It might have been a man's or a woman's voice, and she could not distinguish the words. The other was Perpetua's, thin, high, and precise, and as she listened she heard her saying on an irritated note

"But I tell you I don't want any. We use aluminium ones, anyhow. Please go away, I can't buy any today."

The deeper voice sounded again, a flood of words. The tone at first had sounded persuasive and wheedling, but now a threatening note had crept into it. Miss Reed hesitated for a moment and then went downstairs herself to the back door. She was just in time to see a big middle-aged woman in the doorway. She had a basket over her arm, and her red scarf, her wild hair, gold earrings, and gaunt brown face proclaimed her a gypsy. But the coal-black eyes with an orange light in their pupils were the eyes of a very angry gypsy. Miss Reed hurried to her friend's help.

"This night it'll be," the gypsy was saying. "You'll see." She hitched up the basket, slammed the door, and strode away down the alleyway leading to the street.

Perpetua was very pale, and trembled as she looked at the door shut in her face.

"What was she saying?" asked Mary. "She seems to have been

quite frightening you. Are you feeling faint?"

"Oh...nothing, really," said Perpetua. "A lot of superstitious non-sense." She laughed unsteadily. "But did you see her eyes? That ex-traordinary look? They—they frightened me—a bit."

"What happened, anyway? What did she want?"

"Oh, well, this woman was trying to sell clothes-pegs, you see. I said I didn't want any, but she kept on and on, so in the end I said I'd call the police if she didn't go away. And then she got very angry and dreadfully quiet. She said in a horrible sneering way that as I'd been so kind she'd tell my fortune for nothing. And she did. She said," continued Perpetua shakily, "that I was going to lose the dearest thing I had this very night before the sun set. And John's in London. Do you think he's got run over? Of course I don't believe in that sort of thing, but you should have seen her eyes. She really looked—well, terrifyingly queer. I almost felt I believed her."

"I am told gypsies have a certain amount of natural hypnotic tech-nique," said Miss Reed crisply. "In fact—"

"Just a minute," said Perpetua. "I must go and see if Perdita's all right."

"You shouldn't go to her till you are in a calm and relaxed state," said her psychological adviser. "Come and sit down for a minute first."

"But I do want to see her, Mary. I'll be all right. Please let me come by. I *will* see her."

Perpetua almost pushed past her out of the kitchen, and ran down the little hall to the front door, and out into the front garden. She looked quickly up both arms of the street. No one was in sight; that was a relief. And Perdita had stopped crying, was perhaps asleep. She tiptoed across and peered into the perambulator.

Many minutes later Mary Reed found her standing there numb. Perdita had disappeared.

Such had been the story of that afternoon. Perpetua Link told it fully in her own way, but in the telling her voice lost its precision, and at the end of the account broke and was silent. Richard and Clare sat very still for a moment saying nothing. Then Clare slowly shut her notebook, put the pencil back in its sheath, and stood up. Richard made as if to speak, but his mind was working too fast on what he had heard to find any words of comfort that were not banal.

"I'll keep in constant touch with you," he said. "You've given me a lot of useful lines to work on, and I feel very hopeful. Good night."

He covered her clasped tense hands for a moment with one of his large brown ones, and then he and Clare let themselves out, without speaking another word.

CHAPTER FOUR

"OH, DEAR," said Clare as they emerged into the quiet moonlit street. "Is it always as harrowing as that?"

"No, not always," he said, "but quite often it's easier to comfort the dumb, simple type, though. Mrs. Link's too clever to trust the police implicitly, as some people do. I hope John will be back soon. You can see that that baby meant everything to them. I bet they talked about it every minute of their spare time."

"It seems a funny way to bring a baby up, doesn't it? But I suppose they just wanted to give it every possible advantage, and it was really frightfully self-denying of them not to pick it up when it cried. Well, what do we do now?"

"I know what I'd like to do," said Richard, putting his arm round her.

"Don't have me with you on the case if it's going to distract you," she said quickly. "I'm happy enough to wait, with things as they are."

"No, I want your help. Truly, I do, Clare. You'll see a lot of things I don't. Besides, you know your Oxford better than I do now. And, anyhow I want you. I'll be very good and sensible. You won't think that's insulting, will you?"

"Goodness, no! I think it's an absolutely terrific honor. I'll be very good and sensible too. Now, what shall we do?"

"I want to sort out the notes first, and think them over. Could we go to your digs?"

"Darling, I'm so sorry, but it's late and I've got rather a demon landlady. Could we find a quiet corner in the Mitre, do you think?"

They set out with speed and resolution, and were soon cooling their passions with hot coffee in an empty writing room. Clare quickly scribbled a longhand version of her shorthand notes, and then handed them across and sat with pencil poised, waiting for more.

"Suspects," began Richard. "This is going to be extremely unrewarding. Where on earth shall we start?"

"Let's go through all the people that had anything to do with the infant Perdita today. I gather that it was a wildly social day for her, because she isn't generally taken out of her own garden. So we might get some clues from considering all the outsiders that have come across her today."

"Right. Well, the morning's out; the baby was in the back garden from ten-thirty onwards.'

"Yes. And in the afternoon she was taken out by that nice nanny," said Clare, "Surely you don't suspect her?"

"Why not?" he replied. "How do you know she's nice? Have you ever thought what a gamble it is engaging a nanny? They come down and apply for the job, and generally you just like their faces and engage 'em on the spot. Or if you go into their references, all you know is that they've looked after other people's children for a few years previously, and seemed to make out all right. You don't know anything about them—what their parents and friends are like, how they've lived, and what sort of record they had before they left home. This girl may have been beaten by a lunatic parent every night during her formative years…"

"Pretty hard-wearing material if so. Still—"

"Or she may be keeping a cad lover."

"Now there we have something." Clare sat up eagerly. "I don't believe that good nannies are the type who'd commit a crime for their own advantage. But she would do a lot to keep somebody else out of trouble, if she was fond of them—father or lover or what not. Look, supposing this hypothetical somebody is desperately short of money, couldn't nanny have arranged for the baby to be kidnapped and held to ransom by someone or other? Not one of her charges, as she might get into trouble for that. A baby for whom she isn't responsible, but whose timetable she knows very well?"

"Do keep the list of minor characters down," said Richard ironically. "This isn't a British film. We've got a hypothetical demon lover and a hypothetical accomplice already. Why the latter, by the way?"

"Because nanny was minding her own children next door from five till seven. She couldn't have taken the baby away herself."

"Stupid of me—yes, of course. Still, I haven't actually come across a case of kidnapping for ransom in England since I went into the Force. Lots in America, of course. But here people tell the police at once, and the money doesn't get paid, surely?"

"I wonder," she said slowly. "You only hear of the cases where the police are called in. Well, we can't possibly know until and unless a demand for ransom turns up. But I do think we should look into nanny's references and family life, don't you?"

"Yes, or get the sergeant to do it. We might leave him to do the more asinine parts of the donkeywork. Now: another suspect?"

"This Dr. Field that met them in the Bestiarick Gardens and seemed so interested in the baby?"

"Oh, Field," said Richard impatiently. "Tedious man. We all know about Field."

"You'll all have to tell me then," said Clare. "I don't remember. I only stopped being an undergraduate last year, and these things are still too high for me."

"Field is a prophet to some people and a figure of fun to others. I know a bit about him from Peter Toms. Field's attached to his college in a loose kind of way, I believe. Anyhow, he has lots of stories about him. He sounds like a blameless eccentric. He's Reader in Post-Embryonic Psychology."

"In *what* psychology?" said Clare, opening her eyes very wide.

"Post-Embryonic Psychology. The job was specially created for him by the P.P.S. Board. He has some bee in his bonnet about *real* human nature—thinks it is only observable in its pure form in savages and very young children and some of the higher apes. All that exists in the more complex types is an irrelevant accretion and blinds us to the true issues."

"I see," said Clare with distaste. "Poetry and Reason and Morals take your mind off the grand facts of Hunger and Fear and Pain, so they are opiates and must be discarded."

"Kept in their place, anyhow. He thinks a working plan for society can't be made till we have got right down (notice how he uses 'down' always in a laudatory sense) to the fundamental urges of the race, as he calls them."

"Oh, well, he never will," said Clare, with relief. "So he can't make a plan."

"Can't he just? You underestimate the man. It's said that he's prac-tically completed a form of government for chimpanzees which can afterwards be applied, with slight modifications, to any kind of anthro-poid society."

"Dear heaven! And you call him a blameless eccentric!" She threw up her hands. "A fanatic of the most destructive sort I should say."

"Oh, well," he replied temperately, "he denies some of the things you and I hold most precious. But I don't think we ought to argue from that denial to his being a criminal and a baby-snatcher. That would be wickedly fanatical of us. You'll be talking about good men and bad men in a minute, if you go on like that." He looked at her severely and she subsided.

"As a matter of fact," he continued, "Mrs. Link has told us that he lives off Merton Street in a small house with a single servant. Furthermore, that he lives a regular and quiet life, works like a beaver, and goes away to attend conferences more than anyone else in Oxford."

"A pernicious habit," she interjected. "People who go to conferences have no friends. I still say he ought to be locked up. Still, let's be moderate and put it like this: No discernible motive, no more opportunity than anyone else, alibi, if any, not known. Grounds for suspicion, general tediousness and known interest in post embryos. Why did he want to measure this one, anyhow?"

"Oh, science," said Richard vaguely. "They're always measuring things. But we meander. I'll interview him later. Meanwhile, I've got a much better suspect for you next on the list."

"Ha! Which is it to be, the Mysterious Foreign Intruder or the Cursing Gypsy?"

"The M.F.I. first. The C.G. later. Oh, lord!" he groaned, running his fingers through his black hair with a hunted look. "Have I got to track down another harmless little man just because he's a persecuted refugee? They hardly let me do anything else at the Yard but round up these tainted wethers of the flock on the chance of their being goats. And they're mostly sheep at that, and generally very frightened ones, because innocence hasn't been much good to them in the past once they came up against the police."

"I know," she said. "I'm a pro-Semite, too, by pure reaction. But he's probably quite easily cleared, in any case. People are always walking about one's house in Oxford, you know. Very few front doors are locked, and very few householders are on their own—nearly everyone has some sort of lodger."

"Do they really? Things have changed a bit since I was up, I suppose. I remember even then, wondering why there weren't far more robberies in the colleges. Everything was left open and the town was full of tramps, and even if you were discovered in someone else's room you could always say you had mistaken it for another. I believe you could clear twenty pounds in loose change any afternoon by just picking up unconsidered trifles from the rooms while people were out, and yet I never heard of its being done."

"Yes, and why stop there? Why not steal letters or clothes, too?

Oxford must be an amazingly honest place—"

"I suppose it is," said Richard, "but that only gives a better chance to the dishonest. This man may have been Nanny's accomplice spying out the land and making sure that the coast was clear before he stole the baby."

"And he may equally well have been just what he said he was."

"Tell me," said Richard, "to give me an idea how general this habit of barging in can be in digs as distinct from colleges—how many unknown persons have burst in on you this term?"

"Only three," she replied tranquilly. "And only one was difficult to get rid of."

"Was he?" growled Richard threateningly. "Wish I'd been there."

"Not a he, darling, a *she*. Trying to get me to sign petition for equal pay for women. Of course I couldn't."

"Why not?" he asked, with interest. "Aren't you in favor?"

"It isn't that," she replied seriously, "but I never sign things, you see, because of the Revolution."

"What? Have you made a vow never to sign anything, drink wine or cut your hair till the Great Red Dawn has shone?"

"No, silly. When there's a revolution they will dig up all the records and they might find one's name in the lists. And then, if it was the wrong party, one would be done for. So I never associate myself with anything involving petitions or lists of supporters. Don't you think that's sensible?"

"I think," he replied, laughing, "that it is as cautious as the White Knight's mousetraps and just about as much good. My poor love, you will be frightfully compromised by marrying a policeman—for I suppose we shall go down with the established order, whether it's shot to pieces from the right or the left. But this conversation isn't getting us anywhere. You agree that we ought to look into the case of the Mysterious Foreigner?"

"Yes. We don't know his name, though, or where he comes from," she objected.

"We have our methods, Watson. The press, the BBC, the Home Office lists of aliens. We'd make the sergeant do all that. And now"—Richard brightened up—"we come to the Case of the Cursing Gypsy. Here, I may say, I am in my element, because I know a hell of a lot about gypsies."

"You look a bit like one yourself." She considered his lean brown face and his rough raven hair. "Have you any gypsy blood?"

"The best black blood, as they call it? No, I don't think so."

"Or are you a second George Borrow? Oh, not in character, heaven forbid, but in habits? Do you sit on the steps of caravans in your spare time, conversing in the authentic lingo?"

"Wagons, not caravans. Good lord, no!" He chuckled. "I hardly know about anything at first hand. I'm the sort of idiot that knows the signal flags of the Merchant Navy and the ritual program of the Polynesians and so on, and that sort of knowledge gives me intense pleasure. But it's all from books. I know masses of Romany words, but I haven't an idea how to pronounce them. Still, I might be able to bluff a bit, don't you think?"

"And make them think you're a 'half-blooded fellow?' Well, it would be fun to try. I could linger on the outskirts of the camp getting off with the men, and you could penetrate into the center and mutter charms to the queen."

"There's only the millionth chance that she'd be the Queen of Little Egypt." Richard was showing off. "But it's quite true that the real boss of any camp is the old woman."

"First, find your gypsies," said Clare warningly. "How's that done?"

"It shouldn't be too hard," he answered, "but we'll have to wait till the morning. The best part—I use the term advisedly—of the Oxford City Police are snoring in their beds. There's just an old man and a boy at the station. And that's quite apart from the well-known difficulty of seeing in the dark. But tomorrow morning early, we can find out which of the villages round about have gypsy camps near them. Then we'll get them to give us a car, and we'll go all round till we find a middle-aged cursing gypsy of terrifying aspect. We'll have a proper adventure."

"It does occur to me to wonder," put in Clare, "why you suspect her and what you're going to ask her."

"Bless you, my dear," he answered placidly. "I suspect her upon instinct. So did Mrs. Link, you notice. Gypsies and fairies are the only two classes of the population who make a regular practice of stealing babies. Don't be so pedantic." He rose and shook himself. "I must go down to the station and put the routine inquiries in hand.. Who was seen near the house? Who last saw the baby in the pram? All that stuff."

"You can't see small babies in prams unless you peek right in," said Clare. "They're just humps with blankets over them. However Come and see me to the corner."

Friday

CHAPTER FIVE

ON THE following morning early, before the dew was dry, Clare set out from her lodging and began walking down Parks Road in the sunshine to meet Richard. But his gallantry did not suffer the reverse of being caught on his own doorstep. Before she had gone a third of the way, she saw his tall loping figure running to meet her in the distance. He was beside her almost at once, not at all winded, though he had been going very fast. After a minute, Richard became practical.

"Darling, have you had breakfast?"

Clare nodded. "And you?"

"Yes, in a manner of speaking. Let's go down to the police station then, and pick up our car and our sergeant. My dear, we are going to have a lovely day."

"It makes me feel rather heartless, though," said Clare. "That poor little Link woman's tormented with sorrow and anxiety about her baby. And yet, I can't help being happy. I don't see how anyone could, with you about."

Richard flushed, looked down and up again mischievously. "On the contrary," he said, "you should have seen their faces when they were giving me breakfast at the Mitre.

> " 'I am down before anyone's up in the place,
> That is, up before anyone's down.
> The domestics are awed by the shape of my face
> And they tremble in fear at my frown.'

But you don't seriously say that it's a duty to be miserable? Remember 'like as May month flowereth and flourisheth in many gardens, so in like wise let every man of worship flourish his heart in this world.' "

"What's that? It sounded nice."

"Malory. My chief guide to conduct, though you wouldn't think it, would you? Judging by results. Well, come and flourish your heart in the police station, and let's go out with all our banners flying. They've given me a sergeant to help us, and a car. I've got a list of the encampments within ten miles of Oxford, but I don't know yet which of them are gypsy ones."

They passed hand-in-hand through the glories of Radcliffe Square, crossed the High, and came by shabby little byways to St. Aldate's. After the fresh morning left outside, the police station with its brown paint seemed dark and airless. Richard announced his arrival, and they stood and waited in the sun outside the main door. Very soon their sergeant came rolling out to them. He was a fat man with a drooping mustache and the small melancholy eyes of a bloodhound.

" 'Morning, sir," he said. "Plummer's the name. It's very kind of you to help us out. We're up to the eyes 'ere, what with the cycles and Americans, and all our best men are busy. There's on'y old chaps like me left now." He looked up sadly at Richard's face as though waiting for a pat on the head. Suddenly something like a smile spread outwards from the mustache over the pond-like surface of his features. "See you before, sir, 'aven't I? Never forgets a face."

"Really?" said Richard, bending down for a closer look. "Where was that? Your face does seem vaguely familiar, but I don't connect it with police work."

The sergeant looked up at him with bloodhound's eyes. "It'd be some time ago, sir, before you was in the Force. When you was one of the young gentlemen." He paused. Richard's memory focused suddenly.

"Good lord! It wasn't you who got me by the seat of my bags when I was climbing into college!"

"On'y at, first, sir, if you remember. I thought you was breaking and entering."

"And when you found it was my own college you gave me a leg up."

"That's right, sir," said Plummer, delighted. "And you sat there on the windowsill singing 'Rule Britannia.' "

"And well I might. You'd saved me seven and six."

The sergeant looked puzzled. "I oughtn't to a took it, I know, sir. But you gave me—"

"I know. But it would have been ten bob to the Dean if I'd called out the porter. I should stick out for more next time, if I were you. Not," he added, sighing, "that there'll be any next time for me. 'Presume not that I am the thing I was.' Oh, well, this is very pleasant. But look, I must introduce you. Sergeant Plummer, Miss Liddicote. I'm spending my leave here to see Miss Liddicote—or was, rather. I don't suppose there'll be much of it left when this case is over. So now she's coming round with us to see how we do things in the Force."

"What a shame, miss," he said sympathetically if obscurely. "And you're only young once, as they say."

Richard stiffened and seemed about to put the man in his place, but Clare smiled into the innocent canine eyes.

"I'm looking forward to it," she said. "It'll be a detective story come true. I'm longing to see how you set about this sort of thing."

"Well, s'matter of fact, miss, so am I," he replied confidentially. "I've never been assigned to a Yard case before. We've got one of the new cars, sir. Very nice, she is; we've on'y just finished running her in. I'll just bring 'er round, if you don't mind waiting a minute."

"Richard, what an extraordinary policeman!" said Clare when he had bustled out of earshot. "I always thought they had enormous boots. But he's got the most ridiculous little feet. He looks like a humming-top."

Richard laughed. "They were a bit apologetic about assigning him to me, as a matter of fact, but he was the only one they could spare. They said he wasn't very bright, but apparently he's a wonder—with drunks—that's why they keep him on. I think they've got a sneaking affection for him, too. Anyhow, he'll do all right for us; we only want someone to drive and stand by to run messages. I'll supply the brains."

"Touch wood," said Clare, enjoying the vigor of his pride. "Anyhow, Plummer remembered your face and you didn't remember his."

"How could anyone? You might as well try to remember a Victoria plum." Richard ran a finger down his own fine nose. "I was a bit drunk at the time, actually. I hope he won't babble the story all over Oxford."

"Don't worry, Richard, dear. He looks too nice to do that. Tell me, where are we going to?"

"Well, there's a camp in one of those green lanes out at Little Haseley, beyond Wheatley. I thought we might try there first. It's a district that gypsies like."

"Lovely. Show me the photograph of the baby again to refresh my memory, and I'll look at all the babies we see." Richard handed over a small snapshot of a white sausage-shaped bundle with a dark mop at one end of it. "Goodness!" she said. "I hope all babies don't look like that. It makes me quite nervous about marriage."

"Doesn't look very human, does it?" he agreed. "Look, here's the car."

Plummer drove with surprising skill, and Richard and Clare sat in the back seat, Richard leaning forward every now and then to give him directions. They swept down the spacious curves of the High, over Magdalen Bridge, and through the long drabness of Cowley. Once well out of the town they turned off the main road and drove between green hedges past fields of buttercups and young corn. They passed through four villages which Richard named from his map, turned down an even smaller and bumpier road, and arrived at last at the policeman's cottage at Little Haseley. The policeman was planting out cauliflowers in his garden, but came hurrying to the road when he saw the official car and Plummer's uniform.

"It's not far out o' the village," he replied to Plummer's question, "Just past the little wood there's a turning to the right. Go down that a bit and the camp's on the left. It's only a step."

"Then we'll walk. I think we'd better keep the police car out of this," said Richard. "You stay here, Plummer, and we'll go along by ourselves and explore. They'll only be alarmed and secretive if they know we're the police. I'll whistle if there's any trouble."

They passed the little wood and went up the narrow lane. Soon they saw on their left one of those grassy green roads which must once have been a pleasant feature of the English countryside. This one, like most of its kind, had thick hedges grown up with trees on either side, which had gradually drawn closer and closer together till most of the road had become choked up, and you could only push your way up it with difficulty. A footpath ran beside it outside the right-hand hedge through the plowland, and was now used instead of the overgrown roadway, which was no more than a wide wooded ditch. But just at the mouth, where it branched off the road, it was still broad and open, an oval space of smooth green turf enclosed by hawthorns and young ash trees. Here they saw a ragged brown tent, a shabby red caravan, an old horse grazing, and four people moving round a fire. Someone was making a deafening noise hammering metal. Richard followed the sound and found a horny-faced man with a sack over his shoulders sitting on a box behind the tent and hammering a round plug on to a black iron saucepan. He looked up as their shadows fell across his work, but said nothing.

"Good morning," said Richard. "Does this road go anywhere, d'you know? We started down it and it seems to be choked up."

"D'no," said the man. "Never been down." He spat and returned to his hammering.

"I thought it might run across to Haseley," shouted Richard, determined to draw him out.

The man stopped hammering. "Never been down," he repeated.

He raised his hammer again. Clare plunged in desperately.

"That's a good strong saucepan," she said. "You don't often see them like that now."

He laid the hammer right down and took out his pipe.

"Ah," he said with enthusiasm. "Lots more wear in 'er. Alyminium," he spat vigorously. "Bloody silver paper, that is. Ah! Don't 'ardly need a tin-opener. Come apart in yer 'and. You got any pots to mend, lady?"

"No, I'm afraid I don't live here," said Clare "Why, are you a tinker?"

"Ah." He jerked his chin to the two women and the old man by the fire. "That's right."

"We thought you were gypsies at first, when we saw the caravan."

He said nothing, but spat again and looked wooden and impenetrable.

"Are there any gypsies about these parts?" asked Richard. The man shook his head and resumed his hammering. They looked despairingly at each other and crept away, followed by the wary and stolid gaze of four pairs of eyes.

"It's like talking to saurians," said Richard, "or waiting for a pebble to come down a glacier. I'm no good with tinkers obviously. Still, I am at least convinced that they aren't gypsies."

"Why?" said Clare. "Do they look different?"

"Oh, yes! Wrong sort of hair and too stiff and stocky. Anyhow, gypsies never are tinkers. Tinkers are a different breed altogether, though they're nearly as ancient and exclusive. Tinkers have a language of their own, too—or had if it's not died out—but they're much more quiet and law-abiding than gypsies are and much less interesting."

"Hark at the voice of the Law!" said Clare. "Oh, dear, I feel very flat. When a chap keeps spitting at me and says 'Ah' it simply ruins my self-confidence. Let's go on quickly to the next place. Where is it?"

"Right the other side of Oxford," he said. "It would be. Place called Mayfield on the outskirts of Wychwood. Oh, yes, and there's a caravan reported at Ducklington. We can take that on the way."

They found Plummer and the village police constable passionately discussing the growing of vegetables, and avoided Plummer's wistful eye as they bore him away. Back they went with another horrible view of Cowley on the way to Oxford, and much more traffic this time to

contend with in the town. The grotesque Station Gothic of North Oxford, decently veiled behind a multitude of flowering trees, and the staring little villas of Summertown gave way to flat fields and low hedges
as they turned westwards for Witney and Ducklington. The "encampment" turned out to be a single motor-trailer caravan housing a don and
his wife who had foolishly given up their house in Oxford in order to go
abroad during the war and serve their country, and now had nowhere to
live. The caravan was large, but overflowing with books and cooking
utensils. The husband had already gone out for the day, and the wife, a
fair fat young woman in a blue smock, brushed her hair out of her eyes
and did her best to be helpful. They had seen no gypsies. "But of course,"
she said, "my husband has to be in college most of the time, which
means he catches a bus to Oxford early in the morning when he's half
asleep, and I quite often go with him to house-hunt. Not that it's any
good, but I'm having a baby in December so we have to keep on trying.
So we aren't really in touch with local affairs. Excuse me." She suddenly went green in the face and dashed to the hedge. Clare was about
to follow her, but Richard whispered, "Come on! Let the poor thing be
sick in peace!" and led her firmly away.

"How did you know?" she asked in awe.

"I've been a P.C. in my time, you know. Once I only just escaped
having to deliver twins. The woman threatened to commit suicide if I
left her before the nurse arrived. Which, I may say, she only just did in
the nick of time. Lord! I was glad to see her."

"Well, it's nice to think that one of us will have some experience
already," said she. "Where are we going now?"

"Mayfield, up in the hills."

The car passed back through Witney and soon began to climb up
narrow roads into the heart of the Cotswold country. There were small
steep hills slanting one across the other in high humps, with narrow
hidden valleys between them. The fields were smaller and had bigger
hedges, and there were frequent dark copses. It was a beautiful but
secretive countryside. The hills and woods pressed closely down, and
the travelers could never see farther than the slope above them. Over
the hill or in the center of the wood, one felt, the possibility of panic fear
might lie, for all that the sun shone so warmly.

"Queer country, this," said Richard. "They were not far wrong
when they named it Wychwood."

"Funny," said Clare. "I was going to say that."

They did not, however, talk any more, as they had to read the map and direct Plummer. They stopped, after many twists and turns, not at Mayfield, but at Harton, the village next before it, for Mayfield, though it had its own church, did not run to its own policeman. The constable was in his garden putting in his late peas. He told them that gypsies were encamped in a clearing on the edge of a wood, just beyond the village.

"I did 'ear they were 'aving a funeral there today. One o' the gippos. They was over 'ere on Wednesday ordering' the coffin. Mr. Benson, that's the carpenter, 'e told me it was for a child o' three—an awkward size. 'E 'ad to make one specially, 'e said and 'e charged 'em a tidy price. But they paid up without any fuss, brass 'andles and all. It's surprising where they gets the money, ain't it?"

Richard looked interested. "What time is the funeral?" he asked. "I don't want to go there and find them all in church."

"Ten o'clock it was, I believe. Funny time for a funeral," he said disapprovingly. "Yes, they're a queer lot, them gippos, and no mistake."

"This is lucky in a way," said Richard when they were in the car again. "The funeral must be over by now, and they'll all be in the camp, if they're true gypsies, because they have a custom of fasting between a death and a burial and they'll be cooking their first meal since at least Thursday. So they're sure to be about. Sergeant Plummer, will you drop us outside the village and wait for us there? I think we'd better keep the uniform out of it for the present."

When the car stopped, Richard turned out his pockets. He handed his wallet to the sergeant, together with his watch and his silver cigarette-case. He kept one pound note which he tucked away in an inner pocket.

"Have you got any valuables?" he said to Clare. "We shall have to let them pick our pockets if we are to get on good terms with them, and my idea is to let them have some loose change and no more."

Clare turned out her handbag and handed over a shagreen cigarette case, a powderbox, a pearl necklace, and a small purse. Richard's last letter to her was there, too. She hesitated over this, but could not bring herself to part with it.

"Here's five bob in loose silver," said Richard. "Don't worry, it all comes out of your rates and taxes."

Clare took the money without argument.

"Now, my plan is this," said he. "We go into the camp on the pretense of your wanting to have your fortune told. One of the younger subordinate women—if there are any—will probably be told off to do this. She isn't likely to get it right, so don't worry. Fortune-telling for money is usually just clever patter—the real clairvoyants will only do their stuff when the spirit moves them, and even then it's generally for special friends. Meanwhile, I, using my alarmingly theoretical knowledge (how do you pronounce the stuff?) will try to establish contact with the oldest woman there—who is the real boss of the show—and see if I can get information about the gypsy who came to Merton Street yesterday. It's a pretty forlorn hope and it may take a long time, so spin your interview out as much as you can, will you, darling?"

They found the encampment by the roadside in a cleared place that had been woodland. Behind it a forest of great knotted oaks stretched away as far as the eye could see. One of them had its roots in a deep still pool. There was a strange assortment of vehicles: two shabby wagons, a light open cart, and two very old cars. Smoke was rising from the chimneys of both wagons and there was a smell of cooking in the air. There seemed to be three or four gypsies. They could only see one child among them—a boy of about five years old.

A dark young man with gold rings in his ears, rather like Richard in physical type but not so tall, was sitting on the ground before one of the wagons. A thick stake about a foot high was driven into the earth in front of him. A heap of dry willow-wands, peeled and cut into five-inch lengths, lay at his side. He had an old kitchen knife, much shortened and sharpened, in his left hand, and with this he was making clothes-pegs. He rested his left hand with the knife in it on the stake, and moved the peg against the knife with his right, whittling it with great speed and dexterity. The chips flew, and it was done. He tossed it down on his other side and was reaching for a new sliver when he saw Richard and Clare watching him.

Richard immediately advanced. "*Sarishan?*" he said, and stretched out his hand. It seemed to Clare standing behind him that he was shaking hands in a complicated way, but she could not see how it was done.

"*Sar'shan, bor,*" said the gypsy surprisedly. "Who taught you to shake 'ands like us chaps do?"

"That's a long story," said Richard evasively. "I'm Richard Ringwood. Maybe"—he was bluffing in the grand manner—"you've heard of me. I've brought this lady along because she wants to have her fortune told. Have you a wife here who can *dukker?*"

He took a couple of half-crowns out of his pocket and handed them to Clare. "Here," he said, "you must cross her palm with silver, you know."

"But I've got lots of money on me already," said Clare, playing up splendidly. "I don't need any more. Oh, well, just for luck, then!"

This seemed to decide the young man, who had been looking doubtful. He asked them to wait and swung himself up into the nearer wagon. They could hear him speaking in a low voice. Another voice answered him, resonant and husky, whether a man's or woman's they could not tell. The person inside the wagon seemed to be scolding and arguing, and the young gypsy to be giving soft answers. Finally, the person inside appeared. She was a gigantic woman with strange smoldering eyes in a gaunt face. She might have been any age from forty-five to sixty. Clare heard Richard catch in his breath sharply. She glanced at him but his face was impassive. The gypsy woman came unsteadily down the steps of the wagon and Richard greeted her too with a strange word. She replied almost absently, "*Kusko divves,* brother," and leaned against the steps.

"My name is Richard Ringwood," he said. "You are Mrs.—"

"Buckland. We're all Bucklands here," put in the young man.

"You hold your tongue, Jack," said the woman sharply, drawing herself up. "Well, what can I do for you, my fine gentleman, and your pretty lady? She has a lucky face," she went on almost automatically. "Cross the poor gypsy's palm with silver and it'll bring you luck."

The mechanical begging whine jarred on Richard for a moment, but then he looked up again and saw her standing with one arm across her breast, ragged and battered and yet extraordinarily majestic. She looks like a mother of slaughtered kings, he thought. But I'm a policeman. I must stick to my business. Yet there was involuntary respect in his voice as he asked:

"Would you be the widow of Plato Buckland?"

"And who was he, then?" The strange eyes mocked him, but at least did not disregard him.

"Why, Plato Buckland that had the fine Romany funeral," said Richard readily, thanking heaven for his esoteric reading. "At Reading it was, and all the Bucklands were there. Both his wagons were burnt, in the old way, and everything in them."

"Aye," she said, with bowed head, as if to herself, "and we should have burnt the horses, too. There's no luck in a dead man's horses…" Her voice sank to a mutter, and then she threw up her head and squared her shoulders.

"Petronella!" she called across the clearing. "Come here now, and be quick. Take the pretty lady to your wagon and *dukker* her *drey*. As for you, young man"—she turned back to Richard with no trace of her former servility, but like one assuming a right—"come in here. Where did the likes of you see Plato Buckland?"

She led the way up the steps into the wagon, moving heavily and steadying herself with one hand, and sank on to the far end of the bunk which ran along one side. Richard followed and sat at the other end, his elbows on his knees. The wagon was clean but intolerably hot because of the cooking stove. The stove burned fiercely under a simmering black pot, which gave out a rich aromatic steam. There was a black bottle half-full on a shelf, and the old woman drank a draught and passed it on to him. He took a cautious taste. It was hot and heady. It was rum. He passed the bottle back. Out of the tail of his eye he could see Clare and the young gypsy Petronella going into the other wagon.

"I never met Plato Buckland myself," he said, "but I heard of the funeral from the Herons." (The Herons were a Yorkshire tribe, so he hoped that he was on safe ground.) "That was the last of the real Romany funerals, they say."

"And what do you know of Romany funerals, young man?"

"I know of the death tent," said Richard, who felt like one walking on a razor edge, "and the burning. I know of the candle at the head, and the long watches through the night. I know of the holy bread, and the thorn tree on the grave. Is that enough for you?"

He devoutly hoped it was, for it was almost the sum total of his knowledge, acquired as lately as a month ago; and he looked up under his brows to see how she was taking it.

For answer there came only a belch—a primeval belch, very deep and hollow—and the woman reached for the bottle and drank again. Lord, he thought, is she drunk? And if she is, can I get any sense out of her? Then he felt her eyes on him again, and was obscurely ashamed of his thoughts under the uncanny sadness of her look.

"Why do you talk about funerals, young man? What brings you here?"

"It was just luck," he said. "We were passing by and we saw the wagons, and the lady with me asked to have her fortune told. I don't know why. Perhaps the spirit moved her."

She started at his last words and looked uneasy. Richard realized that he had unwittingly shaken her by the manner of his expression, for her people believed, he knew, that spirits thronged the air at a funeral season, and perhaps she had taken his last words literally. Perhaps the fasting or the drink had increased her fancies. His own head was beginning to swim with the heat and the strange smells.

"I buried my grandchild today," she said slowly and as if unwillingly.

"I'm very sorry," he replied simply. "Was it a boy or a girl?"

"A little girl, a mite of two months." The toneless words were slurred and thick. "Only two months she lived, and always sickly. I saw it in her little hand the day she was born. And there's no more to come. No more. She was the last."

The woman sat with bowed head, as still as a mountain.

"It's hard. Yes, it's hard to lose her, and hard to pay for her burying."

"Have you tried," said Richard, forcing himself to the question, "to sell your pegs and baskets in Oxford? It's a big place, and you could sell plenty there."

"Yesterday," she said dully. "Yesterday it was I walked there. A big place, a hard place. I didn't sell the half of them." Then, with a sudden, shocking return to the begging whine, so spiritless that it could not even have been effective: "Help the poor gypsies, kind gentleman. Help the poor old Romany woman to bury her daughter's child. It'll bring you luck."

Richard never knew whether his next action was prompted by real compassion or by his sense of outrage at seeing her dignity so lowered—the impulse at least was wholly towards her, and he remembered this later when he was trying to account for what followed. He pulled the single pound note from his pocket, and then, feeling it was too little, undid his jacket, ripped open the lining, and drew out the five-pound note that he always kept sewn inside. He offered her the money without a word.

She stretched out a hand and took it gropingly, but her eyes did not follow her hand in the natural way. They were fixed unwaveringly on his face—or rather, he felt, not on his face but on his very being, searching it with a strange and awful light. She seemed to have become nothing else but a naked power of vision, seeing his fraud, his justice, his sympathy, his suspicion—seeing it all impersonally, without a shadow of judgment. As those eyes beat upon him he tried with all his power to turn away his own, but he could not; yet it was not fear that held him, but a terrible curiosity; his mind was perfectly clear, every sense unnaturally alert.

The eyes came nearer; she must have leaned forward, for he could smell her odor of hay and sweat and see a vein standing out on her forehead. Then she spoke.

"I'll tell you." The voice had deepened to the tone of a plucked cello string. "I'll tell you the truth, young man, no *hokkiburen*, for your great-grandmother was one of us and the *dupper* is on me. Listen!"

It was strange and terrible to hear her. She began by speaking of his past life. He could not always follow the voice as it throbbed or failed or fell into outlandish utterance; he knew—he could still reason well enough to know—that the language was ambiguous and held many meanings. Yet there was his life unfolding as he had never unfolded it even to himself. Griefs buried many years rose again before him. Then she seemed to speak of the future. She foretold marriage, children, a fight, a sudden death. He sat like a stone, awed as even a rational man must be by the thought of his own future. And then he heard her say, "And we know why you are here, yes, we know..."

"God help me!" groaned Richard in his heart. "That is evidence." His head cleared a little and he was able to draw into himself and listen more coolly, sifting and weighing the blurred unequal utterance.

"Yes, we know. A loss, a precious thing lost...Ah, but it's out of man's keeping—all for a *mullo mas*! But there's danger there, stowed away—away from the white breast, to the dark. Augh!" Her nostrils widened, she choked and made blind pushing movements with both her hands. "*Devel*, the stink, no more! And she lacks her own, she lacks her own..."

She was in tempestuous motion now, weaving with her arms and moving her shoulders as if she were trying to shake something off her back. Her hair uncoiled and tumbled about her as she tossed her head. But then her movements were stilled and she lifted her head and spoke in a fuller, clearer voice.

"What is lost will be found. A single loss, a double find, one for you and one for another. It will be the same if you find it today or tomorrow or the day after. No man keeps it from you."

She suddenly fell back, her eyes shut and her hands slack beside her. Richard thought that she had fainted, but when he approached and lifted her upright she opened her eyes and looked at him, though in quite a different way. He saw that she had old, tired eyes like dull black pebbles and her jaw was sagging.

"You haven't told me enough," he said. "You say you know why I'm here?"

"Give me a drink, young man." She took the bottle and drank deeply.

"Well?" he repeated impatiently. "Why have I come?"

"Wait. I'm tired. I can't remember...for the lady, was it. That's right, for the lady's *dukkerin.*" Then she saw the banknotes beside her, and memory came back. "Ah, and you gave us money for the funeral, God bless you. And you talked Romany, but you couldn't say it right," she added, with a ghost of the old mocking look.

"Yes, but after that? Where's the child that's lost? You told me yourself. Where's the baby that was stolen yesterday?"

"I don't know. Never heard of no baby here, only our poor little girl that's dead—dead and buried. Eh, I'm tired. Leave me to sleep."

He could hardly hear the dull, slurred phrases.

"Were you in Merton Street yesterday afternoon?" He took her by the shoulder, shaking her a little.

"Eh? I know no such place. Let me be. I haven't touched a bite of food since yesterday morning. Let me be, I've had enough of troubles."

She shut her eyes again. Either she had no memory of all she had said, or she regretted it and was shamming drunk and stupid. He did not know which, but it seemed clear to him that nothing could be gained by questioning her at present. Her fatigue at least was genuine. He decided to leave her, at any rate, for the time. Besides, he doubted if he could stand the atmosphere in the wagon a moment longer. With one last look at the huddled, untidy figure dozing against the wall, he turned and began to clamber down the steps to the ground.

"The dear God bless you!" said her voice behind him. He turned quickly, but she seemed to be asleep. And yet, curiously enough, he felt that she had meant it.

CHAPTER SIX

CLARE WAS standing a little way off, in desultory conversation with Petronella, Jack, and an old man. She disengaged herself, however, without difficulty and came over to Richard.

"Richard, are you all right?" she whispered anxiously. "You're looking frightfully pale. What's she been doing to you?"

"I'm all right. But don't talk to me just yet, darling, if you don't mind. I've got a lot of stuff in my head and I must write it down before I forget. Sorry."

They left the camp, went down the lane, and turned the corner in silence, Richard walking with long nervous strides and Clare almost running to keep up with him. Round the corner was a field gate, set slightly back from the road. Richard turned into this little haven, sat down in the hedgerow, and began to write absorbedly in his notebook. Clare sat down too, and watched him with controlled impatience, wishing she had brought her cigarettes. Richard looked up for a moment, pulled a cigarette and box of matches out of his pocket, and tossed them across to her. Then he returned to his writing. She lighted a cigarette and sat very still with averted eyes. It was so quiet that she could hear the pencil moving over the paper.

Richard shut the book with a snap and Clare started violently and looked up. Richard moved over to her. "Hallo, Clare!" he said. "Are you cross with me?"

"Hallo, darling!" she replied rapturously. "Look, we shall get ants down our necks if we go on like this. Have a cigarette."

"*Sordida rura*," sighed Richard, sitting up. "All right. But I want to hear about you first. How did you get on? Where's the matches?"

"You're sitting on them. Oh, well, I had my fortune told all right. I wasn't frightfully convinced, I must say. I gave her a few false clues, just for fun, and my dear, she swallowed them hook, line, and sinker. In fact, she built up the whole story on them. Do you know what? I love a fair man across the sea. I think he's left me, but no he's coming back. In fact, he's going to marry me and we shall be frightfully rich and have one child. Oh, yes, and I shall have many lovers."

"Rather a comment on present-day ideas of good fortune."

"Yes, isn't it? But I must say, she did it very well. And my pockets and bag were neatly cleared out by the child in the wagon with us—at least, I suppose it was the child; I didn't see a thing go. But I got my own back while I was wandering round waiting for you to come out. I found the remains of a fire, and the ash looked a bit odd—black and crumbly, you know, not like wood ash. So I poked about a bit with my toe. And then I bent down, ostensibly to brush my shoe, and look!"

She held up a small strip of white knitted wool. Richard took it delicately in the palm of one hand.

"What d'you think it is?" He did not look as impressed as she expected.

"Well, it might be the top of a baby's sock, don't you think?"

'Good God! Yes, I suppose it might. Well, you've done better than I have. I just don't know what to make of my interview." He stowed the piece of knitting carefully away in an envelope.

"Oh, do tell me about it! Was she the same woman that came to Merton Street yesterday?"

"Yes. Yes, I'm sure she was. She's just like Mrs. Link's description, for one thing—figure, clothes, voice, everything. And what's more, she admitted that she was in Oxford yesterday."

"Well, then, what are we waiting for?"

"Oh, Clare, it isn't as simple as that. Though I admit I'm a bit shaken by your finding that sock—if it is a sock, and if we can trace it to the Links. But I don't think she would steal a baby, somehow. You see, half the time she was just a poor old woman who'd buried her only grandchild, telling a tale of woe with a good deal of caution and a bit of an eye on the main chance. But the other half—well, it was a different dimension. Like the Sibyl or something. She really is a prophetess of sorts. She told me things I've never told anyone before. And the queer thing is that in the course of this prophecy she got on to the baby. At least, I think she did. I can't quite make it out. I wish you'd read it and tell me what you think."

Clare began to read. She frowned and looked up. "*Spoke of Mother's death and also of loss of Andrew.* Who was he?"

"Andrew was a great friend of mine who was killed in the war. But go on to the part about the baby."

"*Was drinking a good deal of rum.* Who was? You or she?"

"She was, of course. I had one sip for politeness."

"H'm. Was she drunk?"

"I don't know. Yes, maybe a bit. Well, by the end, perhaps. I don't know. I can't decide where Bacchus stopped and Apollo took over."

Clare looked at him, again with a shade of concern, and then shrugged and returned to her reading.

"Why does she say '*we know why you have come*?' Why not *I*? Doesn't that suggest that all the gypsies were in the conspiracy?"

"I never thought of that. Yes, I suppose it does. I took it to mean her and her spirit of prophecy. That seemed to fit better, somehow."

"Oh, Richard, come off it!" said Clare, laughing. "What has she done to you? Be your age!"

"Yes, I can see that it all sounds absolutely bats to anyone who wasn't there. Though if you had been, perhaps you too…Well, look! Would this be a fair way to work it? Could we approach the matter on two levels? One, the oracular. Treat it as a genuine oracle, like the chaps at Delphi, and try to get the inner meaning."

Clare made an impatient little sound.

"Two," continued Richard, "treat it as an attempt to throw us off the track, but assume that since she was drunk she let out a few truths inadvertently."

"That's better," said Clare. "Richard is himself again. Well, now, *we know why you've come*. That's an admission. And *a precious thing lost*. That might be their baby, I suppose. But have we any real evidence that they lost one? They told me, they told you, they ordered a coffin. That's all."

"They must have had a death certificate. And if the worst comes to the worst, there's the churchyard. We can exhume."

"What's all this about a *Buller Mass*?"

"I'm not sure. That's what it sounded like, but I don't know the word. After that she seemed to be smelling something absolutely foul. Her face worked and she kept on saying 'the stink, the stink!' "

"Oh, nuts. She'd probably got to the sick stage, after all that rum. Now, this next bit is interesting. *A single loss, a double find*. Do you think they lost their baby and stole another? But if so, why double? Or did the other baby die on them, too, leaving them with a couple of corpses?"

Richard stared at the ground. He seemed to be rearranging his ideas.

"Could be. And if, as I believe, her trance was genuine—"

"Or if she was really drunk, which seems a likelier explanation."

"She might have been involuntarily confessing to it. Lord, yes, she might. But then what d'you make of this part about stowed away in the dark, in no man's keeping?"

"Why, the darkness of the grave, surely. Oh, Richard, how awful!"

"Yes, but look, aren't we being unnecessarily gloomy? Here's a more sensible line. Suppose the baby was kidnapped by the gypsies. Well, then, let's write it down." He did so, as follows:

(a) Motive.—Grandchild dead, mother for some reason unable to have other children. A girl-child needed by the family. "Girls are the breadwinners, you see; the boys do less work," Richard explained. *Quarrel with Mrs. Link provides emotional motive.*

(b) Opportunity.—Mrs. Buckland on her way out from the back door could easily have leaned over that low wall and scooped the baby out of its pram. Mrs. Link did not see her off the premises, and the gypsy was the last person seen at the house before the crime was discovered.

"Richard, oughtn't we to have searched the camp?"

"We saw it pretty thoroughly between us. Besides, if we give the alarm…Oh, Clare, I've just remembered something odd. The village P.C. said that the coffin was for a child of three. That doesn't square with the story about a baby dying, does it?"

"N-no. But here's another thing. The woman who told my fortune said she was 'that bad with the milk fever.' She did look rather ill, and she kept touching her bosom as if it hurt her."

"Yes. Yes, of course you're right. She was that shape, too, now I come to think of it. I ought to know a nursing mother when I see one, after that year in Limehouse. So it must have been a small baby. But then why was the coffin so much larger than it need be?"

"Lord knows. And why did the old woman have to talk about babies at all?"

"I keep telling you," he said, "only you won't believe me. She was in a trance. She had to tell me the truth because she's a born clairvoyant and the fit was on her. But notice the wording. It's worded to remove suspicion from herself as far as possible. *In no man's keeping.* In a woman's? Or in God's? You can't tell. It's like the Delphic Oracle; you know, 'wooden walls' instead of 'ships' and so on."

"Yes, and look farther on," she said, turning the page. "*It* (whatever *It* is) *will be found again. It does not matter if it is found today or tomorrow or the next day.* Does that mean it's dead and will stay quietly in its grave, or it's alive and you'll find it?"

"Lord, I don't know. I expect I'm an idiot to take anything she said seriously, except the admission that she was in Oxford. No sensible policeman would." He dropped his head in his hands for a moment. Then he stood up with impatient energy.

"Anyhow, there, are various things to do, and that's something. I'll go and see the doctor who gave the death certificate, and the carpenter who made the coffin, and the parson who took the funeral. I may not be able to think, but I can at least enjoy the illusion of doing a spot of work."

"There, don't worry. It'll be all right. You'd like to do these interviews on your own, would you? Yes—well, then, shall I try to scratch up a picnic lunch? It'll be late to lunch in Oxford, and, anyhow, it's such a lovely day, it seems a waste not to have a picnic."

Like most of his sex Richard hated picnics, but like a lover he agreed heartily to her proposal.

"I'll get Plummer to drive you back to Harton, shall I? There's a shop there."

"I think I'll walk. It's so lovely, and it'll fill up the time. I'll just come and collect my valuables first, though, and tidy up."

They set off together down the lane, and separated at the car.

The vicar was in his study writing his parish magazine, smoking an ancient pipe, and looking, as Richard afterwards said to Clare, more like Three Nuns than any priest should. He was distressed to hear of the kidnapping but delighted to meet a real detective.

Yes, he had buried a gypsy baby that morning, of two months old. Yes, the coffin had been rather large for the probable size of the baby. "But then," he said, "the grown-up gypsies have very large coffins, too, I've noticed. We get a good many gypsies coming to this church, for burials and marriages—it's rather a tradition of ours. The sexton always complains of these large coffins. They like to be buried near the edge of the churchyard, too. I don't know why."

"I believe it's a survival from the old custom of wayside burial," said Richard. "Which, of course, they aren't allowed to practice now. Do they like a thorn tree planted on the grave, too?"

"Bless my soul," said the vicar, "this is just like Sherlock Holmes. Yes, they do when they can afford to pay the extra for it. This time they couldn't, so we put the grave under a may tree that grew in the churchyard hedge. The poor old grandmother was so terribly distressed, one wanted to comfort her as much as one could."

"Can you tell me how they behaved at the funeral?" asked Richard. "Did they seem fidgety at all?"

"Oh, no, very well on the whole. At any rate, they didn't smoke, as the bargees did in a canal parish I was in once. Of course, they aren't used to being in church and so they are rather awkward and embarrassed—but not more so"—he sighed—"than a good many of my own people. They were very quiet and reverent—all on the edge of tears but restraining themselves admirably."

"You don't take the view that the gypsies are a lot of rascals?"

"Of course they are!" said the vicar, with a beaming smile. "They got one of my cockerels only yesterday, I'm sure, though I can't prove it. But there! We are all rascals, aren't we? Dear me, what a way to talk to a policeman! Forgive me."

Richard laughed. "I don't think we're exempt from the primal curse," he said. "But none of these gypsies struck you as outstandingly criminal types?"

"Oh dear, no," said the vicar, rather surprised at Richard's theological turn of expression. "No, they struck me as a very nice lot. The old grandmother is a bit uncanny, but I didn't think she was malevolent. More a sort of white witch, if that isn't too fanciful. Or perhaps just a very forceful personality."

"Well, thank you, fa— mean sir," said Richard. "You've helped me a lot. I mustn't waste any more of your time. Before I go, I don't suppose you could tell me which doctor gave the death certificate?"

"There's only one—Dr. Lane-Smith, from Harton. As matter of fact, I met him coming home in his car, and he mentioned he'd been out to the gypsies. You might catch him if you go over at once."

Richard took his leave and walked away through the churchyard. He had no difficulty in identifying a new small grave under a may tree. There were other graves, too, by the hedgeside. Some had thorn trees planted on them, and over a few there were pieces of red rag tied to the branches. Richard knew that these must also be gypsy graves, piously visited by the families with their yearly offerings of scarlet deckings, for that is an ancient custom of the race. How characteristic, he thought, that red should be their mourning color.

He regained the car and Plummer drove him back to Harton. The doctor's house was of decent gray stone with a neat garden in front. He was shown straight into the dining room, where the doctor was hastily demolishing a large cold pie. He was a small bald man, wrinkled and spry and birdlike.

"Sit down, sit down. Sorry I can't stop lunch and come out and see you—very tricky confinement—not sure the first stage'll last much longer. Have to be back. Police, eh? Well, what can I do for you?"

Richard explained that the death of the gypsy baby might have connections with the case on which he was engaged, and asked for the cause of death and any unusual details the doctor might remember.

"Cause of death?" said the doctor, passing to chocolate blanc mange. "Perfectly simple. Pulmonary pneumonia. Too far gone for me to do anything. Predisposition owing to malnutrition—the mother had insisted on feeding it herself and she's had trouble with her milk. They'd been dosing it with concoctions—herbs and snails—Lord knows what. They have their own remedies, y'know—all right for colds and bruises, and light complaints like that, but they never discovered the sulfonamide group. Ha, ha. Quite a clear case. No doubt whatever."

"Thank you," said Richard. "Now could you just tell me one thing more before I go? Who laid the body out? I gather they didn't have an undertaker."

"I know. Very tiresome. These gypsies won't wait the usual four days for the funeral. Must get it over quickly. I got old Mrs. Fox at Mayfield to see to it for them. They got the coffin from Benson, the carpenter. What's the time? Good God!" Cramming an immense last mouthful of blanc mange into himself, he nodded speechlessly and rushed out of the room.

The carpenter's cottage was Richard's next port of call. This interview was soon over and confirmed what the constable had said. The coffin had been ordered for a child of three and paid for and carried away on their cart by the gypsies. This was no news.

Mrs. Fox at Mayfield, however, was much more interesting, though whether her remarks had any bearing an the case Richard could not decide. She, too, had been surprised that so large a coffin had been prepared for so small a baby.

"I didn't like it at all, sir, I can tell you," she said, "going among them heathen gippos. I got young Lino, that's my son, Lionel's his real name, but we all calls him Lino—I got young Lino to wait be'ind a bush near by, for I was fair terrified to go in by meself But I couldn't refuse, not for a baby." She sighed sentimentally. "Only two months old! I always did like to 'ave the layin' out o' babies."

"I am sure," said Richard grimly, "that it has many attractions. Did anything particular strike you about this one, apart from the outsize coffin?"

"Well," she said indignantly, "I wouldn't a' gone if I'd a known their heathen ways. I tell you, sir, that pore little mite 'adn't been let die in peace. They'd washed 'er an dressed 'er in 'er best clothes afore ever she died—in 'er last agony as you might say. They said as much too, as bold as you please. They wouldn't let me do no more than sponge 'er little face and close 'er eyes and put 'er little 'ands quiet on 'er breast. An' watching me all the time, like wolves they was. But wouldn't touch 'er themselves. Oh, no, wouldn't demean 'emselves," she snorted. "Made me lay 'er on a piece of carpet on the ground in a little tent they'd rigged up, so they could put 'er in 'er coffin, carpet an' all, w'out touchin' 'e r. I did 'ear," she added, "as they kep' a candle burnin' in the tent all night. Lino, 'e was coming back pretty late from the Mayfield Social an' 'e said it gave 'im a fair turn when 'e passed to see the candle and two men watching by it."

"But you weren't there when the coffin was screwed down?"

"No, sir. They said as they'd attend to that themselves jus' before the funeral."

"Did you go to the funeral, by the way?"

"Not likely, not at that time. 'Ow could I get into me blacks first thing in the mornin'? It's against nature."

"It is indeed," agreed Richard with the emphasis of incomprehension. "Now just one thing and I'll leave you to your cooking. Did you see or hear any other young baby in the camp?"

"No, sir," she replied with decision. "There was a little boy—about five, I'd say 'e was, but skinny. But I don't think they'd got no other babies there."

Her eyes were beady with curiosity, but fortunately she was enough in awe of Richard—or rather of Richard's beautiful shoes and well-cut clothes—to refrain from asking questions. He complimented her on her excellent memory and answers and left the mausoleum-like little front room in which she had received him. They drove out of the village and found Clare sitting on a bank about half a mile along the road.

She had managed to buy bread, beer, cheese, fruit, and a lettuce which the woman who had sold it to her had kindly washed, and on this fare they all three feasted in the corner of a field, Clare with great pleasure, Richard with complaisance, and Plummer with polite but mournful submission.

CHAPTER SEVEN

THE DEPRESSION of the sergeant, though decently concealed, made itself felt. Richard, who was a good officer to his men though not to his superiors, set himself to lighten it. His sergeant was hot, uncomfortably seated, and deprived of his usual square meal. Material conditions could not be improved, so one must interest him in the work and thus help him to forget his discomforts. Richard embarked on a short account of the morning's interviews, confining himself, however, to the barest bones of the scene in Mrs. Buckland's caravan which had moved him so deeply at the time, for Clare's common-sense remarks had since made him feel rather foolish and credulous. Obviously, he had let the situation get out of hand. Now he gave a conventional summary of the objective facts, while Plummer, sweating profusely and eating twice as much bread and cheese as anyone else, kept his eyes fixed on his superior with flattering attention. But he was still looking depressed and even rather embarrassed. The cure seemed to be ineffectual.

"So that's how it is, Plummer. Not much to go on yet, afraid."

Richard got out his pipe and waited for comments. Plummer carefully brushed a great many crumbs from his tunic—his contours attracted them—cleared his throat, and at last uttered, "Well, sir. Well, it

seems a bit unpleasant, don't it? People don't like it, there's no denying
that, and as for getting in the papers—well, the less said the better, as
the saying goes. But there, what must be must be. It isn't for us to
grumble. I suppose you'll go back and apply straight away, sir?"

Richard's match burned down till it singed his fingers. He dropped
it almost absentmindedly. Was there something about the air of the
place, he wondered wildly, or was the oracular manner catching? What
on earth did Plummer mean? But before he could frame a question, the
sergeant was off again.

"I've never 'ad one, sir, not in all my time in the Force. Makes you
think, don't it? And"—he dropped his voice to a hoarse but resonant
whisper—"it's not very nice for the young lady, is it? But never mind,
there's bound to be a bit of delay, on account of getting the hands together."

"The hands? Whose hands? Plummer, what on earth are you driving at?"

Plummer, with an uncomfortable glance at Clare mumbled something about its being a lot of digging.

"Digging!" said Richard in loud triumph. "Got it! You're talking
about exhumation orders. Thank God! I thought I was going mad. You
think we should dig up that coffin, do you?"

Plummer nodded miserably, stealing a glance at Clare who was
sitting very still with a set expression on her face. But Richard was for
the moment unaware of her, intent as he was on a practical problem
which did not seem to him at all out of the ordinary. To exhume or not to
exhume, that was the question. He had often had to decide it before.

"And you don't much like the idea. Well, is it really necessary,
anyhow? What good would it do? M'm?"

"Seems," said Plummer still unwillingly, "seems there might be two
of 'em in that coffin, don't it, sir?"

"Well, what evidence have we got that there were ever two babies
in the camp? A bit of white knitting in the fire and the likelihood—that's
all it is—that Mrs. Buckland was at 50 Merton Street yesterday. And
perhaps it was rather odd that the coffin was so big and no one saw it
screwed down. But then, again, the layer-out, Mrs. Fox, said there
wasn't another baby in the camp—and she's an observant old misery,
you know. Really, I don't think we're justified in exhuming— not yet,
anyhow. The gypsies'd hate it, and as you say, the public don't like it,
either." He turned to Clare with a twinkle. "Wherefore, they ask—with
far less justification than the poet, who really rather enjoyed it—where-

fore all this wormy circumstance? Why linger at the yawning grave so long? A fair question. No." He stretched himself like a cat. "No. There are other means of solving the problem of the coffin."

Clare revived. "X-ray?' she asked interestedly. "Or dowsing with a hazel twig?"

"Intelligence, madam, pure intelligence. Supported, of course, by the usual stultifying routine work. I have some ideas, and they might click if only these damn flies'd leave me alone. Come on, let's get back to Oxford. We've got to question that nursemaid, and I'd like a word with Link's bank manager. That means I'll have to call on the Chief Constable—no, I mean his deputy. D'you know when the chief'll be back again, Plummer?"

"He's on holiday, sir."

"That's fishy. He's probably kidnapped the baby himself. Well, off we go."

Plummer rose with alacrity and bustled off to the car. Clare and Richard followed him and got into the back seat. The sound of the engine gave them a little cover for private conversation.

"Bless him!" said Clare, with an affectionate glance at Plummer's fat back. "Isn't he a poppet?"

"Who? Oh, him. Yes, he's nice, isn't he? Not very smart, though. Why specially a poppet now?"

"Oh, I don't know—sort of comforting." Clare suddenly saw that she could not be grateful for Plummer's attempt to spare her feelings without an implied criticism of her lover. And that was unthinkable. After all, a policeman's wife has to take exhumations in her stride. Still she changed the subject, saying flatly:

"I think I'd better fade out for a bit when we get to Oxford, don't you, Richard?"

"Fade far away, dissolve, and quite forget? And only the day after we got engaged? Why?"

"Well," said Clare sadly, "you can't take me tagging along to the police station, can you? There are limits."

"But won't you be frightfully bored?"

"No. Well, yes, of course, but you oughtn't to expect me say so."

They both laughed. Then Richard said, "Would you like to do a bit of investigating on your own account?"

"My dear, I'd simply adore to. What?"

"Well, actually this thing might be a bit tedious. Only it isn't a job for an ordinary policeman."

"You know I'd adore it, whatever it is. Tell me."

"Well, if you'd go to the Bodleian…"

"And shut myself up for two days waiting for a book? O.K. Love will find out a way. Come and look for me in a week or so."

"Good heavens, is it as bad as that? How the place decays! Well, Love will find out a way because I'll give you a grand official note in the name of the Law. Then you ought to be done by teatime."

"Fine. And I'll make you tea in my digs. Well, go on. What do I do?"

"I want to know about gypsy burials. Would you find out about them? I'll give you a list of all the standard books I know, and you may find some others as well. I'm afraid the bits about funerals will take some looking for. It won't be arranged in a very orderly and systematic way, but that isn't very surprising, really—I mean, gypsies aren't, either."

"Should I look out for anything special, or would that be cheating?"

"The main thing is dates and places. If you find accounts of particular gypsy funerals with all the trimmings, make a note of where they were and how long ago. You see, if there haven't been any lately, or only in frightfully remote places, we should have fair grounds for suspecting that the Bucklands were just putting on an act with all their traditional stuff. It may just be cover for something they want to hide, a sort of picturesque smoke screen. And another thing. See if they've got the details right. Because if they haven't, that makes it look more like an improvisation."

Clare looked out of the window and saw that they were just passing the road to her lodgings.

"Hey! Here's my turning. I'll get off here."

"Nonsense. We'll drive you to your door at least." He gave Plummer the well-known address to which he had sent so many letters in the past year.

When he reached the police station, he was told that the deputy of the Chief Constable was in conference—needless to say, about the traffic problem—and was afterwards due to attend a meeting about the bicycle thefts. Richard, wondering dispiritedly whether the first step in dealing with the crime wave in Oxford might not well be the prohibition of all wheeled traffic, left behind him a brief written report and had himself driven to 51 Merton Street to question the nurse there. The chimes slowly tolled out a quarter past two as he stood waiting on the doorstep.

The door was opened by a woman in her late thirties or early forties—plump, placid, with a mild autumnal beauty that rested the eye, the sort of beauty that bears children easily and makes good bread.

"I'm so sorry," she said in reply to Richard's question, "afraid my nanny isn't here today. She lives out, you see, with her sister. And she hasn't turned up at all today, has she, darlings?"

Richard was puzzled by her last words, till a little face peered out on each side of her, at about waist-level. "This is Pippa," continued the woman, "and this is Widdy. I'm Mrs. Luke."

Richard bowed slightly (he was not at his ease with small children of his own class, though he had liked the street Arabs of Limehouse) and introduced himself.

"It was so unlike her not to let us know," continued the slow soft voice, without a hint of reproach. "There were the children in bed waiting for her to get them up, and there were my husband and me fast asleep."

"We're not allowed to wake Daddy up," explained Widdy. "And we didn't get up till nine o'clock. Just think of that, nine o'clock!"

"I got up at half-past six," said Richard like a martyr.

"Lucky you! We're not allowed to get up till a quarter to eight."

"And so," Mrs. Luke went on undisturbedly, "we're all just going up to Nanny's house to see if she's ill or something."

"Oh, don't do that," said Richard. "Let me go. I've got a car, and I must talk to your nurse, anyhow. She might have noticed something yesterday evening, you see. I can be your messenger. Shall I ring you up after I've seen her?"

"How kind of you, isn't it, darlings? Of course I always think policemen are so kind, only my husband says you're not a proper policeman—I mean, detectives are like professors, aren't they, who are always rather fish out of water?...But so kind all the same. Now we can go for a proper walk, darlings."

"See the monkeys," said Pippa at once.

"Yes, if you like. Go and get your sun hats."

"There is just one thing," said Richard. "The girl's address. I've got her name already: Gladys Turner. Is that right?"

"Yes, such a nice girl. We're all so fond of her. I do hope she won't have to give evidence or anything. If you'd just see if there's anything we can do, and of course find out when she's coming back. But not if it's a bad cold, or it'll run all through the family, and my husband does

get such sore throats with all that Anglo-Saxon. That is kind of you."
She beamed on him.

"Not at all. I'm going up to...where was it?"

"Thirty-four Jersey Street, off Walton Street. How lucky you asked
me, wasn't it? Well, goodbye, and thank you again. We'll be back about
four. No, Pippa, your sun hat, not your Sunday hat. Well, I'll come and
look myself. Excuse me, won't you? Goodbye." She shut the door gently.

Jersey Street was in the heart of that part of Oxford called Jericho,
generally classified as a slum. Yet although it is overbuilt, overcrowded,
and overpoor, the district has its charms. The streets run down towards
the river and look across it to the great wooded hump of Wytham Hill,
green and solitary. It is true that most of the houses are meanly built and
stand flush with the pavement, yet here and there one finds a cottage
with its own front garden, a fragment of marooned village architecture.
Number 34 Jersey Street was an endearing little house; behind its
wooden railing the small garden was bright with marigolds and sweet
williams. The knocker and the door handle were newly polished, and
the lace curtains were white in the front window. Richard used the
knocker and a large lady in an excessively flowered apron opened the
door.

"Good afternoon. Does Miss Gladys Turner live here?"

"Yes, but she's out at work. 'Course, I could take a message if you
like."

"She's not at Mrs. Luke's, I'm afraid. That's why I've come here.
Could I have a word with you, perhaps?"

"Well, I don't know, I'm sure. It depends what you want, see."

"I'm from the police."

The woman's jaw dropped, and she looked nervously at her neighbors' windows as she hurried Richard inside. Sure enough, one of the
next door curtains moved slightly.

"Now, then, what's all this?" she said, sitting down on part of the
three-piece suite and causing Richard to sit on another. "I've never
been mixed up with the police, nor Gladys neither. You must have come
to the wrong house."

"Don't worry," said Richard. "I only wanted to ask Miss Turner if
she'd seen anything unusual in Merton Street yesterday. I'm sure *she'll*
be quite ready to help me." There was rebuke in his emphasis.

"Well, so am I, sir, I'm sure. Anyone would be. But she's at work,
see. She won't be back till six o'clock. Why, what's happened in Merton Street, then?"

"Someone's missing. Bur Miss Turner *isn't* at work, you know. I've just come from Mrs. Luke's, and she hasn't been there all day. Did she take a day off, or something? Mrs. Luke thought she must be ill."

"Oh, no, she's never ill. She's not the sort to give way. Let alone taking a day off without notice. Well, I don't know, I'm sure."

"Did you see her this morning?"

"No, she leaves ever so early to get the children up. And she has her breakfast at work, see?"

"Well, did she sleep here last night?"

"That I wouldn't know, sir. She makes her own bed, see. And I was in bed and asleep last night when she came in. She stayed on late for Mrs. Luke—they were going out, see, and Glad stopped on to mind the children. Ever so fond of them, she is, and of course Mrs. Luke's very considerate, and gives her a bit extra if she asks her to stop on."

"Yes, yes. But Gladys *isn't* at Mrs. Luke's today. Have you any idea where she can have got to?"

"Well, I never. She isn't at work today?" said the woman with surprise.

"*No!*" said Richard. 'Now tell me, Mrs.—"

"Harman is the name."

"Mrs. Harman. Have you noticed anything unusual about Gladys's manner and behavior lately? Anything happened out of the ordinary?"

"Oh, no! Glad's a steady girl, she knows what's right. Now, if it was Ive, it'd be different Why, only last night—"

"Yes? What about last night?"

"Well, I am worried as a matter of fact. But there, perhaps I'd better not talk about it."

"You'd better tell me and get it off your mind. I'm very good at keeping secrets, and I want to help you. We'd better have all the facts in the open, you know. It's very queer, Gladys disappearing like that."

"Yes. And it's very queer Ive disappearing, too," she said in the same stolid weary voice. "Very queer."

"Ive. Who's Ive?"

"Why, Gladys's sister Ivy, of course, like I was telling you. I was ever so worried when I'd found she'd gone this morning."

"Gone?"

"Gone with the wind, as they say. And after all those goings on last night, too."

"Last night?"

"Well, yesterday evening. She was acting ever so funny, kind of excited and upset all at once. And then she went up to her room quite early, and I heard her crying. But she wouldn't let me in when I went up to see what was the matter. Wouldn't even have a cup of tea. And another thing. She took the ink up to her bedroom."

"The ink?"

"Yes, the ink off the kitchen dresser."

"What would she do that for?"

"Why, to write that note to her sister, of course. She must have put it on the kitchen table when she went out."

"Went out?"

"Well, she must've gone out, mustn't she? Her bed's not been slept in and she didn't have her breakfast this morning. She has her breakfast with me, see. And I do her bed. I can't trust her to turn the mattress. She's not like Glad."

"And is the note still there?"

"Oh, no. Glad must've taken it this morning."

"Then how do you know it was there? She put it out after you'd gone to bed, didn't she?"

"Yes, but I came down to let the cat in, see. She was yowling to come in so, she woke me up. And there was the envelope on the table. She'd taken whatever was inside."

"And was there a light in either of the girls' rooms?"

"No."

"What time was this?"

"Getting on for two o'clock by my alarm, it was."

"Well, now, when you heard Ivy crying. What sort of noise was she making?"

"Why, just crying."

"I mean, was she sobbing, or wailing, or what? What did she sound like?"

"Well, that's a funny question. Let me see. It was like a kiddie, sort of."

"Like a kiddie? Like a baby, you mean?"

"Well, yes, I suppose a bit. Ivy, she cried easy, not that awful sobbing some do. She's just a kid, really, although she was twenty last month. Just a kid. You can't help being fond of her."

"You don't think she could have had a child in her room, crying?"

"My goodness, no! What would she do that for?"

"Or a small baby?"

"Police or no police," said Mrs. Harman, rising majestically, "this is a respectable house, sir, and I can't sit here and listen to talk like that, nor Gladys wouldn't like me to." And she made the motions of sweeping out.

"Mrs. Harman," said Richard. "Can you keep a secret? An official secret?"

She paused by the door and then nodded, half against her will.

"The reason I asked about a baby is that there's a baby missing— a very young baby—and I'm trying to find it. That's why I was so interested in the noises in Ivy's room last night. Don't ask me to tell you any more, because I mustn't. But try to cast your mind back. Could Ivy have had...I mean been hiding a baby in her room last night?"

"I don't know, I'm sure. Poor little mite, what a wicked thing! Whatever will they think of next? I don't know what to say, I'm sure."

"It didn't occur to you that the crying sounded like a baby's?"

"Well, I never give it a thought, see. But now you mention it, sir, I wouldn't like to take my Bible oath—no, nor sign my name neither. You can't be too careful, can you?"

"But you think it might have been a baby?"

"Well, there again, you never know. I'd rather not say one way or the other, reely. I was in a hurry, like, and the cat was going on so."

"The cat?"

"Yes, sir. It's that tom next door, sir, it's a disgrace, they ought to have got him attended to. We can't hardly hear ourselves think, sometimes."

"M'm. Oh, well," said Richard, "I won't press you for an answer now, Mrs. Harman. But you might think it over again, would you? Now will you take me upstairs and show me the girls' rooms? Then we can see if all their clothes and things are there. If they haven't taken anything away, then I don't expect they'll have gone far."

She conducted him up the narrow staircase on to the tiny landing, and opened the door on the right.

"This is where Ivy sleeps," she said.

It was an untidy little room. Soiled and torn underclothes were piled on the single chair. There was a heap of film magazines stuffed half under the bed and a jungle of dusty cosmetics on the chest of drawers.

"No sponge or toothbrush, I see," said Richard at once. "Was there a toothbrush yesterday?"

"Oh, yes, and a face flannel too, and a nail brush. She didn't have a sponge, and you can't wonder, the price they are. Still, Ivy's a one for keeping herself nice, I will say that."

"Is she?" said Richard a little incredulously. "Well, now, will you look about and see if any of her clothes are missing? I'll see if there are any papers."

There were no letters, and the quantities of scattered newspaper cuttings which Richard unearthed all turned out to be articles on Home Beauty Treatment.

'Well, I never!" said Mrs. Harman. "There must be something Going On."

"Why?" said Richard, looking up from the top drawer, his nose slightly flexed in distaste at the stale smell.

"She's taken her new costume, and her new shoes, and both her nighties. And the basket trunk. And her dance frock. And her black beauty satin. Well, I never."

"All her best clothes, in fact? H'm. Will you show me her sister's room now?"

It was smaller and darker, with a damp patch on the ceiling. Richard suddenly remembered the damp patch on his own night nursery ceiling, which used to turn into a live hippopotamus as dusk came on and drive him nearly mad with fright. What had made him think of that? Of course, this room was just like a night nursery or a school cubicle, so clean, so bare, with the white honeycomb counterpane and the brush-and-comb bag hanging from the right-hand knob of the looking glass. A child's jersey on the chair, too. Or rather, a half-knitted jersey, a back and half a front. There was a double photograph in front of the mirror. (I only had my mother's, thought Richard, and I used to take it into the bed with me. Sometimes I hurt myself on the corners.)

"These her parents?"

"That's right. They both passed away. Her mother, she was killed by an unexploded bomb after the war was over. But I must say, Gladys has been as good as a mother to Ive. Can't do enough for her."

"Well, it looks as if Gladys has left her toothbrush and things, anyhow. Can you look and see if she's taken anything else?"

Mrs. Harman rummaged vigorously, revealing unnaturally tidy drawers. After a few minutes she said:

"It looks to me as if she's gone off in her working clothes with her coat over them and a scarf. I don't think she's taken nothing. Look, here's her case under the bed with her winter clothes in it, same as usual. She always puts them away, turn and turn about."

"What about money? Did she have a bank account?"

"No, I was always going on at her to put it in a savings book—the lady comes round for the stamps, see, so it'd be no trouble—but she said no, she didn't hold with it. She used to put some aside every week, though, in a little black cashbox. Here it is."

Richard took it from the back of the top drawer. The lid opened at a touch. It was unlocked and empty, and the landlady gaped with dismay.

"Don't worry, Mrs. Harman. I expect she wanted it in a hurry and just took it. It isn't your responsibility. Try to think where they might have gone. Have they got any relations? The parents are dead, you say?"

"Yes, their mother lived at Bristol. That's why Gladys gave up her job where she lived in, see, and came here to make a home for Ive. Ive wouldn't go into service, so Gladys said, well, at least she shall have a proper home to come back to at nights. She's only a kid, see, although she's twenty."

"And how old is Gladys herself?" asked Richard, touched by the story.

"She's twenty-four, sir, but she's got, a lot of sense, she's not like some. She'd do anything for Ive. Why, there was a feller down by the Willow Walk, one of these bottom-pinchers, waiting there for Ive, and Glad, she gave him a black eye. He didn't come round no more after that."

"Well, well, what a girl! But tell me, have they any friends or relations out of Oxford? Do they ever go and stay with anybody?"

"They've got an aunt at Weston-super-Mare that lets lodgings, but they've only been there once. She's generally full up in the summer, see, and Glad has to take her fortnight to suit Mrs. Luke. Let me see… I can't think of anyone else. They went to a holiday camp last year, and Ive said it wasn't bad, but Glad didn't want to go again. No, I don't think they've anyone else to go to. Alone in the world, as you might say."

"What about boyfriends? Are either of them fixed up that way? I'm sorry to be so inquisitive, but it's the only way to find them."

"That's all right. I quite understand," said the woman with another temporary return to formality. "Well, Glad did go with a young feller, but he was killed in the R.A.F. She hasn't seemed to take up with no one since then. But Ive—well, she is a one for the boys and no mistake. Only one at a time, mind you, but they don't last long and that's a fact. She's just a kid, see. Her latest says he's in

Atomic *Ree*search. Mind you, I don't think he's a high-up. But he works in that atom place at Harwell. Nasty things, I don't know how anyone can. But he won't last long. He's due to go back to Canada months ago, only there was some mistake about his draft. He said he was loaned here temporary."

"He's a Canadian, you say? What work is he doing?"

"I don't know, sir. I did ask him, but he started talking about security and I didn't half feel embarrassed."

"What did you think of him? Did you like him?"

"Well, he was all right, I suppose. He came in for a cup of cocoa after the pictures once and he was ever so nice, you know, American style. But I do think he might be a one to take advantage."

The tired blue eyes met Richard's, and he nodded.

"Mind you," she went on, "I don't think no harm's been done yet, but Glad and me, we've been a bit worried. It's just as well he's going back to Canada soon."

"M'm. Where does he live?"

"He wouldn't say, he said security reasons again. Ive was always on at him to tell her, she was that disappointed she couldn't get it out of him." She chuckled. "Ive's a one, she is."

"What was he called? Leslie Gray? I'll just note that down. Now I don't think I need bother you any more. You've been most frightfully helpful and I'll let you know as soon as I get any news for you. I say, I suppose you haven't a photograph of either of them, have you?"

Mrs. Harman rummaged out a very small snapshot of a slim fair girl and a thicker darker girl in cotton dresses, with the sun in their eyes and their faces almost illegible. Richard took a closer look at Gladys's photograph of her parents and tried to memorize the features. But he did not feel they told him much. Both were very ordinary faces, the mother stronger, and the father's perhaps better-tempered. With thanks and comforting phrases he eased himself out of the house.

In the car, his pent-up impatience cracked.

"The station, sergeant. I believe I'm on to something at last. No, not the police station, you…not that, the G.W.R., dash it. I mean the British Western Region, and don't let's waste any more time."

But the men in the two booking offices had not been on duty the night before. Richard cursed himself for feeling disappointed. Of course, they wouldn't be. These things were done in shifts. But he could at least insist on seeing the stationmaster and enlist his weary cooperation. The booking clerks in question would be back that evening at eight o'clock, and Richard engaged to come down then and show them the photographs, in case they remembered selling tickets to the originals.

"You can ask, of course," said the stationmaster gloomily. "But we get thousands through this station. Stands to reason, we can't be expected to notice them. Why, you'd think people had nothing to do but go by train, the crowds we get."

"They can't be doing it for pleasure, obviously," said Richard acidly. "Well, I'll come back this evening."

He returned to the car and to Plummer, who seemed prepared, like the unhappy Theseus, to sit eternally, but without the least sign of boredom.

"Plummer, have you heard of a place where they do atomic research—Harwell or something?'

"Nasty dangerous things. They ought to take a vote before putting them down in the district. Yes, sir, that'll be 'Arwell."

"Well, will you ring up their office and ask if they employ a man called Leslie Gray, believed to be a Canadian—medium height, brown hair? And get all the details you can—nature of work, character, home address and soon."

"Very good, sir."

"And then you'd better have some time off. You've had long day and not much food. Couldn't you get home for some tea?"

"Easy as easy," he said, brightening at the thought. "My old woman had our bit of beef she was going to make a stew for me dinner. And it'll hot up for tea beautiful." He, let out his belt two holes. "Are you sure you don't want me, sir?"

"Not till half past five. I'm going to see Mrs. Luke again, then Mrs. Link, and then I shall go to Miss Liddicote's house to collect some information she's been getting for me at the Bodleian. Perhaps you'd pick me up there at five-thirty. You can have the car to go home in."

Plummer beamed. He had never met this attitude in a superior officer before, and if he had had a tail he would have wagged it right off.

CHAPTER EIGHT

THE LUKES' house in Merton Street was still empty, and Richard, remembering that the children had asked to go to the Bestiarick Gardens, decided to go there too. If, after all, he did not meet Mrs. Luke there, he would pass the time pleasantly enough, till four o'clock, when she had promised to be home. So off he went, at his usual headlong pace, and was soon passing through the turnstile in the great classical gateway.

Once within the gardens, his steps grew slower. He had not been there since he was an undergraduate—never, in fact, since that golden day when he and Andrew had planted the Bear. It was a huge stuffed bear, and they had smuggled it out of his father's club in London—a feat in itself—driven it to Oxford in Andrew's car, and secretly introduced it into the Smaller Mammal House. They had placed between its paws a bloodstained human skull borrowed from a medical student, and wonderful alarms had ensued, though no one had been able to explain the affair. Childish, no doubt, thought Richard. But what fun it was! Other memories came flooding back into his mind, all memories of things that he and Andrew had done or talked of together, and indeed they had hardly been a day apart. It was odd how fresh those memories were. Odd, too, how he had never had any other intimate friend except Andrew. His death had left an enormous gap—the gypsy had been right there.

Then he remembered how the gypsy had spoken of a single loss and a double find. Double? He was only looking for one baby.

"Wonder if she meant old Andrew?" he thought, his heart lifting for a moment. "We never actually heard his death was confirmed. Just lost in the prison-camp muddle."

But then his depression returned. The thing was impossible. The gypsy's sayings were strange and had moved him deeply at the time, but did not such creatures live on man's appetite for hope? He passed slowly through the main gardens and out to the open ground by the river, where the new ape house stood. He halted there, frowning and preoccupied.

He looked up and found himself face to face with a gorilla in an outdoor cage, sitting grimly in the attitude of Rodin's *Penseur.* The gorilla was also frowning and preoccupied. It passed a hand over its receding brow and sighed deeply. Richard's black eyes met the gorilla's brown ones and they gazed at each other abstractedly.

"Never mind, darling," said a tender childish voice at Richard's elbow, "it'll soon be time for your tea."

He turned sharply, but was relieved to find that Pippa was addressing these consolations to the gorilla and not to herself. Mrs. Luke and her two children had come round the corner behind him.

"Hallo!" she said. "You have been quick, hasn't he, darlings? Or has my watch stopped? Did you see Nanny? What's happened?"

"I'd rather like to have a word with you alone," said Richard. "But I suppose you can't leave your children."

"Oh, yes, it's easy. You see there are two nannies we know here, at least not nannies, really, Italians, if you see what I mean. Pippa and Widdy wanted us to go and talk to them, only I thought it was rather unfair, because I'm sure they want to tell each other how awful life is in England. Look, Pippa, John's got a ball like yours. Let's go and see it."

She sailed across the lawn with her daughters to a group of children and nurses under a tree, and presently returned by herself. The wind that ruffled the treetops seemed to let her hair and dress alone. With her, it was always halcyon weather, and her voice was as slow and calm as the Merton chimes.

"Do you mind if we go into the ape house? It's rather smelly, but I don't think there's anyone there. And if the children can't see me, they won't come and interrupt us."

He followed her into the building and they stopped in front of a cage with six chimpanzees in it.

"I'm afraid it isn't very good news," Richard began. "Your nanny and her sister both seem to have disappeared. They went last night. Gladys, I mean your nanny, hasn't taken her clothes, and perhaps that's a good sign. But no one has any idea where they've gone. I'm sorry."

She opened her eyes a little. "How extraordinary! I wonder what can have made her do that?"

"There's an obvious answer to that question," said Richard. "So obvious that I hope it can't be right. But just look at the facts: A baby next door to your house is kidnapped between half past five and six. Your nanny knows that baby's very rigid routine, and she knows you and your husband will be out. Her sister comes off work at a quarter past five, when her shop closes, and doesn't reach her lodgings till a quarter past six. She then goes straight up to her bedroom unobserved, and refuses to let anyone in. Sounds of shrill crying are heard in the house. The moment your nanny comes off duty, she and her sister disappear—though we don't know if they went together or separately— and go off to an unknown destination. Putting motive and character aside, doesn't it look as if she'd kidnapped the baby, using her sister as an accomplice?"

"Oh, no," she said, with mild reproach. "Our dear nanny'd never do a thing like that. Besides, why should she want to?"

Female witnesses, thought Richard. Why can't they keep to the point?

"Though, of course, one does do the most awful things sometimes, doesn't one? I once stole a toy for darling Pippa, it was a most heavenly woolly kangaroo with a baby kangaroo in its pocket, at a children's party, and Pippa couldn't bear to let it go. So I just slipped it under my coat. Of course, I felt dreadful about it the next day."

"So what did you do?" Richard was fascinated in spite of himself.

"Oh, I made it a little jacket and took it back again, and nobody minded. Pippa had forgotten about it, you see, so it didn't matter."

"Yes, I see your point. Repentance does cause a lot of bad feeling. Still, to get back to the case. I want you to tell me all you know about this girl Gladys Turner."

She gazed at a chimpanzee who was putting both hands over a notice saying DO NOT FEED THESE ANIMALS, and looking at them fixedly.

"Aren't they human!" she exclaimed delightedly. "Oh, yes, about Nanny. Well, she started with the Pettigues. She'd had a little training in one of the government nurseries, but Marian Pettigue said it didn't seem to have spoilt her a bit. She was with them till her sister started giving trouble, two years ago, after her mother died. They were very sorry to lose her, but they had to have somebody living in, and Nanny wanted to be a daily, you see, so as to make a home for her sister, so Marian Pettigue very kindly put her on to me. And I must say, she's an absolute treasure. Besides, we don't go out much in the evenings. Harold likes to work then."

"You say her sister was giving trouble? How was that?"

"Oh, well, she's very pretty, you know, and rather silly, and at Bristol she insisted on being an usherette at a cinema. Still, she came home at nights. But then the mother died, poor dear, and Ivy insisted on living in lodgings by herself. It wasn't bad at first, because Nanny found her a respectable family. But then she moved, and Nanny thought she was getting into bad company, and didn't like to leave her on her own. So in the end, she got Ivy this job in Oxford, left her own job, and set up with her sister in Jersey Street. That's how she came to leave the Pettigues, and I know it was a struggle for her. She was so fond of the children. They're twins, you see."

"But I still don't see what's the matter with Ivy. Why get so worried about her? After all, lots of girls do live alone. Is she unbalanced, or something?"

"Oh, no, I don't think so. Just silly, you know like girls are."

"H'm! Are there any other relations?"

'There's an aunt at Weston, I think. I believe they went to see her once."

"Anyone else?" She hesitated and Richard pressed the question. "A black sheep in the family, for instance?"

Mrs. Luke looked at him hard, and he found himself ridiculously wondering when he had last washed hands. It was that kind of look.

"Will you have to tell anyone else if I tell you?"

"I won't tell anyone unless it's really necessary. I can't say more than that."

"Nanny told me in confidence, you see. Well, she's got a brother."

"Younger or older?"

"Younger. Between her and her sister. I heard about it last year—last autumn, I think it was. Nanny came to me—I could see she'd been crying—and asked me in that formal way they have when they're upset about anything. You know, they sound cross, but they aren't really."

"Yes. What did she ask you?"

"She said, 'Could you make it convenient to give me a month's wages in advance, Mrs. Luke, as I have an unexpected bill to pay?' Well, I worked it out in my head and it came to about ten pounds. So of course I said I'd lend her ten pounds and she could pay me back two shillings a week."

"Not much 'of course' about it. Still…What next?"

"Well, that seemed to upset her worse than ever, poor child. But it was just as well in a way, because she had a good cry and told me the whole story. Her brother worked in a garage, she said, and he'd been stealing money out of the office. Not much, just odd silver, but it had mounted up to about ten pounds before they were sure it was him. They'd noticed the losses, you see, and kept an account. Well, the man who owned the garage said he'd overlook it if it was paid back. And so Gladys's brother wrote and asked her for the money. He lost the job, of course, but still, that was better than going to prison, wasn't it?"

"H'm. Why didn't Ivy contribute?"

"Oh, Nanny specially didn't want Ivy to know. Ivy thinks he's in Yorkshire, I believe. Nanny doesn't want them to meet, you see, because the boy really does seem to be a bad influence. I gather he's always getting into trouble. Nanny said she'd told him he'd got to keep away from Oxford or else she wouldn't ever help him again."

"And has he kept away?"

"I don't know. I expect so. Nanny doesn't talk about him much. I think she's rather ashamed of him. I did ask her once or twice, but Nanny just said he'd got a new job or was out of a job. I think she must still be sending him money now and then, because she never seems to have any new clothes."

"Do you know where he is?"

"No. I didn't ask, and Nanny didn't tell me. She's seemed more cheerful lately, so perhaps he's settled down now. I do hope so."

"Now, I want you to think very carefully before you answer this question. How fond do you think your nanny was of this brother of hers?"

"I suppose it all depends on what you mean by fond," she said slowly. "She wouldn't let him get into trouble without trying to help. But she won't let him near Ivy. I mean she doesn't really think he's nice, you know. But she'd do anything for him."

"*Anything*?"

"Not anything wrong, no, of course not. I don't mean she wasn't fond of him, but you see it was her duty to be, in a way, I mean, she really was frightfully devoted to him, but I think it was because she thought she ought to be. But, oh, dear, I can't put it very well. You tell me what I mean."

Richard was not at all averse from expressing the matter clearly, and indeed, nothing is more flattering than to be asked to tell a woman what she means. It happens so seldom.

"You mean, don't you, that you think all her feelings are guided by a sense of duty, like Cordelia's, and none the less strong for that. Therefore, she wouldn't commit a flagrant breach of duty out of love for her brother, because love and duty are completely bound up in her mind, and there would be something monstrous to her in violating one for the sake of the other—a kind of division in nature."

He looked up with perhaps a touch of triumph, to find her gazing dreamily past him at the patch of sunshine in the doorway.

"Oh, yes, how clever of you," she said slowly responding. "How well you put things! Harold would be interested. Though she'd be rather large for Cordelia, I think."

Irresistible laughter bubbled up in Richard, shaking him from the diaphragm to the back of the nose. To cover it he turned to the cage before them. But the chimpanzees' amusements had now become so specialized as to be embarrassing. He strolled along, to the next cage, where there was a single ape sitting still in a corner.

"Poor thing!" said Mrs. Luke vaguely. "He looks like Dr. Costard in the vacation when the college kitchens are shut, so lost somehow. Do you think I ought to get a temporary? I mean, do you really think you'll find Nanny? And if you do, will she be able to come back to work? The children are so fond of her."

"I hope we'll find her," he said seriously. "It isn't easy to hide from the police without a good deal of practice. But I can't possibly tell you whether she's innocent. If she has kidnapped the baby, her only motive will be to get a lot of money for its ransom. We can guess why she might want the money. So long as money isn't being asked for, it looks hopeful for her. And no demand has been sent to the Links yet, at least I don't think so. I think they'd have told us if it had."

"Oh, dear, yes, don't worry about that for a minute. I'm sure they would. Of course, if it was me, I'd pay out anything, on any condition, to get my baby back, but Perpetua's so public-spirited, you see. She wouldn't dream of it."

"What's she like? I suppose you know her fairly well?"

"Oh, well, neighbors, you know...But I'm so bad at explaining. She's got a sense of duty, too, but not like Nanny's. It's more a sort of idea that she must cope with things, and know all the up-to-date methods, and be efficient. The way she brought up her baby, for instance..."

"I gather little Perdita had a sort of Board of Directors, didn't she?" said Richard, with his sidelong half-smile.

"Oh, yes, and was fed on the stroke of the hour, and she read up textbooks by the dozen before she was born. Poor Perpetua! She's exactly the same about her marriage, too; she never just sits back and enjoys her husband."

"How do you mean? Does she deal with him by up-to-date methods, too? Poor John!"

"Oh, my dear!" said Mrs. Luke, looking rather roguish. "You wouldn't believe all the books she has about it! Do you know, I once went in there and found John all by himself in the sitting room, and Perpetua with her hair in pincurls pressing her clothes, upstairs. And she said it was such a pity, it was John's only free evening that week and she had to spend it ironing, because she hadn't pressed her skirt and it said in her book that a wife must be well groomed if she wished to keep her husband's interest. So silly, you know, because they're obviously devoted to each other and hate being apart."

"I don't think that's a sense of duty."

"Well, not like Nanny's, I know. But it's the Links' special brand.

But they're very sweet, you know," she added earnestly, "and they simply adore their baby. I do hope they'll get her back."

"So do I," he said. "But I've never had a more puzzling case. It's a sort of fight with shadows, and I don't see how to tackle it."

"I'll hold my thumbs for you," she said. "Now I must go and find the children, or they'll never get any tea. Goodbye, Mr. Ringwood. I'll let you know at once if I hear anything of Nanny."

She went away, leaving Richard comforted and encouraged, though he could see no reason for it. He took out his little book and began to make notes, leaning against the bars of the cage. Presently he felt a plucking at his coat, and turned round. The ape had sat down behind him and was trying to explore his pockets. Richard rather liked its sophisticated melancholy face with bulging cheeks and scanty reddish beard. It looked like an unsuccessful art dealer.

"I can't offer you much," he said apologetically, "though I can see you're a deserving case. Wallet? Well, better not, perhaps. Handkerchief? No, no! Haven't you heard about germs? Matches? Cigarettes? Hallo, you're an addict, are you?"

The creature was uttering low vehement grunts and stretching out the bald brown hand of supplication. Richard half-opened the case.

"Now, then, Percy!" said a voice behind him. "Don't you bother the gentleman! You ought to know better."

Richard saw a stocky young keeper approaching.

"Is he a smoker?" he asked. "He seems very interested in my cigarettes."

"Ah, he used to be, but he knows better now—No, Percy! The missionary that brought him up used to let him smoke regular, but that was out East. We had to stop him when he came here. It might have irritated his chest, you see, and you can't be too careful, not in this climate."

"Oh, he was brought up by a missionary, was he? I thought he seemed very meek and mild. I suppose that's why."

The keeper smiled. "Oh, no! The missionary was a very lively gentleman, sir. When he used to come and see Percy, I didn't know if I was on my head or my heels, he used to go on so, the missionary, that is, not Percy. No, orangs just are quiet, that's their nature like. Unless they're frightened. Then they can be devils. Just look at that, now!"

A chimpanzee in the next cage had flown into a temper and was bouncing up and down, shaking the bars and using what was evidently appalling language. The ape Percy rose up, moved over to the remotest part of his own cage, and huddled down with his hands over his ears, looking harassed.

"There, you see!" said the keeper. "He doesn't even like the others carrying on. Though his own temper's just as bad in a way. Sulk! My goodness, can't he sulk! I've known him not look at me for days together, not even to take food. I will say this for the chimps, they come round easier after a row."

"Perhaps he's lonely. I suppose he's the only orang you've got."

"No, we've got another. But it's not on show at present."

"Oh, nothing wrong, I hope?"

"Nothing wrong," said the keeper, with a fatuous paternal smile. "You never saw a finer specimen, Mishandled, that's all. Mishandled, not to say insulted. And not by us. I name no names, but there's some visitors ud be better in the cages than the monkeys, the silly ideas they have. Ah, animals always know, don't they?"

The ape was by now extracting imaginary fleas from Richard's hair, and Richard looked up indignantly to defend his personal hygiene. But the keeper continued courteously:

"I can see he likes you. It's a sure sign, that scratching is. He'll scratch me by the hour sometimes. Well, sir, I must be getting on."

"Good lord, so must I!" said Richard to himself, looking at his watch. "Four o'clock. Not so bad. Nice time to call on the Links before I go to Clare's."

CHAPTER NINE

JOHN LINK had reached home in the small hours of Thursday night. It would be difficult to say whether the husband and wife had derived a greater degree of comfort from each other's presence, or distress from the sight of each other's grief. They passed a wretched, wakeful night. Every now and then the cry of an owl, or some other soft nocturnal sound, would make Perpetua start up instinctively, thinking that her baby was crying for her; each time, the realization of the truth, which followed a second later, was harder to bear. Yet she had shed no tears, and when at last she rose to go about her household tasks, the reminders of her child that met her eye everywhere still did not melt her frozen grief. It was not until they were washing up after breakfast, and she dropped the teapot with a sharp shocking sound on the tiled floor, that she suddenly burst into hysterical weeping. John carried her upstairs and laid her on the tumbled bed, but nothing would stop her tears, till at last she fell into an uneasy, exhausted sleep. Then John stole downstairs and rang up his neighbor, Mrs. Luke.

She came quickly. The sound of the front door awakened Perpetua. She called out, and Mrs. Luke hurried up the stairs at once. She stayed upstairs for half an hour, and then came down in search of John.

"How is she? Is there anything I can do?"

"Let's put a kettle on for some tea," she said. "Then we can talk while it's boiling. Oh, yes, I think she'll be all right now that she's had a good cry. She's been frightfully good, really. I was just asking her about her milk, you know. She mustn't lose it, because it might make all the difference when you get Perdita back if her mother can feed her, mightn't it? I know a very nice maternity nurse, and I'm sure she'll come along if she's free and tell Perpetua what to do. Poor darling, she must be in pain, though I've done what I could. But of course a real nurse is much better." She made the tea with slow gentle movements, "And John. Do try to spare her any worrying news you can, won't you? There! The tea's ready now. You take it up. I must get back. I'll tell you as soon as I've got a nurse."

And so by Mrs. Luke's skilful management (of which she herself could certainly have given no rational account) the greater anxiety was for the moment swallowed up in the lesser, and the parents found relief in the possibility of action. Mrs. Luke engaged a nurse who would come at two o'clock to give treatment, and who meanwhile gave instructions that would keep Perpetua occupied. John did some sketchy housework and prepared a makeshift lunch. As he was heating a tin of soup, the flap of the letterbox clicked and something fell softly onto the floor of the hall. He went and picked up the one letter in its flimsy envelope. He drew out a sheet of cheap lined paper, inscribed in a childish backsloping hand. He gave a great gasp as he read it, and turned red and then pale again.

"What shall I do?" he whispered, clutching the edge of the gas stove. "Oh, my God, what ought I to do? Shall I tell her?"

."John, dear, d'you want any help?" called his wife from her bedroom.

"No, it's nearly ready. I'm just bringing it up. You stay there and keep quiet till the nurse comes."

Then he realized that his problem was shelved until the nurse had come and gone, and putting on the most cheerful face he could, he carried the tray upstairs, and devoted himself to his immediate responsibilities.

The nurse, a big cheerful woman, had gathered up the tools of her trade and bustled away. John turned from shutting the front door to see his wife dressed and coming downstairs.

"I'm all right now, really I am," she said in reply to his protest. "I'd rather be downstairs. The detective said he'd probably be coming in this afternoon. I'd like to see him."

"Did he?" said John distractedly. "When? Do you really feel quite well now?"

"Oh, yes. The nurse has shown me what to do. I feel ever so much better. But you're looking awful, my dear."

"Well—oh, dear, I don't know. Are you really feeling better? Well, perhaps I ought to tell you. Look, this letter came just before lunch. It's all right, it isn't bad news."

Perpetua read it. It ran as follows:

DEAR SIR,

I know a man saw your kid pinched this afternoon, he has plenty of gen but won't hand over under £50, he says send it in £1 notes to I. Sidney, post restant Oxford Street Post Office by return or it will be too late.

If you tell the cops he don't think he can save the kid.

Yours sincerely
A. WELL-WISHER

"Oh, John!" She flung her arms round his neck. "John, it's going to be all right! Have you sent it off?"

"Sent it off? You mean to the police? No, I haven't. I thought as Ringwood was coming this afternoon—"

"To the police? But, John, it says they can't save her if the police are told. Have you been to the bank and got the money?"

"But, Pettie, surely we ought not to send it off? I mean, naturally the writer'd back his demand for money with threats, wouldn't he? Surely it's the police we have to trust."

"John, the police haven't done any good at all so far. But the man who wrote this letter knows something, you can see he does. We can't risk losing touch with him. He says we must send the money by return or it will be too late. For God's sake—go out to the bank and draw the money now. Go on, quick!"

She pushed at him with both her hands. He still looked miserably uncertain and did not move.

"The bank's shut, anyhow. Do be sensible, my dear. Of course I want to do everything to get her back, of course I do, but don't you see? This may be a hoax. It may just be someone who's read about Perdita being taken. It can't be an honest man. And surely, surely, it's our public duty to report this. Why it's practically blackmail."

"Our public duty!" cried his wife hysterically. "What's that got to do with it? I wish the bank wasn't shut. How can we get the money?"

"Do be sensible, Pettie. Surely we ought to show the letter to the police. It's a valuable clue. If we don't say anything and just send off the money, we may hear nothing more, and then we'll have lost the chance. Not to mention fifty pounds."

"D'you mean you wouldn't risk the money? Oh, John, it can't be that! You *can't* be thinking about money at a time like this!"

John winced and turned pale, as if she had struck him with a knife. Tears of pain and indignation came into his eyes.

"How *can* you!" he whispered in a choked voice. "How *can* you say such a thing?"

The doorbell rang and they heard the front door handle turn.

"Hullo!" said Richard Ringwood, strolling into the room. "Hope you didn't mind my coming straight in. I've got such a lot to tell you. When did you get back, John?"

Perpetua had slipped the letter into her pocket. The envelope still lay on the arm of the chair. They both stood tongue-tied.

"Have I come at a bad moment?" Richard had immediately felt the tension and had noticed John's pallor and the unshed tears in his eyes. "I can come back later if you like."

"No, don't go," said John, trying to speak normally. "We're—we're upset, of course, and my wife isn't very well. She's just had a nurse with her. But of course we want to hear everything."

Richard sat down. He picked up the envelope that was lying on the arm of his chair and turned it abstractedly between his fingers as he spoke. The two parents also sat down, on the edges of their chairs.

"Well, you may not think it's good news, for we haven't found her yet. But we're working on three lines, and two of them seem fairly promising. We haven't traced the man with the foreign accent that you found wandering about the house yesterday, Mrs. Link…"

Perpetua released her pent-up breath with a hardly perceptible sound.

"…but we found the old gypsy woman. And Mrs. Luke's nanny has disappeared, and her sister too. We're following that up now."

Richard felt, he could not tell why, that the Links took little interest in the gypsy and the nanny.

"Where've they gone? London?" asked John.

"I wish I knew. Why London particularly?"

"I don't know. Just an idea." To cover his confusion, John changed the subject. "We're so grateful to you for taking the case on. I ought to have said so before. We know that if anyone can find Perdita, you can. But tell us—please, before you start on details—do you really, honestly think you can? Because if not—well, I don't know. It just doesn't make sense. Even if we have another baby, it won't be the same—and how do we know she'd be safe, either? One feels so helpless. It's—it's—"

"Poor chap," said Richard. "It's the uncertainty, isn't it?"

"Yes, and feeling it's not in our hands. Oh, I don't mean that, Richard, old man. You know how grateful we are, we're sure that if anyone can find her, you can, but…" He was plucking feverishly at the stuff of his armchair.

"Well, if you want my personal advice," said Richard, "I can only say wait, and don't let it get you down. There really is a chance, you know. And surely it's better to wait for a bit than to make up your mind to the worst. But I think what you really want is my professional opinion, isn't it?"

"Yes! Yes, please. Your absolutely frank opinion."

"Well, this is actually the first case of kidnapping that I've dealt with. Don't look alarmed. I know the general pattern; we read each other's' reports, you know. There are three classical motives for kidnapping. First, ransom money. If this is the reason, you'll be asked for money soon. Don't pay it. Let us know at once. You're much more likely to get your baby back if you do. Secondly, desire to possess a baby. Bereaved mothers or childless women with a strong maternal instinct have been known to steal other people's babies. That's why I went to the gypsy camp—gypsies still think babies are worth having in bulk. But I drew a blank, as I'll tell you presently. Thirdly, lunatics. In that case of course it's not done from rational motives at all, so it's harder in a way to trace—only they don't usually take very efficient precautions, so they very often give themselves away."

"Do—do you mean a—a lunatic may have got hold of Perdita? Oh, God!"

"It's only a remote possibility, and it doesn't necessarily mean ill treatment, you know. Most lunatics are only violent towards people they're afraid of. And you notice I put it third on the list. Money is at the bottom of most crimes. Now I want to ask you some questions. You can help me a lot if you answer them carefully."

"Yes! Yes, of course. Anything."

"Well, first of all, have you any enemies? Think carefully."

"I—I don't think so. I've always been very careful to keep on good terms with everyone, you know. Of course there was Peter Longman—he was in for my Fellowship. But he got one at Cambridge only a term after."

"Yes. Anyone else? Did you ever get anyone sacked from his job?"

"N-no. I voted for cutting down the college servants, but not conspicuously. More than half the Fellows did the same. It was quite uneconomic, the way we were running things."

"Are you on good terms with your family—and your wife's family?"

"Yes. Oh, yes. We don't see them much, you know, but there haven't been any rows. Just a difference of outlook."

"I see. You've given them help when they've needed it?" Richard remembered that Link had been a poor undergraduate.

"Oh, yes. I got my father into a very well-run Home only last year, when my mother died. My sisters can look after themselves, and so can Perpetua's family. They're in business."

"And you're sure no one has a grudge against you?"

Link looked alarmed, but stood his ground. Yes, he was sure. Of course he couldn't pretend everybody liked him, but who could? He'd always rather made a point of getting on with his colleagues.

"Know any mental cases?"

"Not now, no. I had a pupil last year who had a mental breakdown, but he was sent away and I believe he recovered. Of course, *eccentrics*—"

"No, I don't mean eccentrics. We'd be shutting up half the dons at that rate."

John Link's laugh was forced. Richard said:

"It's no good saying I know how you feel, because obviously I can't imagine it. But I'm damn sorry. Now, shall I tell you the details of my investigations so far?"

He told them clearly and systematically, and they both listened with strained attention.

"And so," Richard wound up, "the first thing I shall do is to try to find those girls. I've got their descriptions out already. I've got to wait till eight o'clock this evening to question the booking clerks at the station. As I say, we haven't picked up the foreigner we found wandering about your house, but I hope we shall. If there's any more investigating to be done at the gypsy camp—it can wait. We've done all we usefully can there at present, and they'll be watched."

John looked up.

"Are there any known criminals in Oxford, by the way?"

"Only one bogus financier, as far as the Yard knows. Mrs. Link, I wonder if you can make anything of this?' He rose, took an envelope from his pocket and brought over to her a strip of scorched white knitting. "No, don't touch, it's rather fragile."

"It's—it's—oh, John, it's one of Perdita's little booties, I think. I made her a pair with that pattern. Where did you find it?"

"In the gypsy camp, on the edge of the fire."

"Oh—oh, dear. And Perdita wasn't there?"

"I'm sorry. But will you try to remember? Was Perdita wearing it yesterday?"

"No!" she cried in surprise. "No, of course she wasn't. She had her pink ones on. I made a list of what she was wearing yesterday, as you asked me. Here it is. Those white booties ought to have been in the wash. Wait a minute. I'll go and look in the airing cupboard."

She ran out of the room, and came back with a single tiny sock in her hand. It corresponded in pattern with the fragment.

"Look," she said, "this is the pair to it. But there's another odd bootie in the cupboard. And there's a vest gone, too."

"Where were these things yesterday?"

"On the line by the back door. I know, because I never leave anything over. If it was from the day before, I'd have put it away yesterday."

"Did you hang the things in pairs?"

"I don't know. I usually do, but I suppose I might have made a mistake. Why?"

"Well, if they weren't in pairs somebody—say the gypsy—might have pinched two odd ones thinking they were a pair."

"But why burn them?"

"I've got somebody working on that now"—he drew a deep breath at the sudden inward vision of Clare—"and I'll be able to tell you this evening, perhaps. But if your baby wasn't wearing this sock, its presence in the gypsy camp doesn't necessarily lead us in the right direction." He frowned, and then realized how discouraging he sounded and cast about in his mind for something to comfort their bewildered grief.

"You know how it is in scholarship," he said at last. "You're faced with an apparently insoluble problem. You keep working at it. Sometimes you read round it and sometimes you just stare at it and sometimes you collect parallels. And then suddenly, you see your way right through?"

John's face lightened somewhat. "You did, Richard. I could never see why you gave up your classical stuff. You'd have had your pick of the jobs."

"Well," said Richard, who disliked this sort of remark, "it's just the same in detection, you see. We have to get all the pieces first and then fit them together, and then there's good hope of a solution. By the way, I wish I knew more about your college."

"Why? You surely don't think they're got anything to do with the kidnapping?" exclaimed John in surprise.

Richard laughed. "No, of course not. But they're your most numerous neighbors. One of them might have noticed something. And I like to fill in the background of a case. It's very often in the background that one finds the important point. You couldn't take me into Hall, could you?"

"Yes, do!" said his wife. "Why not tonight? It's your evening for dining in Hall, isn't it, John?"

"I'd rather stay with you, my dear. I don't want to leave you alone."

"I won't be alone. The nurse is coming."

"Well, it would fit in rather well, actually," said Richard. "I've got to hang about to see the booking clerks at the station at eight. And I may not be free after that."

"All right," said John dejectedly. "I mean, of course. I shall be delighted. We dine at seven-fifteen. Will you pick me up in my room at ten past?"

"Thank you, I will. Sure there's nothing else you want to ask me—or tell me?"

He paused, trying to gauge the quality of their silence. "If we think of anything," said John at last, "I can tell you this evening, can't I?"

"M'm. Or ring up the police station. There's no time to be wasted, you know. Well, till then."

The slam of the door and the sound of his own footsteps drowned the flood of whispered conversation that his departure had released.

It was not long after half past four when Richard left the Links' house and began to walk to Clare's lodgings in North Oxford. His way lay past Blackwell's, that noblest of bookshops, and he could not resist dropping in to buy Clare a present. In fact, he became so absorbed in choosing it that when he noticed the time, he hastily bought the four books under his arm and ran all the way from the Broad to Bradmore Road, arriving at the door on the last of the many strokes of five o'clock, thankful that the chimes of Oxford will always give a minority vote to justify a late arrival.

Clare took him to her room at the top of the house. There was a carpet the color of blackberries, and the curtains and covers were striped white and blue. Venetian glass glittered like golden bubbles on the shelves and mantelpiece. She pushed him gently into a big chair and fed him China tea and thin triangular sandwiches. He had much to tell her.

"But how maddening for you not to know where to start looking for that nanny!"

"She'll turn up in the official filter in the end. Though not before we've got scores of wrong ones. But I want to get her now. Time's everything in a case like this."

"Yes. How were the Links taking it?"

"They're absolutely shattered—all on edge—and she was ill, too. They'd had a nurse there. And yet, I don't want to be fanciful, but I felt there was something else upsetting them, something they didn't tell me. I must get at John's bank manager tomorrow. Or tonight. God! Tomorrow may be too late!"

"You'll find the baby, darling. I'm sure you will. Your Sibyl said you would, don't you remember?"

"*Stowed away in the dark, in no man's keeping.* Ugh! Well, if you find that encouraging—"

"Gypsies, by the way," said Clare, producing her notebook.

" 'Ratty, my generous friend,' " said Richard, quoting from *The Wind in the Willows*, " 'I am very sorry indeed for my foolish and ungrateful conduct.' "

" 'Bless you,' " she replied in character, " 'what's a little wet to a Water Rat?' Have you noticed how we have all the same favorite books?"

"Oh, books, yes. I bought us some books today, they're on that chair, but you mustn't look now. I want to hear the results of your valuable research, and time is getting short. Go on and tell me, there's a good child."

"Child! I like that. Why, a Theosophist told me only last week that I was an Old Soul."

"And went on to remind you that you owed him a fiver from a

previous incarnation, I expect. My dear Old Soul, my young and rose-lipped cherub, we really must get on."

"Here it all is," said Clare, taking up some sheets of paper. "First of all, there have been traditional funerals, right up to the war. Here's a list. The best one seems to have been a funeral at Reading in the nineteen-thirties, when they burned a wagon and everything in it, and there's something rather interesting there. Because the man was called Buckland, like the gypsies at Mayfield."

"Yes, that was Plato Buckland's funeral. They're a very ancient stock, aren't they?"

"Yes, so I suppose they'd be conservative about keeping up old customs. Do you know about their burials? It's very curious."

"Remind me," said Richard evasively.

"Well, death is thought of as a pollution. So they do their best not to let anyone die in the wagon, because the wagon would be unlucky after that, you see. They generally rig up a tent nearby and move the dying man into it when they think he can't last much longer—ghastly, isn't it? And they burn the tent afterwards."

"That fits in with what that awful old Gamp at Mayfield told me. Go on."

"They're afraid of handling dead bodies, but also afraid of undertakers—they don't want the privacy of their dead to be infringed—so they often wash and dress the dying man all ready for burial before life is extinct."

"Oh, good for you! This all bears out Mrs. Fox at Mayfield."

"After the body has been laid out," she continued, reading from her notes, "it is often placed on a strip of matting or sack, so that it can be lifted into the coffin at the last minute without being touched. It lies in state in the death tent until the funeral, which is generally as soon as possible, with a candle at its head, washed continually by relatives."

"What?"

"No, *watched*—sorry, couldn't read my writing. The relatives fast before the funeral except for a little bread and water. Now here's something I thought rather beautiful. They often lay a crust of bread on the dead man's breast. It isn't food for the next world. They just think that bread is a holy substance and they often carry a crust about with them to protect them against bad spirits. They call it 'the dear God's bread.'"

"Like Herrick. How does it go? '*In your wallet*'—no.

" '*In your pocket for a trust*

Carrie nothing but a Crust;
For that holy piece of Bread
Charms the danger and the dread.'

It isn't only gypsies. But don't let's get sidetracked."

"Disposal of property," read Clare. "Gypsies do not leave their personal possessions to relatives. Everything except money—and occasionally snuffboxes—is publicly burned. If they aren't burned, then the coffin is made larger than usual and the dead man's property is put in with him."

"Oh, good! I knew there was something to account for the big coffin, only I couldn't remember what it was. Thank goodness we didn't exhume."

"Yes, but that may be cover for something worse, mayn't it?"

"It may. But I'm sure they'd been fasting too. They had that sharp clear look about the eyes. I wonder if they'd have gone so far as that if they were just play-acting."

"But then, what about the sock?"

"Bootie, darling, according to Mrs. Link. Yes, that was Perdita's, sure enough. But the gypsy seems to have taken it off the line."

"But why did she steal it if the baby was dead, already? Could they have stolen it so as to give their baby plenty of ghostly booties in the underworld?"

"I think it was just instinct. Gypsies steal upon instinct. I don't take this point seriously."

"Well, what do you take seriously? When will the key point emerge?"

"It probably has already," he replied wearily. "Real intelligence consists in seeing what's under your nose. I just have intellectual astigmatism, that's all. Is there someone at the door?"

Clare looked out of the window. "It's your sergeant," she said. "Oh, dear, must you go? When shall I see you again?"

"I don't know, darling. I've got so many lines out and there may be a bite any moment. I haven't made a proper report at the station, and I ought to do that. But I'm dining in Hall with Link, because I want to look at his colleagues and see if I can pick anything up there. And I must see the railway people soon after eight. Shall I ring you up some time after dinner?"

"I expect I'll be in," said Clare in an offhand way which did not attempt to conceal sudden and choking anger. "If not, they'll take a message. Better not kiss me, it'll make you late."

She shut the door on him and herself walked blindly into the tea table and fell, breaking some china.

"Are you all right, darling?" said his anxious voice behind her.

"Perfectly, thank you," she replied with difficulty from the floor. "Please don't wait."

She was pulled to her feet violently and held at arm's length.

"Do you think I like it either?" His voice shook. "Do you think I prefer police stations to punts and constables to courtship? It's my job. Shall I give it up? I will if you want me to, but I should be ashamed to the end of my life, and you'd despise me forever. What do you want, you unreasonable creature?" He gave her a gentle shake and she came into his arms.

CHAPTER TEN

PLUMMER WAS sitting at the wheel of the official car when Richard came out, and began zealously disentangling his stomach from the steering wheel and opening the door, his object being to spring out smartly and salute. But Richard had put his head through the left-hand window, so Plummer, with one leg hanging out, had to twist round and try to salute over his own shoulder.

"Hallo, Plummer," said Richard, leaning his arms on the window and smiling. "Flies bothering you? Had some tea?"

Plummer repacked himself into the seat. "Yes, lovely, thank you, sir. There's a message come by phone to the station, sir. It's from the station."

Richard clutched his hair with one hand and held out the other for the typewritten slip that Plummer was offering him. On it was written: "From the stationmaster, G.W.R., to Oxford police. The booking clerks come on duty at 6 P.M. and not at 8 P.M. as stated by an oversight."

"He was ever so sorry, sir. He says there's been so many changes lately, it slipped his mind."

"That's all right." He got into the front passenger seat. "It fits in rather well, really. We'll go to the station now."

Plummer appeared to understand at once, and drove off. At the railway station, Richard tried the down side first, as it led to more seaports. The booking clerk on the down platform had one of those noses that grow straight out of the forehead in a single line of solid bone, and in England always go with impenetrable stupidity. Richard had often wondered whether the Greeks really had noses like that, and if so, how they had managed to be so intelligent. No doubt they could get away with anything. The booking clerk, at any rate was no exception to the English rule. After backing and filling for some minutes, he looked at the photograph. It was upside down. After about eighty seconds he turned it right way up, gazed at it for another minute, and then said, "No, I never see them. But I wasn't here yesterday, sir, of course."

"Where were you, then?"

"On the up side, of course."

"Then who was here?"

"T'other chap, of course." He moved his great head in the direction of the lines. "Chap on the up side."

Richard guessed that the clerks must take it in turns to be on the up or down sides of the station. Having had his guess confirmed, after a pause for thought by the clerk, he crossed the lines by the subway and went into the other booking office. The man there looked quite human, and there was a promising indentation where his nose met his forehead, but it soon became clear from his conversation that he only exercised his mind off duty. People who bought tickets bored him. There were too many of them. They were always in a hurry, and they never had any change. As he delivered himself of these sentiments, looking from time to time at the photograph, the telephone rang beside him. It did not seem to bother him, but presently he picked up the receiver.

"Hold on," he said, and laid it on the table.

"You don't remember an American or Canadian accent?" Richard asked,

"Can't say I do. Wait a minute, though. Come to think of it, there was an American last night, tried to pass off some foreign coin on me for a shilling. I gave it back to him double quick. He didn't like me spotting it, neither."

"Youngish, brown hair, medium coloring?"

"Might be. Can't say I reely looked."

The telephone receiver was emitting loud angry barks.

"I say, hadn't you better answer that thing?" said Richard. "I don't mind waiting."

"I expect he'll ring off in a minute. They mostly do. I do remember one thing, though. He wasn't a black."

"Well, that's something. Do you remember how many tickets he took and where he was going?"

"I'm ever so sorry," he said after a pause. "I just can't remember.

It's no good. They all come at me one after another and I just can't tell the difference. What a shame, I might have had my picture in the paper, mightn't I?"

"Oh, well, they might not have had room. There's always the international situation and the local weddings. Let me know if you remember anything."

"I sure will." The telephone receiver was now silent. He replaced it on its hook, and the bell rang again.

"Hold on," he said, and laid it down.

"I forgot to tell you, sir," said Plummer, when Richard was back in the car. "I rang up 'Arwell like you said, and they said there wasn't anyone called Leslie Gray on their books. Seems funny, don't it?"

"It makes me all the more anxious to find those girls. I don't like the sound of that chap. Let's just go to the other station, too, and show them the photograph. Though I don't believe that anyone who was traveling to Cambridge or Bletchley could possibly be a crook. Still, we'd better make sure."

But no one at the other station remembered the girls. It was now nearly seven o'clock. Richard left another report at the police station, and then told Plummer to drive him to John Link's college.

"I'm dining here, Plummer, with Mr. Link, in the hope of picking up some odds and ends of gossip. I'm afraid you'll have to stay at the station in case any identifications come through. I'm sorry."

"That's all right, sir. It's a nice change after the traffic. Did Miss Liddicote enjoy her day? She's an Oxford lady, isn't she, sir? I've often seen her about. I never forgets a face."

"She's here in term, yes. She lives in Somerset, quite near my father's place."

"Ah," said Plummer in a very deep manner. "Should I let you know if she rings up, sir?"

Richard met his eye, but it was guileless as a cocker spaniel's.

"Thank you," he said, with dignity. "And let me know if they pick up the girls or Gray, won't you? The porter will send a message through to me."

He was just in time to join Link in the procession of the dons into Hall. They shuffled under an arch and up a short stone staircase, and came out on the dais at the end of the dining hall where the High Table stood, bathed in the soft light of shaded table lamps. Half-reflected on the glossy damask of its surface stood great pieces of College plate, ancient saltcellars and tankards with those sapphire shadows that silver acquires after two hundred years of faithful polishing.

Richard, as the only guest that night, was placed next to the Provost in the place of honor. John Link was on his other side, and opposite him there was a very old man and a very young one. The seats were too widely spaced for him to hope for talk with any but these four. Everyone stood at his place and silence fell. The Provost made a signal to the undergraduate at the head of the scholars' table, and he recited a long Latin grace. Then they sat down to the subdued roar of young men's voices, and Richard and the Provost were introduced and began to make polite conversation.

The Provost, a bachelor in his middle fifties, had earned his present laurels by a distinguished career in the civil service and had only recently returned to academic life. His manner was as smooth and impersonal as plate glass, and he talked most readily about administration. Richard elicited from him four criticisms of the way the police force was managed, and agreed with three constructive suggestions, the last abut salaries, on which the Provost was well informed. He thought the country would save money if young policemen were paid less and family allowances for married men were increased.

"I'm glad you're in favor of policemen having families, sir."

"I didn't say that. I said family *allowances*. The point is, that if you step up family allowances you're making a concession which offsets the lower pay for bachelors, but in fact a saving is effected, because no one is going to have any more children with the cost of living on the upgrade."

"Oh, I see." Not families, family allowances. Not children, child guidance. Not houses, housing. Richard realized that the personal details he was hoping to pick up about life in the college would not be learned from its Head, and felt, the whitebait having been removed, that he had at any rate done his duty by the Provost. The Provost thought so too, for he turned to his other neighbor and was soon deep in a discussion about government grants for research.

"I say, John," Richard whispered. "Which are sheep and which, are goats?"

This was an expression they had both learned from the tutor they had shared as undergraduates. Sheep represented the older and goats the newer branches of learning. Their tutor used to say that the sheep had no original ideas and the goats stank, so he was being perfectly fair all round.

"Two goats to your right," said John, with a dreadful forced jaunti-
ness. "Mostly sheep opposite and at my end. Or do mathematicians
count as goats?"

"No, sheep, sheep."

"And Robin Shawyer opposite you. He's a doctor."

The very young man opposite must have had acute hearing, for he
looked up, saying:

"What's this, John? Are you washing my dirty swabs in public?
Shame!"

"It's not as bad as that," said Richard, hoping to start a conversation. "I was asking John which were the scientists and which were the
literary gents."

"Oh, no, you weren't," he replied merrily. "You were asking which
were sheep and which were goats. I know all about Blodger. Don't
count me as a goat, that's all. I'm not, am I?" He appealed to the very
old man beside him.

"My dear Robin"—the voice seemed to well up richly as though
through an immense vat of the oldest College port—"I will vouch for
you absolutely. You are our brightest hope in this increasingly wicked
and cheerless society. You never question the kitchen accounts; you
voted against providing a ladies' lavatory in College; and you have, for
your years, a remarkably sound taste in wine. Have you tried this Burgundy? Do, do. It is young, but noble, and if you appropriate its description to yourself you will do yourself no more than justice. We'd better
have another bottle."

Under eyebrows like mustaches he shot an exploratory glance at
Richard.

"And you, sir? May I introduce myself? I am known as Old Costard. Yes, I am commonly reputed to be eighty-nine, but I should warn
you from the age of forty upwards I have enjoyed a spurious venerabil-
ity, thereby ensuring indulgence for my weaknesses and respect for my
opinions. Try this Burgundy. *Siccis*," he continued, pronouncing in the
anglicized manner, "*omnia nam dura deus proposuit!*" He was somewhat the better for wine.

"Thank you," replied Richard. "Though I suspect that *mordaces
sollicitudines* are the breath of life to a real progressive." He could
hear the Provost telling a great story of mismanagement on his left.

"Well, God bless you, if I may say so without committing myself.
How delightful. Link, my dear man, is this a fellow of King's, Cambridge? He must be. You won't find a man under fifty in this miserable

place who could take a Horatian allusion."

John glanced at Richard, who nodded slightly.

"No, indeed," said John. "He's a detective-inspector of Scotland Yard. We were up together."

Costard chuckled. "*Odora canum vis*, are you? Well, my life is an open book, though not perhaps a book for beginners. You must sit next to me at dessert, and eat a black market banana. You shall tell me about the criminal classes and listen to me vilipending my colleagues. You find us tonight in a particularly happy situation. At least half of us aren't dining."

He applied himself to the *crème brûlée*, which was ambrosial. Richard turned to the Provost and remarked that the rumors of sumptuary legislation in his college seemed to have been greatly exaggerated.

"I didn't know there were any cooks left in England who could come up to this standard."

"Technically, yes, he does very well, but I believe there is a lot of waste, and it is needlessly elaborate. I'd rather have somebody who understood bulk buying and paid some attention to dietary values. But of course that's the Bursar's business. It seems to me that the luxurious standard of living here is quite outdated and militates against efficiency. No government establishment would stand it. I suppose everyone's finished their wine?"

He addressed the last remark to the table at large and took up a small ivory mallet which lay beside his glass of water. Everybody rose (since Richard had already done so), though Dr. Costard seemed inclined to rebel and put on a great show of decrepit senility struggling to his feet. But at last he, too, was standing. The Provost rapped with his mallet and said grace in an authoritative but detached manner. John Link had eaten hardly any dinner and had been looking increasingly wretched and impatient, so Richard whispered to him to go home. He could, in fact, though of course he did not say so, work much more freely without him, and his presence was embarrassing, as he had, it seemed, told no one in College about the kidnapping. John, with obvious relief, handed over his guest to the care of Costard and slipped away to his wife.

Costard led Richard, by a kind of invisible hand, to the common room, and did not relinquish this mysterious grip until he had settled him in one of a pair of armchairs at the window end of the semicircle. There were little tables of fruit in front of them, and the decanters began to go round. Outside, the last of the evening sunlight lay caught in the luminous green of the Fellows' skittle-alley, as it glimmered up between its black box hedges.

Costard's pungent periods ceased as they poured and savored their port. Then Richard glanced up and met his inquiring look.

"You approve? I laid this down myself, twenty years ago, when I was common-room steward. Got it from Chiswick's cellar."

"It's admirable. Though by next year—"

"You're perfectly right. We are not drinking it fast enough, and by next year it will begin to go off. Barbarians, barbarians! But not you, my dear fellow. You, if I may say so, are a man after my own heart. I am sure you are wasting your talents in London." This was Richard's opening, and he took it not very adroitly.

"I wonder if you would think it out of place for me to ask your advice about a case?"

"On the contrary"—he was now in a state of ponderous benevolence—"like the ancient Persians, I prefer to give counsel at night. Unlike those misguided Asiatics, I am averse from revising it in the morning. Say on."

"I am engaged upon a criminal case," said Richard, unconsciously falling into his partner's Gibbonian manner, "in which the crime seems to be inexplicable unless committed from motives of personal animosity. John Link's baby has been kidnapped."

Costard looked blank.

"I should need to have drunk rather more or rather less than I have," he said in a colorless voice, looking away, "to feel as I should about this news. But, of course, if I can give you any practical help—"

"Indeed you can. That's why I ventured to introduce the topic. Port, sir? Yes, as I say, apart from personal animosity, I can't understand it. But Link swears that he hasn't got any enemies. Do you think that is really so?"

Costard settled back more comfortably and reflected.

"His independent actions, on the one hand," he said, "could never make him any enemies, since to the best of my belief, they do not occur. On the other hand, his part in joint actions, such as voting, and his philosophical support given to this or that school of thought, may have earned him dislike in some quarters. Still, one could hardly imagine revenge taking so violent, and, I may add, so inconvenient a form, especially in England. On the continent, now, somebody might have thought Link's little *volte-face* in Congregation was a personal matter. But here, everyone of any importance realized that he had merely gone over to the more influential party. He is not without charm, that young man, but also not wholly able to conceal his perfectly natural ambition."

"What was the *volte-face*?"

"Oh, he helped me to defeat a P.P.S. measure a week ago. You've heard of P.P.S.? Our new Honor School, you know—Psychology, Politics, and Sociology. It is a shortcut to highly paid bureaucratic employment; one starts place-hunting three years earlier than the others. A detestable abuse of university studies. Well, a powerful faction in P.P.S. were trying to introduce experimental psychology, and they wanted to use undergraduates as their guinea pigs. Yes, that was their monstrous proposal, to obtain unlimited license to manipulate the minds of their wretched pupils. I was against it, of course. But I was the worst possible man to oppose it openly. I have a certain reputation as a diehard, despite the fact that, as you see, I am dying quite easily and pleasurably—but that is by the way. I therefore selected Link as my protagonist, since he was known to have left-wing sympathies and an austerely social conscience. But I knew he was a good fellow at heart. I selected him, I say. I gave him some good port and introduced him to one or two of my friends—in short, I persuaded him to oppose the measure. He made a speech along the lines I had indicated, but better, my dear fellow, far more eloquent than I had dared to expect!"

"He knew his Cicero pretty well when we were up together."

"Just so, just so. A good rhetorical training is never lost. How right you are! Well, as I say, he defeated the motion. And since then I have had cold looks from the P.P.S. But I don't suppose anyone is fool enough to blame poor Link." He chuckled.

The common-room scout approached Richard at this moment and whispered to him that the police wanted him on the telephone. Hope and excitement rose in Richard as he took his leave.

"I'm afraid I must go," he said. "Something new has come in. Will you lunch with me at the Mitre one day soon and go on with this very interesting conversation?"

"The conversation," he said, with a pontifical nod, "I would gladly continue. Luncheon, I fear, I must decline. My brain is not at its best till later in the day, so I confine myself to teaching during the morning. You must come and drink with me some night soon."

It was Plummer on the telephone, rather flustered and loud.

"Hallo! Hallo, sir? Is that Inspector Ringwood?…Can you hear me, sir?…This is me, Sergeant Plummer. Mrs. Luke has just rung up, sir. She wanted you particular…No, she wouldn't leave a message. She said would you ring her back?…Very good, sir. I'll bring the car round at once."

Richard rang off and turned to the porter. "Could you get me Mrs. Luke, 51 Merton Street? It is rather urgent, or I wouldn't bother you."

The porter manipulated the various knobs of the complex machine, and handed Richard the receiver in a remarkably short tune.

"Oh, is that Mr. Ringwood? I wanted to tell you that Nanny rang up." The slow warm voice was quite undistorted. "Yes, about five minutes ago."

"Where from? What did she say?"

"Well, she didn't say anything. I thought it was so queer. The telephone rang and I answered it, and they told me to hold on for a call from Liverpool. Then I heard Nanny's voice. She said, 'Hallo, this is Nanny. Is that Mrs. Luke?' and then there was a sort of click and the line went dead. She sounded so worried."

"Did you notice the time?"

"Well, Harold did, and he told me to write it down. It was eight twenty-five by our clock."

"You're sure it was her voice, are you? Good. Well, thank you very much for letting me know. I'll have the call traced at once. Goodbye."

Richard rang up the exchange and asked them to trace the call from Liverpool and report it to the police station. Then he went out into the street and found Plummer just driving up in the car. He jumped in and had himself taken to the police station at once.

He had not waited very long when the exchange told him that the call had been traced to a public telephone box in Liverpool. "And Liverpool's on the line for you now. Will you hold on to take the call?"

"You bet I will," said Richard blithely. "Plummer, is there plenty of petrol in the car? Go and see, there's a good chap. Yes, Inspector Ringwood speaking—shut that door, blast you!—yes, I can hear you."

It was the Liverpool police. A man and a girl, corresponding to the official descriptions of Ivy and Gray, had taken passages on a small cargo steamer that was to sail for Lima at four-thirty that morning. The clerk had sold them their tickets before being questioned by the police, so no one had kept track of them. The ship was called the *Santa Rosa*.

"This is the sixth couple corresponding to the description that we've had reported to us," said Richard, "but the girl's sister seems to have just rung up from Liverpool, so it looks as if you'd scored the bull's-eye. I'll put the name of the chap who spotted it in my report. Now listen,

I'm coming to Liverpool at once, and I hope to arrive before the *Santa Rosa* sails. But I want that ship watched. Get the passenger list, and check the passengers in. You'd better station a man on the wharf, and give him a warrant to look over the ship first. Where is she berthed, and how do I get to her? Right, I'll be with you as soon as I can."

Next he dialed Clare's number and told her the news.

"So goodbye till tomorrow. What are you doing now? I want to imagine you."

"I'm reading the books you brought. The natural history one's frightfully good."

"Yes, I thought it could be the foundation of our nursery library. Which do you want first, a boy or a girl?"

"Both. Twins. Darling, you won't drive too fast, will you? And come back soon."

He went out to the sergeant.

"Plummer," he said. 'We're going to drive to Liverpool Yes, now. Have you had any food?"

"Not since my tea, barring a cup of cocoa."

"Well, go to the nearest pub and get lots of sandwiches and put them in the car. I believe we're on to something at last."

CHAPTER ELEVEN

THEY WERE all ready to start and Richard had one leg in the car when he slapped himself on the forehead.

"Maps! We want road maps. Do you know the shortest way to Liverpool? I don't."

"There should be some maps in this pocket, sir."

"Berkshire, Hampshire…No, that's no good. All right, I'll go myself."

He dashed back into the building and presently returned with one of those books of road maps where you lose your place every time you turn the page. But at least it covered the right counties.

"Got it out of the lost property," he explained briefly. "Now, we'll take it in turns to drive. What's your bedtime, Plummer?"

"About half past nine, sir, as a rule. My old woman's got a bad leg, see, and it plays her up a bit by the evening. Saves the light, too, if we go up in good time. But don't worry, sir, I shan't get sleepy till after eleven. I generally hears it strike before I go off."

"Well, you'd better take your turn first, while you're fresh, and I'll be working out the route. Drive as fast as you can."

"I once got up to sixty on my motorbike, sir, when I was a young chap. Ah, I was half the size then, a regular shrimp. I've had to give it up now, of course. Too much wind resistance, as they say." He belched. "Pardon. Ah, it's a treat to have a car like this to drive. You needn't be afraid of me getting sleepy, not with a job like this."

He did drive very well and made good time, though Richard longed to go faster and sat nervously fidgeting with the map. Plummer slowed up conscientiously for crossroads and built-up areas, sat bolt upright, and used the horn frequently. He looked blissfully happy. At eleven o'clock Richard told him to stop.

"Try to get some sleep," he said. "I don't expect we'll get to bed tonight. I'll wake you up when I've had enough."

He took the driver's seat, and the car was like a horse changing from a canter to a gallop. It tilted as it roared round corners, it seemed to leap into the air as it skimmed over humped bridges, it darted perilously through narrow places, while the headlights picked out a lightning succession of bushes, cottages, and trees that looked flat and oversimplified, like stage scenery, against the blackness behind. Richard drove with all his attention, remembering the map which he had been at such pains to learn by heart while Plummer was driving, and always going rather faster than he dared. In the back of his mind there was the feeling of his little mare under him, galloping, galloping over the treacherous Quantock Hills with their potholes and hidden streams, the unexpected hedge looming at him, his desperate looking along it for a gap, and his father's eye on him watching for the jump, the sickening moment when the mare's back rose almost vertical and her hind legs left the earth, the sharp flints on the ground the other side of the hedge with the cold light lying wickedly on them; then down again and on, and his father's eye still on him, and he riding faster and faster for fear they should think he was afraid. He always left the other little boys far behind, but his father never praised him. Still now in his police work, and particularly at times like this, he would be that boy again, hurling himself forward trying to reach his own impossible standard, and never, as he thought, doing quite well enough. And then suddenly, above his own intense conscious effort and above the unrecognized subconscious ache, he heard Clare's clear childish voice over the telephone. "You won't go too fast, will you? And come back soon."

He smiled, relaxed his pressure on the accelerator and looked at his watch. It was nearly two o'clock, and there were lights ahead. A sign advertised coffee and snacks all night, and he stopped the car outside the hut, and looked at Plummer. He was sleeping like a baby, with his small fat hands folded across his stomach. Richard nudged him.

"Is it bad again, my duck?" Plummer murmured drowsily. "Never mind. I'll make you a nice cuppa tea." He struggled awake, and looked up surprisedly. "Sorry, sir. I thought I was…Did you want me to drive?"

"What about a cup of coffee first? It's getting cold now, and we've got plenty of time in hand."

They went into the hut, empty except for the proprietor, a rheumy despondent man fiddling with a defective wireless set that moaned and whistled. His jaw dropped at the sight of Plummer's uniform, and he served them quickly and timidly with a hot tasteless drink made with treacly coffee essence. Richard paid. They drank it down in silence and returned to the car.

"Think he had some real drinks under that counter?" asked Richard casually, as he eased his long legs into the passenger's seat.

"It's feasible," said Plummer. "But ordinary chaps like him, they don't like the uniform. I've noticed it before. It makes them feel funny like. Don't mean no harm necessarily."

"No. I suppose we've got to get used to being feared by half our fellow men and despised by the other half," said Richard bitterly. "Part of the job, what?"

"Ah, but it's only before they gets to know you, sir, isn't it? Now my dad, he was a butcher's assistant, and would you believe it? He was twenty-six before he could get my Mum to marry him. And it was all on account of him having a humane killer. She couldn't bear to think of it, it turned her up, like. Still, when she did finally come round, he'd saved up forty pounds for the furniture, so maybe it was just as well in the end."

"How old were you when you married?" Richard asked. They must think we're absolutely bats to wait so long, he thought.

"Twenty-one, sir," said Plummer proudly. "But we was lucky."

"Got any children?"

"Two married daughters, sir. We 'ad a boy, but he was killed in the war. At Dunkirk, it was. The Oxford and Bucks got cut off."

"Yes, I remember. Bad luck. Fork right at the next turn."

They were silent, Plummer because he was tired, and Richard because he was uncomfortable to have touched on so sore a subject. Decent working people roused in him a kind of envious admiration; they went straight for life without havering. If he'd been a working man, he'd have asked Plummer more about the boy, and Plummer would have liked to tell him. Yes, and if he was himself a working man, he'd have had a child of ten by now. Thirty-three, and what had he to show for it? Then he suddenly smiled, remembering Clare's thin legs and yellow pigtails when he was twenty-three. So that's why I didn't marry. Good enough.

He sat watching the route and giving directions from time to time, and at three took the wheel again, driving carefully. They had run into the soft misty rain of a west-country night; the wheel was clammy and the headlights blurred. It as not yet dawn when they came into Liverpool, a great amphitheater of dim lights round the dark glitter of the harbor. At the top of the amphitheater was the prosperous district; bourgeois respectability drowned in sleep, streets of yellow-brick villas of the last century with all their windows dark. The bright streetlights picked out here a stained-glass window flanked by imitation arrow slits, there a conservatory with crocketed pinnacles and flying buttresses. Soon they began to wind down the hill, and the town became shabbier, more wakeful, and more beautiful. They saw fewer lampposts and more lighted windows. The ships' sirens sounded near and melancholy. They passed by Great Homer Street and Great Virgil Street, and were soon in the heart of Irish Town, lying on the lower slopes of the amphitheater, where the lovely Georgian houses, mansions of the great slave traders of that time, teeming with tenement life behind their curtainless and broken windows, stood in a square like a beautiful ruined face, with toothless gaps where the bombed houses had been. There they saw a pair of policemen on patrol and asked their way to the dock where *Santa Rosa* lay. The policemen had heard of their search and were interested and full of information. As they talked, the streetlamp spluttered overhead. There was a scream and a burst of angry shouts from the house above them. The policemen took no notice. A lean cat scuttled past them with some dripping abomination in its muzzle, and slipped furtively down an area.

Richard drove on, following their directions, till he came to the waterfront. There was the dock as they had told him. It had a wooden fence round it and a locked gate in the fence. By the gate and inside the fence was a hut. Richard rapped on the gate.

"Anyone there? Police!"

A harbor official came out of the hut and unlocked the gate. Richard, calling over his shoulder to Plummer to lock the car, went through and was met by a policeman in uniform, nearly as tall as himself and perhaps ten years younger.

"Inspector Ringwood?"

"Yes," said Richard, showing his card and returning the salute.

"P.C. Thomas, sir. They put me on to watching the ship." Richard introduced Plummer and they moved away from the hut.

"Didn't expect you yet, sir. You must've come pretty quick."

"We made reasonably good time. Well, any sign of Gray and the girl?"

"Not yet. She's a small ship, as you see, and there's only been nine passages booked. Here's the list. I got it from the captain. You see there's four British—Mr. and Mrs. Gray, Gutch, Mr. Jessop—the rest are foreigners."

"Have you been over the ship?"

"Yes, sir. I did that at nine o'clock. Your couple weren't on board."

"You're sure of that?"

"Yes, sir. I know how to search a ship—my father's in the Merchant Navy—and I went over her thorough, with two other men to help me."

Richard liked his assurance and his stolid ruddy face.

"Four of the passengers are on board already," he went on. "There's a lady teacher, a Miss Gutch—she's middle-aged—and a Greek commercial traveler, and there's two invalids—a Venezuelan who came to England for an operation, and a Mr. Jessop. He's an R.C. priest, and if you ask me, he's got T.B. pretty bad. He's got a friend on board seeing him off. Their papers were all right."

"Did you see the friend's papers?"

"There now, I never wrote down his name. But his papers were O.K., sir, and he doesn't tally with the description. He's a big broad man with a beard. And, anyhow, you can see he's the right sort. He's just come out of the army."

"What sort of ship is it?"

"Mixed cargo. The skipper's from Lima." He grinned. "Had a bit of trouble with him, I did. He's a little man with a big mustache and a hell of a temper, and he's as cross as two sticks because he's had to sail a day late on account of the dock strike. And then there was something about his owner not having turned up. He seemed to think it was all my fault, and he didn't want to let me on board. He don't speak English, either, and the crew are all afraid of him. So I don't know if they really explained properly, though there were plenty of them standing round having a try. I did get one thing, though, because he kept on saying it. Nothing's going to stop him sailing at four-thirty. If he said that once he said it twenty times."

"Oh, well, I don't see why he shouldn't. We're only interested in these two passengers, and you say they're not on board. What's the crew like?"

"Mixed—mostly South Americans, with a Dutchman or two and a few Lascars. Shall I take you aboard?"

Richard reflected. He was sure that the man had conducted the search thoroughly, and though he itched to have something to do, he felt that this was hardly a reason for disturbing the irascible captain further. The ship looked very small—even rather cozy—and lay close to the quay in the deep oily water with two gangplanks fore and aft connecting her with the shore. There were lights behind a few of the portholes and a thread of smoke from the funnel.

"What sort of time will the rest of the passengers arrive, do you suppose?"

"Can't say, really, with these small ships. They do as they like, you see. It's not like the liners where everything's cut and dried. There's one thing you can bet, though. The South Americans will be late. They always are. That's why the captain's so mad. He's swearing he'll go without them if they don't come on time. Well, sir, I don't reckon anything'll happen till it's light. Why don't you go and sit in the hut by the gate there and keep warm? I can keep a look out, and the gate's locked anyway."

"You take my sergeant over," said Richard. "I'd rather stay out here. What about those sandwiches in the car, Plummer?"

"Wouldn't come amiss, would they, sir? I'll get them. But what about you?"

"I'm not hungry."

This was an understatement; the very thought of food sickened him. He hated nothing so much as waiting on watch in the small hours of the morning, and there was much of it in his kind of work. One began with a sense of high adventure, but soon it was replaced by weary impatience, and that in turn led to self-mistrust. He would miss his man, or find it was a wild-goose chase. He moodily watched Plummer and Thomas go into the watchman's hut and turned towards the darkness to wrestle with his hopes and despairs. Tall and hunched like a crow in his gray raincoat, he strolled out towards the water. The lamps were very few here, making yellow oily pools of light on the moist paving stones, with cheerless dark spaces between. He came to the desolate quayside, and climbed down a flight of dank slippery steps until the sea was lapping at his feet. The water was foul with the jetsam of a port. Shining his torch on its surface, he made out an empty ice-cream carton, a bloodied clout, and a sodden Palm Sunday cross.

"Wonderful material for a realistic novel about Liverpool," he thought gloomily. "It'll keep me occupied when I get chucked out of the Force."

He climbed slowly up again and sat on a bollard. He thought about Clare. She seemed infinitely desirable, but so far away that he could hardly imagine her; he could only tell himself that she was like this and had said that. He lit a cigarette. The taste disgusted him at that hour but was somehow comforting. He began trying to recite *Lycidas* to himself, but the gaps in his memory troubled him; he had once known it by heart. A dirty dawn was beginning to break.

There was a knock at the gate and the watchman let three figures through. They came slowly across the paved space towards the ship. One was an Indian, smartly dressed in the height of European fashion except for his turban; there was a moist purplish pit where his left eye had been. Walking by his side with small steps was an aged Chinese man in a long black overcoat with a fur collar turned up round his ears, and his hands tucked into his sleeves, so that his arms looked if they were a continuous semicircle from shoulder to shoulder. A huge pale mulatto came behind them, carrying two suitcases, but presently stopped and stood propped against a lamppost while the other two strolled on. The yellow artificial light caught the whites of his eyes and the pockmarks on his cheek.

"Nothing for me there," thought Richard, "unless you count it as more material for a novel—a thriller this time—when I get chucked out of the Force. The mysterious Oriental, and all that. Of course he may have hypnotized the girl into seeing him as a Canadian. But I doubt if even the reading public would swallow that. Oh, lord, lord, if only something would happen!"

He went over to the watchman's shelter and met Plummer coming out.

"I was just bringing you a cup of tea. It's cold, isn't it? Sit down and warm yourself, now do, sir. I'll tell you if anyone stirs."

Richard went into the smoky warmth of the hut and drank the strong bitter tea.

"Who were those three that came in then?" he asked the Liverpool policeman.

"The Chinese was a passenger. His passport was O.K. He had a friend with him and a Lascar with his luggage. I didn't ask for their papers."

"Quite right. You can't fake up any European to look like those three, can you? What a lot of nationalities for one small ship."

"Well, we get used to that here in Liverpool. My dad said there was only one place to beat it for variety, and that was Marseilles, and he'd been all over the world. It makes it pretty difficult for the police, though."

"Yes, I was in Limehouse for a couple of years, so I know what you mean. I say, how easy would it be to get on to one of these docks without going through the gate?"

"Easy enough from the water, if you can pick up a boat. There's a lot of couples do that and spend the night behind the warehouses, I'm afraid. We can't keep track of them."

"What about the landward side? Are there any loopholes there?"

"I don't think so. There was one weak place in the fence, but I got it patched up. When the gate's open, people might slip through with the luggage; it's a big gate, as you see, but it's been locked ever since I went over the ship."

"You don't miss much, do you? How did you manage to patch up the fence?"

"Brought a bit of wire down on the chance, sir. I knew what to expect."

The ship's engines, which had been running gently, now began to make more noise. The sound brought them both to their feet and out into the open.

"Ah, she's getting up steam," Thomas remarked. "Engines not so good, neither, by the sound of them. I reckon the skipper's worried he'll catch the wind broadside on before he's got enough way on her."

"Why?"

"The wind's dead against her, blowing straight inshore, so the tide won't be running very strong."

"Does that matter, for a steamship?"

"Ah, I remember asking my Dad that question. 'Sonny,' he said, 'they may turn ships into things like tractors and tanks, but they won't turn the sea into an arterial road.' He was in sail when he was young. But I reckon he was right. A man has to study the sea, even under steam. You'll see; he'll try to get off quickly once the tide's with him."

"But they can't go without the passengers, surely?"

"There's not a blessed thing that skipper can't do if he's made up his mind to it. He's properly worked up. If you'd seen him, you'd know what I mean." He grinned. "Why, there he is now."

A small squat figure had appeared on what Richard supposed to be the bridge (or was it the quarterdeck?). From his mouth there poured, like stuttering volleys from machine-gun, the brassy, equally stressed syllables of an angry Latin male. The handful of seamen on deck bustled about where they had lounged till now. Richard looked at his watch and saw that it was a quarter past four.

"Go on board again, will you, and have a last look round? I want to make quite sure that nobody sneaked up with a boat in the night."

"The old man won't like it," said the constable wryly, between amusement and alarm.

"I know. I'm afraid you won't like it much, either. Sorry. I'd go myself, but you're the one that knows about ships, and we've got to be quick, if the captain's really in such a hurry to get off."

The constable saluted, squared his shoulders, and tramped across, watched by Plummer, the Indian, the Chinese, and the Lascar. His feet rang hollowly on the wood as he marched up the forward gangway, and he was greeted by a fresh burst of American Spanish, remarkable in volume and continuity. The Lascar, in obedience to a murmured command from the old Chinese, took up the two big suitcases and carried them up the forward gangway in the policeman's wake. He slid behind him and disappeared into the bowels of the ship. Thomas, after a short and inaudible (on his part) altercation with the captain, followed him. More and more of the crew swarmed over the deck, and the shabby, crazy little ship quivered and plunged to the throb of her noisy engines. A tall thin man in black, with a gray muffler over his mouth and chin and a black hat, came up on deck, supported by a square bearded man in a British warm, who held his arm. They paced slowly to the head of the after gangway and stood there.

"That'll be the priest with T.B., and his friend," thought Richard. "Five more passengers to come."

He beckoned to Plummer, and shouted against the noise of the engines and the clamor.

"Go and stand at the foot of that gangway"—he pointed to the after gangway—"and don't let anyone on to the ship till I say you can."

Plummer trotted along and took up his position. Richard placed himself at the foot of the forward gangway. The ship's siren let off two deafening blasts, and the captain began to shout through a megaphone. Richard could see his great curling mustaches and observe the neck of a bottle sticking out of his pocket, as he held his megaphone in one hand and shook his clenched fist at Richard, and then at the Chinese and the Indian, who were still pacing in gentle conversation. The Indian seemed about to reply, but the Chinese, with a deprecating smile, bowed to him and proceeded with small steps and unimpaired dignity up the forward gangway, his hands still tucked up his sleeves. Richard did not ask him for his papers. Those slanting eyes, those flat cheekbones and thin curving whiskers convinced him even more at close quarters that so fine a national type must be genuine. At the top of the gangway, the Celestial turned, bowed again to the Indian, shook his joined hands in final greeting, and disappeared below.

The captain was now bellowing with all the force of his lungs at someone on land. Richard looked behind him and saw to his horror that the dock gate was standing wide open. A barrow piled with suitcases and hatboxes was being trundled through it, pushed by a porter. Three people followed and approached the ship.

There was a man in his thirties with brown hair and a fair skin. He was of middle height. With him was a woman in black, with a bushy fox fur hiding the lower part of her face. She had extremely fair hair and wore huge dark sunglasses with yellow frames. A smaller, darker man walked behind him. But it was the fair couple that made Richard's heart beat so fast. They corresponded to the descriptions of Ivy Turner and Leslie Gray.

He advanced to meet them.

"I'm from the police. May I see your passports, please?"

"Sure, sure," said the man in a strong American accent. "But make it snappy, carp. We're just about doo. We sail at four-thirty."

He handed Richard a passport and then, rather unexpectedly, began to answer the captain's angry shouts in Spanish. The Lascar who had taken the Chinese's suitcases on board came ashore again and began to carry the new lot of luggage from the barrow up the gangway on to the ship. He used Plummer's gangway, and Plummer, at a nod from Richard, allowed him to do so. But Richard stood with his back to his own gangway, guarding it while he looked at the passport.

The passport was Peruvian, and bore the names of Juan and Pilar Riviero, as husband and wife. The husband's picture was just recognizable as a bad photograph of the man in front of him, but the woman's depicted a black-haired, heavy-eyed girl quite unlike the blonde who accompanied him.

"Take off your hat and fur and spectacles, please." He would have liked to ask her to wipe off the heavy makeup too, and to show her real skin color, but felt that that would be going too far. The woman stood quite still and did not remove her disguises or answer him. The man, on the other hand, came up angrily and stuck out his chin under Richard's nose. He had to stand on tiptoe to do so.

"Say you," he hissed. "Listen. That's plenty from you, fresh egg. Quit foolin' around and gimme my passport, or it'll be just too bad for you."

The captain weighed in with another volley of curses, pleas, and threats, and some sailors, at an order from him, stood by to pull up the gangways. The fair man looked really alarmed.

"Hey!" he called out in ringing tones to the gatekeeper. "C'm arn over and take this carp outa my hair. Tell 'm I'm O.K. Hell, I'm a part-owner of the boat. You can't do this to me."

The man from the gate came running across, shouting: "I've seen him before, sir, he's all right. He often sails in the *Santa Rosa*, and he always arrives late."

"Hell, I do nart," said, the man. "The captain always starts before skedool."

"Do what I ask, and you can leave at once," said Richard sharply. "Hi, you!" he addressed the little dark man. "Your passport, please."

"Hell, he's my typewriter," said the fair man. "O.K., Pedro, give'm your passport and scram up that plank."

"All right," said Richard, checking it and handing it back. "Now, madam, your glasses off, please." Then, as she still did not move, he whipped them off with a light accurate gesture that tilted her hat off her forehead. It was a bitter disappointment. There stood revealed before him a black-eyed woman of well over thirty, with dyed hair, purplish-black at the roots, gazing at him stupidly. Her husband was abusing him, though keeping his distance, and the captain was fulminating from the ship. Richard felt angry and extremely foolish.

"I'm sorry, I'm sorry. A mistake. You can go now. Better hurry, perhaps? Very sorry to have held you up."

He stood aside and they hastened up the gangplank, muttering vengefully. The gatekeeper was mumbling something beside him.

"What's that? Why aren't you back at your gate?"

"I said that gentleman's well known to me," said the man peevishly. "And we've special instructions not to upset the Americans. I wouldn't a let him through if he hadn't a been O.K. I know my job. What d'you think I'm here for?"

"Minding the gate, I hope. Go back at once, blast you! Hurry up!"

The man slouched off, going slowly on purpose, and looking back over his shoulder every third step. Richard heard a creak and a jolt close behind him, and turned. The sailors were beginning to haul in the gangplank behind him.

"Hi, wait!" cried the voice of P.C. Thomas, as he came up from below and pushed his way across the deck to the gangplank. "Let me get ashore, you silly bastards!"

He scattered the simian little sailors and began to lumber hastily down the plank. But it tilted under him, for it was coming away and no longer rested squarely on the dockside. He was scared, and made up his mind to jump for it while there was still any firmness under his feet. He landed in Richard's arms, knocking him to his knees. Richard gripped him hard as he swayed back on the rebound, and only just managed to save him from falling into the water.

As they were still struggling apart and to their feet, both winded, there was a scurry of feet behind them, and over his shoulder Richard saw that a man and a girl were running towards the after gangplank, which Plummer was guarding. The man carried a basket trunk. The girl had on a long dress under her tweed coat. They were both so near the after gangplank that Richard saw that he could not reach it in time himself.

"Stop her! Stop her," cried a woman's voice from the gate.

"Stop them, Plummer!" shouted Richard, without looking round. He saw Plummer stretch his arms wide to bar their passage. "Not like that, Plummer! Use your fists! Go and help him, Thomas!"

But it was too late. The man struck brutally at Plummer's belly with the basket trunk, and Plummer went over like a ninepin, knocking his head on the ground, and lay still. The couple were on the after gangway now, and Thomas had not yet reached it, The siren was sounding a last sustained note. Richard had to make his decision quickly and he decided to stick to the girl, whatever the consequences. He was so sure that the girl was Ivy and she had looked so frightened. The only thing to do was to board the ship himself, since the girl could no longer be prevented from doing so. The gangplank by which he had been standing was pulled more than halfway back on board by now. He made a running jump, leaped the five-foot gap from the quay to the end of the gangway, landed on all fours, and scrambled up on to the deck. But before the swarm of little sailors engulfed him, he had just time to see, with bitter satisfaction, that he had acted unnecessarily. The girl was on shore again, lying, with dangling arms and legs, in the arms of a broad man with a beard, and P.C. Thomas was standing by her. So much Richard saw, and then he turned and began to push his way towards the captain, while the ship moved away from the dock and out across the wide harbor.

It had been the bearded man who unexpectedly saved the situation when the three policemen failed. Standing by the priest chatting at the head of the after gangway, he had taken his leave and was just going ashore, when he saw the hysterical girl being half-dragged across to the ship. He saw Plummer attempt to stop them. He saw him fall and heard the agonized female voice crying from the gate "Stop her! Oh, stop her!" and he acted instantly. He ran down the after gangway and met the couple halfway across. He seized the man as if he were a doll and threw him hard on to the boards behind him. His shoulder struck the wood heavily. The girl staggered as her partner was wrenched away from her, turned, and tripped on her long pink skirt. But the big bearded man had her by the waist. He held her up like a child before him and ran down the gangway with her to the shore. The sailors hauled the gangway in on deck and helped the prostrate man to his feet, and the ship drew off from the land.

The constable looked around him bewildered.

"Where's the inspector? He was there a minute ago. What's happened to him?"

"He jumped on to the ship at the last minute, I think. Shall we shout?" And without waiting for an answer, the bearded man began shouting in an enormous voice, "Come back! Stop!" The constable shouted nearly as loudly, "Ahoy there! Stand by!"

There was a muffled answering shout from Richard, struggling in a knot of sailors, but the captain took no notice whatever, and the ship was swinging round away from them.

"Oh, dear," said the constable, looking young and anxious. "This is a do and no mistake!"

"We've got the girl, anyhow," said the bearded man in a gruff and placid voice. "It was the girl you were after, wasn't it? Hullo, we seem to have got two girls now!"

And indeed he was festooned with dejected female figures, for another girl—the one who had shouted from the gate—had run across the open space and embraced the unconscious girl who lay in his arms, supporting her hanging head and shaking at her inert hands.

"Ivy," she said, again and again., "Ivy, Ivy, duck! It's me, it's Glad. Speak to me! She's my sister, sir. Lay her down and let me see to her."

Between them they lowered Ivy until she was lying on the ground. Her sister sat on the cold stone and took Ivy's head and shoulders in her broad lap.

"Awkward for you," said the bearded man to the constable conversationally. "You'll be wanting to get a man on to the pilot's boat, won't you? I suppose your inspector can come off with the pilot. I expect you'd like to get to a telephone and make sure the pilot doesn't come off without him? You wouldn't like to leave me in charge here, would you?"

Doubt and relief struggled on P.C. Thomas's face.

"Perhaps the other chap'll be all right in a minute." He pointed to Plummer. "Is it any good blowing your whistle to collect a few more policemen?"

"I could try. But I'd best get to a telephone and try and get hold of the pilot's boat, and not wait about. The inspector'll want to be getting back here. It's his case, you see. Will you look after these two for me, till I come back?"

"Yes, I'll keep them here, don't worry."

The constable ran off, pausing every now and then to blow his whistle. As they heard the sound of his footsteps grow fainter, the bearded man turned to the two girls.

"How is she?" he asked the elder sister. "Is she hurt?"

"I can't see any mark on her. She's breathing all right and I can feel her heart. Oh Ivy, Ivy, me dear, wake up! What's the matter with you?"

"Keep her still. I'll get some water." He clambered down the steps and came back bringing sea water in his cupped hands. He dashed it in Ivy's face and she moaned and stirred, but did not open her eyes.

"Rub her hands," he said. "I'll get some more water and try it on the policeman." He fetched water for a second time and poured it on Plummer's head, and this time was more successful, for Plummer raised himself on one elbow and looked about him.

"I'm all right," he said immediately. "I'm all right. What's happened? Where's the inspector?"

"He's on board the ship. He got taken off by accident. But they've gone to fetch him back, and the girl's here with her sister. I should keep still if I were you."

But Plummer was sitting up and staring at the big dark girl. "I say, miss," he said hoarsely. "What's your name?"

"Turner, Gladys Turner. I don't know what's the matter with my sister."

"Well, now," said Plummer, rising shakily to his feet. "It's all right, sir, I can manage," he said to the bearded man and then turned to face Gladys. "I've seen you before. You're an Oxford girl, aren't you? Don't you worry, now. Let's have a look at her. Don't cry, now."

He bent over her and then looked up.

"What's the matter?" said the bearded man. "Concussion?"

"You come and smell," said Plummer darkly. Together they bent over and sniffed,

"Is it poison?" cried Gladys. "Oh, is it?"

"No, not poison. Just gin, that's all. She's passed out, like. There now, there's no call to take it so hard. She's safe, isn't she? And we'll soon have her as right as rain. She just wants a nice laydown." He turned to the bearded man. "But how did you get here, sir? I thought you was on the ship."

"No, I was only seeing someone off. The other policeman asked me to stay here while he went off for help. There's someone coming now, I think."

"I only hope they get Inspector Ringwood back. He'd be proper disappointed. Would you come along to the station, sir, if you don't mind? I think he'd like to see you."

"Inspector Ringwood? It was Ringwood, you said?" He gave a deep chuckle. "Yes, I'll come. I think I might rather like to see him." And picking up the still unconscious Ivy like a child, he carried her towards the gate, and the rest of the party followed him.

CHAPTER TWELVE

MEANWHILE, Richard, with small South Americans clinging to him as he struggled step by step towards the captain, had not thought of the pilot's boat, and hoped for no alleviations of his miserable predicament. As he saw it, he was now bound on a voyage to Lima in company not only with a lot of hostile foreigners whose language he could not speak, but also with a criminal whom he was unable to apprehend. He almost wished that he had studied Modern Languages at Oxford, but he dismissed the wish as unworthy. Surely with Latin, Dante, and French a man might make himself understood anywhere? He could have added an impressive presence, but he was not aware of possessing one.

At any rate, he shook off the small and vociferous sailors, and addressed himself to the even smaller and more vociferous captain. Their attempts to scold each other and to justify themselves were not made any easier by their language difficulties. Richard, having done as much shouting as he felt the situation demanded, modulated to a more dulcet key, and turned to the immediate problem of finding the man Gray, who had disappeared from sight, basket trunk and all. To Richard, that basket trunk was crucial.

"*Ubi est Americana?*" he asked ingratiatingly. "*Non Señor Riviero, altero Americano, Señor Gray? Ubi? Dove? In inferno?*" He made his meaning clearer by pointing to the stairway that led below deck. "*Age duc! Avanti!*"

The captain's brow darkened at the word *inferno* and he made another impassioned speech. All the syllables were equally stressed and poured out like a river, so that Richard had no idea where one word left off and another began. After a while he gave up trying to understand, and attempted to remember stray words of Spanish. When the captain at last stopped, he bowed politely and said:

"*Señor Capitano illustrissimo! Gracias! Salud, amigo!* I'm a policeman." He showed his card. "*Je'cherche l'Americano.* The other American." Then, with a sudden memory of Graham Greene: "*Gringo! Altero gringo!*" He held out both hands appealingly. "*Altero gringo criminal. Gracias?*"

The captain's features softened. The English didn't really want to stop him from sailing. They merely wanted one of his passengers, who had, after all, paid the fare in advance. He had misjudged this man. He made him a fine speech, which began with the necessity for every man to be in control in his own sphere, went on to expound the principles of liberty, and ended by offering to kiss Richard's hands and give him a drink. Richard understood the last part, since the captain pulled the bottle out of his pocket, uncorked it, and held it out. Richard bowed and took a small swig, while the captain barked at some sailors to conduct the stranger below.

"Decidedly," thought Richard, "the Peruvian bark is worse than the Peruvian bite. Though the bark, to judge by the instant obedience it commands, must send the temperature of his subordinates down to zero. I wish I knew Spanish; he could give me some useful tips."

He followed his guide down the companionway. The guide knocked at a cabin door.

"Who's there?" cried a voice inside.

"Police!" shouted Richard.

The door was unlocked, but when they entered, Gray was on the other side of the cabin with his right hand in his pocket.

"Take your hand out of your pocket," said Richard. "I've got you covered. Where's that basket trunk?" He kicked the door shut behind him.

Gray went over to the shelf and pulled the trunk by its strap.

"For God's sake, handle it carefully!" cried Richard. But it was too late. Gray had tumbled it roughly on to the floor.

"Open it, and show me what's in it."

The man fumbled with the strap and lifted the lid. Then with both hands he tumbled out piles of women's clothes. Nothing but clothes. Soon they were all over the floor and the trunk was empty.

"Where's that baby?" asked Richard with no outward sign of his deep disappointment

"She got pushed off the boat," said the man sulkily. "If you mean my wife."

"She isn't your wife. Where's the baby you kidnapped? Open that cupboard!"

He did so, but it was empty, and his own suitcase contained nothing but clothes. There was certainly no baby in the cabin, and the man's bearing had become confident, even a little truculent

"See here, I've had enough of this"—the assumed transatlantic accent did not succeed in veiling a basic cockney—"you leave me alone. There ain't no baby here, and you got no right to come along disturbing me. This ship ain't England."

"So I'd have a right to disturb you in England, would I? Well, I'm glad you admit it. You wouldn't, if you were an honest man. Show me your passport."

The man blustered weakly, and Richard began to hope he would refuse, as this would give legal grounds for arrest, since they were not yet out of harbor. But then Gray suddenly capitulated and handed it over. Richard examined it carefully It was a British passport made out to Leslie Gray and wife (Ivy). The "wife" section seemed to him to be written in fresher ink and not in quite the same hand, and the photograph was nondescript.

"I'll have your fingerprints, too, please. Give me your hand." He took the man's sweating fingers and pressed them hard on the shiny inner side of his cigarette case. Then he wondered what on earth to do next. He could not prove that Gray had broken the law—even the passport would have to be certified by experts before it was proved a forgery. He could not at present prove that Gray and Ivy were not married, and in any case Ivy was past the age of consent and Gray could not be prosecuted for abducting her, if she had gone of her own will, unless it could be shown she was fraudulently enticed. Yet Richard had seen many criminals in his time and was convinced that the man before him was a typical specimen. It was not the shifty eyes or the loud clothes or even the fear; it was subtler than that, a kind of flavor or spiritual smell exuded by his whole personality. Richard decided to temporize.

"Yes," he said, putting remarkable menace into the single word. "Yes. That's all I need at present. I shall be seeing you again. You gave Miss Turner a false description of yourself—yes, you weren't at Harwell, were you? And you got her to come with you on false pretenses with a forged passport. And she isn't your wife. But I won't arrest you—not yet. There's plenty of sea between here and Panama, and of course we shall get in touch with the police there. So you'll be at liberty for the present. Unless you'd like to make a full statement now? You might do worse. We don't have the third degree in England."

The man swallowed, licked his lips, opened his mouth, thought better of it and said nothing.

"Well, you've plenty of time to think it over," said Richard grimly. "Put the things back in that basket trunk. I'll take it with me. You know, a voluntary statement helps quite bit in court, once you are in trouble. And you will be, don't make any mistake about it. You'd better write one during the voyage."

He took up the little basket trunk and went on deck. Mr. Riviero, with whom he had parted in such exacerbating circumstances, was leaning over the rail smoking a large cigar. He looked at Richard with disgust.

"Hell!" he said. "It's the carp again. Are you taking a trip right to Lima? You think my wife is gonna do a striptease right across the ocean, you got another think coming."

"Mr. Riviero," said Richard, with great earnestness and formality. "Please accept my apologies. I was completely wrong. I am a detective—a C.D. man, don't you call it?—and I'm after a kidnapper. A kidnapper of a baby two months old."

"That's tough," he conceded. "But I don't see that it affects me any."

"I had to inspect your wife rather closely," continued Richard, "because she looked as if she might be a girl I suspect of having a part in the crime. You know, blonde, slim…"

Mr. Riviero looked gratified, and Richard pressed his advantage.

"Well, of course I made a mistake and I'm very sorry. Will you overlook it and help me now? You could help me a lot. You speak Spanish and I don't, and I must somehow get the captain to stop and let me off the ship. The baby isn't here. And there's another thing. This is confidential."

"Huh?" He looked gratified but wary.

"There's a passenger in this ship called Gray. The police may want him the other end. Will you keep your eye on him, and will you tell the captain to do the same? And will you find out for certain that there are no stops between here and Panama? We don't want him to slip away."

"Sure, there's no stops. I'm a part-owner, so I ought to know. We're way behind skedool, any rate, we don't aim to top any. But gee, are you tellin' me I gotta make this trip with a *criminal*?"

"No, no! If I could prove he was a criminal I'd take him off with me now, if I can get off But, you see, in England we have to presume people are innocent till they're proved guilty. I'm just asking you to keep an eye on him as a good American—no, I mean Peruvian—citizen. You don't seem like a Peruvian to me."

Mr. Riviero smiled. "Ten years ago I was Johnson P. Rivers, and a traveling salesman for the New World Beauty Products, Inc. Then I met up with little Pilar, who is quite somebody at Lima, and took out my naturalization papers. Now I direct her pop's trading company. You ask me," he continued rhetorically, "do I have any regrets?"

"No, I don't, not just now," interposed Richard. "After we've seen the captain, perhaps."

"Do I have any regrets? No, sir, I do not have any regrets. I aim to carry the flag of American culture to the ends of the earth."

"Fine. But don't carry me to the ends of the earth, will you? We seem to be getting out of the harbor. Could you go and do a bit of interpreting to the captain? Gee, that sure is big of you." He took Mr. Riviero by the elbow and swept him off.

Conversation with the captain seemed at all times to involve considerable discussion of abstract principles; it was rather like the dialogue in *Troilus and Cressida*. There was a speech on degree and another on the theme of delimitation of civilian responsibility. But in the end the cardinal fact emerged. The *Santa Rosa* would shortly be dropping her pilot, and Richard could return on the boat in which the pilot would leave. The captain was very anxious to have Gray taken off too, but Richard explained that he had no legal grounds for apprehending him. He did, however, tell them again about the kidnapping of the baby, which stirred the captain to the depths. He delivered another speech on blood relationships and insisted on having the ship searched again for infant stowaways. Richard at this point found himself making a speech on the beauty of English family life, but mercifully the pilot's boat arrived before he had finished, and with it a policeman to escort Richard ashore.

Saturday

CHAPTER THIRTEEN

THE OXFORD police car in which Plummer and Inspector Ringwood had arrived at the dock was useful for transporting the bedraggled party away from the waterside to the Liverpool police headquarters. They were received there almost as kindly as if they had been stray dogs or lost children. Ivy was tucked up on a camp-bed with a blanket over her; Plummer's bruises were attended to, and there was plenty of strong tea and bread and jam although it was not yet five o'clock in the morning. The Liverpool police took to Plummer at once and were soon talking to him as if they had known him all their lives. And Plummer, once he had some food inside him, stopped telling everybody he was all right and really began to look quite rosy and cheerful again. The bearded man sat warming his hands on his steaming cup. He did not talk much, but looked so placid, and so much at his ease that no one felt he was an interloper in the family party which had somehow come into being. Plummer was anxious about his Inspector Ringwood, but they assured him that he was being taken off, in the pilot's boat, and not being carried to South America. Gladys was extremely anxious about her sister's physical condition, but Plummer assured her that it was only a matter of sleeping it off and sicking it up. After that, she looked less anxious and even more ashamed and miserable. She sat stonily by her sister's side and no one could get her to talk. All agreed that statements should not be taken before Ringwood arrived.

"I suppose"—it was the bearded man's deep infrequent voice—"none of you chaps happen to remember Inspector Ringwood's initials?"

Nobody did. It appeared that initials were not much used in the service.

"How old a chap is he?"

Plummer said he was a youngish gentleman, maybe about twenty-seven or twenty-eight. P.C. Thomas, who came in at this point and was appealed to, said he was a middle-aged man, maybe about thirty-five or forty. They were arguing the question when the girl on the bed stirred and hiccupped.

"Hold up, duck!" said Plummer, rushing to the rescue. "Here's a basin. That's a good girl! You hold her head, miss. That's right!"

Ivy was a pitiful sight, in her shiny pink dress, now mudstained and crumpled, with her fair hair hanging in matted wisps over her eyes. She wore the remnants of a heavy makeup, but the black had run from her eyelashes and the blue had smudged from her eyelids on to her cheeks, and her face was a daub of mingled paint and tears. She lay back exhausted as Plummer took the basin away, but her eyes were open, sullen and frightened.

"There now, Ive," said her sister violently. "That's a nice way to go on, isn't it, being sick in front of strangers? I'm ashamed of you. I declare I'm thoroughly ashamed of you. Anyone'd think that you were a bad girl off the streets to see you now. I've been looking for you all day and all night, and now I'm sorry I found you. I'm fair disgusted with you. Well, what have you got to say for yourself? Going off with a good-for-nothing boy like that, and see where it's landed you! I always told you he was no good. You're man-mad, that's what you are, man-mad. I don't know why I bother with you. You're nothing but a disappointment to me from first to last. Where were you last night, I'd like to know? Tell, me, where were you last night? Ah, Mum'd turn in her grave if she knew I had to ask you that. Well, where were you?"

"I shouldn't ask her any questions till the inspector comes, if I was you," said Plummer. "She'll only have to tell us everything twice. You let her stay quiet a bit longer, and then she can have a bit of a wash presently, and she'll feel better."

"Serve her right, if she does feel bad. It'll teach her a lesson. Drunk, was she? I never thought I'd see my own sister drunk!"

The bearded man put down his cup and stood up.

"You're looking tired yourself," he said, "Do come and have some tea. You'll be the one who has to look after her, so you'd better keep your strength up, hadn't you? Sit down here, and then you won't have the light in your eyes. Is she your only sister?"

Gladys gulped at the tea and tears came into her eyes.

"Yes, sir. And thank you ever so much for what you did. Taking her off the ship, I mean. If it hadn't of been for you, I might never have seen her again."

"I was lucky to be there," he said, seating himself by her with his big hands on his knees. "And I'm glad you're here to look after her. It'll make all the difference for her, having a home to come back to, you know, and making a fresh start. Would you like some bread and jam?"

"Well, yes, please," Gladys said, rather shamefaced. And then added in a lower voice "Should I give my sister a cup, do you think, sir?"

"Perhaps not just yet, she might be ill again. You look after yourself. This has been a shock to you, hasn't it? I can see you're very fond of your sister."

"Yes, I am. I do hope they won't be too hard on her, she's only a kid, really, and she's that easily led. I do hope she hasn't got into trouble."

The bearded man gave no sign of surprise at this emotional reversal. "I shouldn't worry," he said, "She can make a fresh start if you're behind her to help her. Look, she's sitting up."

Gladys darted forward with the basin.

"There, my dear," she said. "Take it easy. Better out than in, isn't it? Don't talk, now, you'll only make yourself worse, you silly chump. You lie down and shut your eyes. I'll see you're not interfered with." She took up her station again by the bedside, and her look dared anyone to remove her. The two policemen and the bearded man sat in silence sipping at their tea, and everybody began to feel very sleepy.

They had been so sitting for some time when Richard Ringwood burst into the room as if he were catching a train.

"Well, there you are!" he said. "You all right, Plummer? I couldn't bring Gray, there was nothing clear enough to charge him with. Why— why—?"

He was staring at the bearded man as if he had seen a ghost. The bearded man returned his look with amusement and affection.

"Well, Dicky," he said after a moment. "Don't tell me you're a policeman!"

"Andrew!" He seized both his hands. "My dear Andrew! Is it really you? I've been praying for your soul for four years!"

"Well, I don't expect that did it any harm. I ought to have written, and then I thought I'd come instead. I've only been in England two days. You heard I was taken prisoner, I suppose?"

"Not even that. Missing, believed a prisoner. But, then you weren't in the lists and nobody could trace you."

"Well, I escaped from the camp. Then I got lost trying to get across

Malaya. I was ill for a while, too. But here I am as good as new."

"Much better than new," said Richard warmly. "And, Lord, look at your beard! But, Andrew, how do you come to be here, in the one police station in all England where I am? Did you follow me here?"

"No, I arrived here this week from India, and stopped on to see after this chap Father Aloysius, who was next to me in hospital out there. He's pretty groggy, and I thought I'd stop on and see him off to Lima. He's got a sister out there.'

"Good lord! So it was you on the boat!" Then the gypsy had been right. This was something more than coincidence. "Did you recognize me there and come along to find me?"

"No, I seem to have got mixed up in this case, whatever it is. And look, Dicky, don't you want to get on with it? Those girls are just about all in, and I won't go away. In fact"—he chuckled—"I've got to make a statement to you, haven't I? But it won't be my turn yet."

"All right, you old criminal. We'll keep our private life till afterwards. I've got a lot of private life just lately, too."

Richard found it difficult to wrench his mind back to the case after such a joyful shock; yet he recognized that now, as ten years ago, his mind worked more sharply and his judgment was steadier for having Andrew beside him. He turned to the bewildered girls with a new sureness and gentleness.

"Are you feeling well enough to make a statement, Miss Turner?" He addressed himself to Ivy. "I'd like you to tell me, in your own way, how you got here, and what's been happening to you since you left Oxford. Mrs. Link's baby's been kidnapped"—there was a horrified gasp from Gladys—"and as you and the baby disappeared the same evening, I followed you here."

"Oh, dear, how awful!" said Gladys. "I swear Ivy didn't have anything to do with that, sir, nor me neither. What an awful thing!"

"I'm sure you didn't. But I want to know more about this man Gray. I don't like the sound of him. You know he gave a false account of himself to you?" He turned again to Ivy. "Yes, he'd never been near Harwell in his life. And his passport was forged, unless I'm very much mistaken. Did you know that?"

"No," said Ivy in a flat, reedy, little voice. "No, that's ever such a surprise. Oo, I have got a headache. Could I go and have a wash, please?"

"Of course. You take her, Thomas, will you? Well, Andrew, tell me about your part in this affair. You saved the situation, didn't you? Come on, now. 'Mr. Andrew Thorne made his statement as follows:' "

"Oh, well, Dicky, it all sounds silly and melodramatic. There was this chap dragging this girl along, and you could see that she was drunk and a bit hysterical. And there was her sister calling her from the gate, not to speak of the bobby here trying to keep them off the ship. And there was me saying goodbye to Father Aloysius right on the spot. So I just knocked the chap out and brought the girl back. Simple, really."

Richard was still staring at him as if he could not believe his eyes. Andrew returned the look humorously.

"It's the beard, I suppose. I didn't do it on purpose, Dicky. It's covering up gory scars. I've had a fine lot of adventures. Hullo, there's that girl coming back."

Ivy had washed her face and combed her hair, and with her pale young face and golden hair looked like a younger sister of Botticelli's Simonetta. She had the same extraordinary purity of line and coloring, the same look of unawakened sensual richness.

"Feeling better?" said Richard. "Now, I won't keep you long, I just want you to tell me about the man Gray. Did he offer you a job or something?"

"Well, yes, he did. He'd got me a job in the films, in Peru. 'Course, I was ever so pleased."

"Will you tell me about it? Don't hurry. And don't imagine that you're talking in public. We can all keep secrets here, and this is just to save you giving unnecessary evidence in court. We can forget about anything that doesn't bear on the case. Just tell us about Leslie Gray, and how he happened to bring you here."

"Well, I hardly know what to say, reely." The ugly flat little voice consorted strangely with the pure full curves of the mouth that spoke. "He seemed ever so nice. I thought he was the most romantic man I'd ever met."

"You haven't met many," interjected her sister robustly.

"That's all you know," she replied, with a flash of pettish vanity, and turned again to Richard with an appealing and fascinated smile. "Well, I say, I thought he was. But he wasn't so tall as you. Oo! I oughtn't to have said that! And he was ever so keen for me to go on the films. He said I was just the type they'd fall for in the south—you know, blonde and glamorous—'course, I bet I look awful now, don't I?"

"When did he say this?"

"Why, the first time I met him, when he came into the shop. Well, anyhow, he promised he'd write to a friend of his out in Lima and ask if

I could have the job, and I had my photograph taken, special, so as he could send it with the letter. 'Course, I must say it was a small photo, it didn't do me justice. Still, he had an answer in a week."

"In a week?"

"That's right, saying I could star as a beautiful blonde spy in a film called *All Things Are Pure* if I could get to Lima in time. He showed me the letter."

"Was it typewritten?"

"Yes, signature and all."

"Was there an address printed on the top?"

"No."

"Did you see the envelope?"

"No."

"Would you believe it! Please go on."

"Oo, don't look at me like that! Well, I went with him a lot while he was getting me my passport—dances and the pictures, and that…No, he never took me to his place. I don't know where he lived. He made a kind of secret of it, joking, like…I thought maybe he had a mansion and didn't want his butler to see me, or a service flat with a porter. But he arranged all about me going to South America. Wouldn't hear of me paying. Well, 'course, I couldn't have paid, could I? But I was going to pay him back when I was a star. I was going to send Glad a fur coat, too, or maybe have her come out to me. Oh, well!"

"But why didn't you tell me about it, Ive?" interrupted her sister. "That's what I can't make out. After all I've done for you."

" 'Cause you'd have stopped me going, that's why. It was always don't do this and don't do that, and save money and be in by half-past ten. I'm sorry, duck, I can see I've slipped up and you was right this time—but if it had worked out O.K., it'd have been simply smashing. Anyhow, I did leave you a letter telling you all about the job, and how I was sailing from Liverpool, and not to worry, didn't I?"

"But what have you been doing all this time, Ive? It's no good telling me not to worry. I'm worried to death."

"I don't want to tire you, Miss Turner," said Richard persuasively. "But if you could tell us about your time here, it might give us some valuable clues. Would you mind?"

"Oo, no. I think you're ever so easy to talk to. Well, Leslie and I got here late off the train on Thursday, was it? Yes, Thursday evening. The ship was due to leave early next morning, but when we went down, he found it was delayed, and Leslie said we'd have to wait till the next day.

So we went to a hotel he knew quite near the docks."

Oh, dear, thought Richard. "Yes?" he said aloud, encouragingly.

"Well, it wasn't much of a hotel, I must say," continued the flat little voice. "It was a bit dirty and there wasn't anywhere to put your clothes. And all the rooms seemed to be full, and there were people going in and out all the time."

"Yes," he said tonelessly. "I know the sort of place."

"And then Leslie could only get one room for the two of us, on account of them being so full. He said he'd told them we were married, and of course I couldn't contradict, you see, because of the passport. He could only get me a passport as his wife, you see, on account of the new restrictions. It did seem a shame in a way—him being so fond of me, too. You wouldn't think it to see me now, with the headache I've got, but he was crazy about me, reely. He would have married me, you know, only he said he must renounce me for the sake of my career, They don't like you to marry till you're a star, see. It's good publicity then. Still, it did seem a shame."

Everybody was now leaning forward in unbearable suspense.

"What seemed a shame?" said Richard.

"Well, I suppose it was a bit hard on him—I thought so at the time. But I—well, I said I wasn't feeling very well and I couldn't stand the journey unless I had a good sleep. So I said, couldn't he get a room for himself somewhere else?"

"And what happened then?"

"Well, it was only natural, I s'pose, but he was ever so nasty, reely. He said ever such nasty things to me. I couldn't repeat them. So then I told him straight, I said, all right, it's all off and I'm going home. But then he was ever so nice again, you know, polite, like you are. And he said he'd just get me a couple of aspirins and then he'd go off and doss down somewhere."

They relaxed, but awaited the rest of the story anxiously.

"Well, he gave me the aspirins and said good night. I felt a bit lonely at first, with all the noise outside, but I locked the door and pushed the bed up against it. I was ever so sleepy, I just rolled into bed. I s'pose it was the aspirins. It was only two tablets, though. Ever such little ones, too."

"And the next day?"

"Well, I woke up feeling awful. It was late, too, because I heard a church clock striking one. The hotel was ever so quiet, though. Gosh, I did feel funny! But I got dressed and presently Leslie came along and I

unlocked the door and let him in. He was a bit cross at first—said he'd
come back in the middle of the night to get something he'd left behind,
and he couldn't get in. But you know what men are. We talked a bit and
he soon got over it. He's a sweet boy when he's in the right mood. By
and by we went out for a snack, and then we walked around a bit and
went down to the ship again. We found it was going at half past four
this morning. So we got the Customs to O.K. us and Leslie left his
suitcase in the cabin. But I didn't leave mine, because I wanted to
change into my dance frock. Leslie said he'd take me dancing all night,
you see, I love dancing. I bet you're a lovely dancer, aren't you?"

"Just ordinary. But I suppose you didn't go and dance straight away."

"Oo, no, it was much too early. We went to the pictures, and then
Leslie took me to ever such a posh place for supper. And after supper
I changed my dress in the Ladies, and we went on to another place to
dance—lots of foreigners and a crooner all in red sequins, ever so romantic, it was."

"Plenty of drinks?"

"Oo, yes, but I wouldn't have any," she said, with a touch of regret.
"You see, Glad and me, we promised our Mum we wouldn't ever drink.
She made us promise in the hospital, just before she passed away. Be-
cause, Dad, you see, he used to…"

Her sister looked at her repressively and coughed.

"Oo, well, let that pass. Anyway, after we'd been dancing for a
while, Leslie said what about a short lemon, that wouldn't hurt a fly. He
said he was getting fallen arches, and he needed support. So he took
me into the bar and we had a short lemon. Gosh, it did taste funny! It
kept making my eyes water. We had ever such a laugh about it. Leslie
said it was a continental recipe from Holland. We had a lot of these
short lemons, and then we sat talking for while in a little sort of nish with
curtains, just outside the bar."

"And then what happened?'

"Well, I don't think the lemon agreed with me. Too acid, or something. Because I felt ever funny. I think I must have fainted or something. I don't remember, reely."

Richard and Andrew exchanged a look.

"When I come round, I was lying on a settee in the bar. 'Course,
the bar was closed, but the boss was a friend of Leslie's. So he gave
me a short orange to pull me round. He said the orange couldn't upset
me. Or maybe it was Leslie said that. I don't remember, I was still
feeling a bit funny."

"And then?"

"Well, we talked a bit more, and then it was time to go for the ship. It seemed so awful, somehow. I felt I didn't want to go after all, and I did miss you, Glad. I didn't want to go. And then Leslie, he got ever so nasty again, you know, cross, and pulling me along. And he wouldn't let me change into my costume, either, and my dance frock kept tripping me up. It was ever such a long way to the dock, and there wasn't no buses nor nothing. And when we did get there, Leslie made me stand behind the fence for ages, till the gates were opened. And then he went dashing in and pulling me along. I had to run ever such a long way and my feet kept tripping me up. And I heard you calling me, Glad. Gosh, I was glad to hear you! I don't remember what happened after that. How did you know where to find me?"

"I went round looking for you, duck," said Gladys. "I'd been to six other ships before I found you. I didn't want to go to the police, you see, in case you got into trouble. So I went round asking for ships that were going to South America. There was ever such a nice old sailor that found out for me."

"But, good heavens!" said Richard. "You must have been walking round all day and all night."

"It was the waiting about between the tides that was the worst, sir," she said, with a simplicity that went to his heart.

"Poor thing, you must be tired to death. Well, we know the end of the story after that. Mr. Thorne knocked down Gray, and jumped off the ship with your sister, just as I was jumping on to catch her the other end. And here we all are. The only puzzling thing is, why Gray should have picked on your sister, and what his game really was. We may know more about that when the Yard have had a look at his photo and his fingerprints. Anyhow, the main thing now is to get you back home and"—he sighed involuntarily—"me back to my case. Are you fit to drive, Plummer?"

"Oh, I'm all right, sir. But there's a chap here, P.C. Dunster, who's got a day off to go to a family wedding in Oxford. He wondered if we'd take him. He said he wouldn't mind driving."

"I don't know. Let's count noses. Two girls, you and Mr. Thorne."

"No, not me," Andrew said. "I've got a few things to see to before I can go, Dicky. I'll come on by train later, if you like. How long will you be in Oxford?"

"I don't know. Do come today, Andrew. I want you to."

This seemed a sufficient reason, for Thorne replied placidly, "All right, Dicky. I'll try and get there about teatime. Where shall I find you?"

"Ring up this number," said Richard, writing down Clare's telephone number on the back of an envelope, and handing it over with a smile even more crooked and mocking than usual.

"What are you up to, Dicky? You look like a gypsy selling a horse."

"Oh, nothing, nothing. That's my headquarters. Ask for Liddicote." Then, more seriously: "Or the police station if, you draw a blank there. You will come, won't you, Andrew?"

"All right, Dicky, 'course I will. I'd better be getting off now."

"If you'd sign your statement," interposed Thomas, who had taken it down. "Thank you, sir."

"Then can we take Dunster, sir? He's downstairs. Thank you, sir."

The Oxford party were all exhausted, and Plummer and the two girls slept most of the way home. Even Richard, who could not usually sleep in cars, fell into an uneasy doze. He dreamed of the old gypsy woman, shrunk to a hand's breadth and hanging up in a bottle over the High Table. Dr. Costard was telling him that she lacked body. But Richard was straining his ears for her voice, which was very faint and faraway.

"A single loss, a double find. One for you and one for another."

"Yes," he said impatiently in his dream. "Andrew for me. But where's Perdita?"

But she was speaking Greek now, and Richard could not make out the words, as Costard had begun talking about diehards.

CHAPTER FOURTEEN

RICHARD would never have believed Mrs. Harman capable of the animation she displayed when he brought the two girls back to the cottage in Jersey Street.

"Well, I declare! There you are! All's well that ends well! Better late than never! Well, I am pleased to see you. What have you been doing? Give us a kiss, Ivy, duck!" she said, laying a broad mottled arm around her. "My word, don't you look awful!"

"Morning, Mrs. Harman." Richard interrupted her flow of words. "Yes, Ivy's not feeling very well. She ought to go to bed at once. Will you take her up? And can I just come in for a minute and have a word with Gladys?"

"You all right, Glad?" She spoke to Gladys in quite a different way, Richard noticed—affectionate, but with the coequal affection of one general on life's battlefield to another. "You take 'im into the front room, then. I'll see to Ive." And she shepherded the dazed girl upstairs.

"Give her some sody bicarb, will you?" Gladys called after her. "You'll find a tin on my washstand."

Then she led the way into the front room and sat down heavily on the sofa; Richard followed her and took a chair. Not an aspidistra leaf had stirred there, it seemed, since yesterday afternoon.

"I won't keep you a minute," he said. "The police will be investigating the case of the man Gray, of course—he was certainly offering fraudulent prospects to your sister. And they can pull him in on that. But that won't be my case. I'm busy trying to find the baby."

She nodded. "I do hope you will. It's a terrible thing to happen. What did you want to know then, sir?"

"Well, first, about Thursday evening. You were alone in Mrs. Luke's house, weren't you?"

"With the children. Yes, sir."

"Did you hear or see anything unusual going on in the street or next door between five and six?"

"No, I don't think so. There was a gypsy come to our door soon after half past five, but I'd just started washing the children's hair, so I looked out of the bathroom window, and when I saw who it was, I didn't go down."

"What was she like?"

"A big woman, dark, you know, with a basket over her arm. She comes round selling pegs and flowers and that, with a younger woman. I've often seen her. But she was her own this time."

"Did you see which way she went?"

"No, Widdy got some soap in her eye and I had to run back."

"And you're sure you noticed nothing else between five and six?"

"Sure!"

"Good. Well, now, I was going to ask you something else—perhaps it isn't so necessary now—still, I'd better ask you. Have you or Ivy seen that brother of yours lately?"

"What, Syd?" She spoke with alarm and horror. "How did you find out about Syd? What d'you want him for? The kidnapping, or Ivy?"

In her shock she had revealed her moral opinion of her brother no less than her concern for him. She seemed to realize this after she had spoken, for she added earnestly:

"Syd hasn't nothing to do with it. I haven't let him near Ivy for close on a year. How did you know about him? Don't tell me he's in Oxford!"

She buried her head in her hands and burst into tears. Richard pitied her from his heart, this decent clumsy girl saddled with so irresponsible a family, and he felt he should have spared her the question. After all, since Gray had not had the baby with him, and the girls' disappearance from Oxford was amply accounted for already, it was very unlikely that their brother, however bad his character, had been implicated in the kidnapping. Richard's question had simply been prompted by that all-embracing curiosity to which he owed much of his success as a detective.

"Don't tell me," he said. "It doesn't matter. Look, here's a clean handkerchief. I was just trying to get a general picture of the circumstances. But it doesn't matter. Don't be upset."

Then, merely to be saying something instead of listening in silence to her attempts to control her tears, he went on, half to himself.

"It's so queer, you see. Why did Gray pick on a girl like Ivy? There are plenty of girls he could get hold of without anyone raising a finger to stop him. I wish I knew what was behind it."

She suddenly raised her head and stared at him through her tears.

"You mean he might have been a friend of Syd's? Yes, he's like Syd's friends. He's like that click Syd went with after he'd come out of the army. That's why I had to get Ivy away. They were bad, those boys, fiddlers and worse, they were. And I'd promised Mum to look after Ivy, see. But he couldn't have done that, could he, sir? He couldn't have got his own sister into trouble on purpose!" she repeated in a horror-struck whisper. "But there was that letter. He wanted her to go wrong."

"What letter?"

"You'd better see it. It's the letter he wrote me when I told him he wasn't to come near Ivy no more, not if he wanted any cash from me. I'll get it."

She went upstairs. Richard did not think that the letter could have anything to do with the case, but common humanity forbade him to leave now until he had heard her troubles.

"Here it is," she said, returning. "It's—it's not very nice, I'm afraid."

She held out a folded letter, and Richard smoothed it on his knee and read it through with an inexplicable quickening of professional curiosity. The letter was written on cheap lined paper in a childish, back-sloping hand, and it ran as follows:

> 14 Grice St., S.E.G.
>
> 10 June
>
> DEAR GLAD,
>
> So you don't want me to polute our little Ives pure mind, don't you. Well thats a nice way to treat youre only brother you was allways a one for family feeling werent you. Maybe Ive hasnt got such a pure mind at that not when we was kids anyhow she was a fair * * * and had plenty of what it takes and I dont blame her.. So do not be suprised if her pure mind gives you a * * * big suprise is the wish of,
>
> Yours sincerly,
>
> SYD TURNER
>
> P.S. Keep your * * * money to suscribe to the purity league.

A sufficiently unsavory document but indignation and pity were both swallowed up, in Richard's mind, by the feeling that he was somehow on familiar ground. The letter ought to remind him of something—something to do with his case. But what? His memory, as often when he flogged it, dug in its heels and stopped like a mule. He recalled his attention with an effort to Gladys, who was watching him anxiously.

"I don't wonder you wanted to keep Ivy away from him, if this is his usual way of going on. Is he always like this? You were all brought up together, weren't you? Did your mother ask you to look after him, too?" Richard wondered whether Syd were not merely reacting more violently than Ivy against their elder sister's Puritanism. She had so far shown more good will than tact.

She laughed bitterly. "Syd? Not likely! Syd couldn't do any wrong, in Mum's eyes. But it was me she turned to in the end. It was me she trusted to look after Ivy." There was passion in her voice. "My father, see, he drank something terrible. Drank himself to death. And Ivy and Syd, they take after him. They don't touch a drop, of course, not after seeing him. Oh, I know last night…but Ivy didn't know it was drink, see. She's just a kid. But she's weak, like Dad was, and Mum knew it."

"And Syd, too?"

"Weak as water, but Mum couldn't seem to see that."

"What's he doing now?"

"Business, he says. He won't say no more. But I don't like it, sir.

He's always dressed up flashy and talking big, but he never has any money. And he's always been getting at Ive to come in with him. He wants to get her away from me, that's what it is. And she'll go one day. I can't seem to do nothing with her lately. Couldn't you speak to her, sir? She'd listen to you."

"It's not much good my talking to her," he said slowly. "The only man who can do Ivy any good will be a decent husband. Try to get her settled. It's the only way with a girl like her."

Gladys had never thought of this. But one could see that she was slowly considering the idea, shocking as she found it. "And now," said Richard, rising, "I must get back to my own case. But we'll be looking after Ivy from now on, don't worry about that. Try and get some sleep."

"And the—the letter?"

"I'll keep that. Nasty thing to have about. Goodbye." He walked down the little path, abstractedly turning the letter in his hands, and his own action reminded him suddenly of the Links' dining room. Why? He stopped and thought hard. Then he remembered.

He had been turning an envelope in his hands there. He had found it on the arm of his chair. It was empty, flimsy, with a central London postmark dated eleven o'clock on Thursday evening. And the writing had been childish and back-sloping—in fact, surely, the same writing. Yes, that was it. Unless he was much mistaken, Syd Turner had been writing to the Links.

Plummer was asleep in the car, his plump cheeks sagging and a look of resignation on his unconscious face. Richard woke him, discovered that he lived in the next street but one, and firmly drove him to his own front door, telling him not to report for duty till one o'clock. Plummer protested feebly, and in vain.

Then, dropping the Liverpool policeman in the center of the town, Richard decided to look into the matter of John Link's bank account. It would be a delicate business, for the bankers, he knew, were not allowed to divulge any information about their customers' accounts except to the Chief Constable himself, and then only for serious reasons. The Chief Constable was away and Richard hoped that his deputy would prove able and willing. He drove to the police station and demanded to see him at once.

He found a smooth fat man with a pink newly shaven face. The sight of him made Richard feel even hungrier and dirtier than he had before. But the man made no difficulties. He began to ring up the banks at once, and, was lucky at the third attempt. Link used a bank in the

High. After some protests, the manager was persuaded to read over to the acting Chief Constable both sides of the account for the last month. Richard watched as the list was slowly transcribed.

"And fifty pounds to his college yesterday. That's the lot? Thank you. Well, here you are"—he turned to Richard—"no large checks to self or anyone else, barring this fifty to his college. There can't be anything wrong with that, can there?"

Richard stroked his rasping chin. "There might be. It's a curiously round sum for battels—dinners and wine, and so on. And, anyhow, surely they pay those earlier on, don't they? Yes, here's a much earlier check to the college for fourteen pounds five and eight pence. Surely that's battels. I say, I think I'd better look into this. Can you give me your authority to question the Bursar's office?"

"Well—yes, if you think it's really necessary. Mind you, I don't see where all this is leading to."

"This man Syd Turner's been writing to Link. I'm sure of that. Getting money out of him, I expect. If so, it is surely connected with the kidnapping. What else?"

"Very well. I'll write you an order. Is that all?"

"I may have to exhume that coffin at Mayfield. Could you get me a gang for that?"

"I'll see what can be done, Inspector. But I can't promise anything at once. We're short-handed, as you know. Is it really necessary?"

"Of course it is!" snapped Richard. "You'll make it as soon as you can, then? By the way, is there any news of that foreigner—the one that was wandering about the Links' house on Thursday afternoon? You advertised, didn't you?"

"Yes, we did, but there's been no answers yet. Queer case, isn't it?" he remarked, feeling Richard's hostility and wishing to smooth things over. "I needn't say how grateful we are to you for helping us out."

"Haven't got anywhere yet."

"I think you've been doing very well up to date. You saved that girl, little as she deserved it Even if it didn't strictly have anything to do with the case."

Richard rose to go before his tongue got the better of him.

"It's a funny thing, Inspector Ringwood. Did you know that there's been another disappearance from the Merton Street area?"

"What?" said Richard sharply. "Why didn't you tell me before? Who's missing?"

"Oh, it won't be anything to do with your case. In fact, don't expect he's really missing at all, he's just not there, probably. It's a Dr. Field. He went off to lecture in London on Thursday evening and should have been back by the late train. But he didn't come back. He should have been at an examiners' meeting on Friday afternoon, and as they couldn't have the meeting without him, they asked after him. Then they rang up London, and it seems he didn't give the lecture on Thursday evening either. So then his college got in touch with us."

"H'm. This is interesting. What time did he leave on Thursday?"

"After tea, I think. They'll tell you downstairs. I expect he just got into the wrong train. These absentminded professors, you know."

Richard scored a real moral victory in forbearing to point out that Field was not a professor.

He went at once to the college to interview the Bursary clerk, who willingly told him what seemed, on the face of it, to be a perfectly innocent story. Mr. Link had come into the office yesterday just before they closed, and had asked whether they could cash him a check for fifty pounds. He had a chance, he said, of acquiring a valuable piece of antique furniture if he paid cash at once, and the banks were shut. Could they oblige him? They could. There were forty-five pounds in the safe, and the clerks had kindly raised the other five pounds between them.

Remembering the mean and dreary modernity of the Links' furniture, Richard thought that John might have found a more convincing pretext. He went straight to 50 Merton Street and attacked him on the subject. John broke down at once, showed Richard the letter, and confessed to having sent off the money yesterday evening. Richard was very angry indeed, and showed it.

"If you'd told me yesterday," he said, "we could have had that post office shadowed and probably caught the man. As it is…did you take down the numbers of the notes? No? Well, luckily, the Bursar's clerk did."

"Then c-can you trace the man, do you think?" John was so utterly woebegone and crushed that some of Richard's anger left him.

"We may be able to. I've come across another letter, in the same hand, that has an address on it. I'll ring up Scotland Yard and get them to send a plainclothesman there at once. And to the post office too, on the chance. He may not have gone there yet."

"Who—who is it, do you know?"

"Don't know much about him. But he must have been in Merton Street on Thursday evening. No one had been told about the kidnapping but us, so early on. He couldn't have heard about it in time to write that letter, unless an eyewitness had told him, and that's unlikely. Either he did it himself, or saw it done, or heard about it from the man that did it. The first hypothesis is likeliest, of course. Now, where's your telephone? I must get on to the Yard at once and not waste any more time."

At the Mitre, aching with fatigue, he dialed Clare's number and his back straightened as he heard her answer.

"Darling," they said simultaneously, "when can we meet?"

"Well, now," continued Richard solo, "I'm just going to have breakfast. I expect you've had yours ages ago, but could you bear to come and have some more? Or coffee, or something? Oh, good! No, I won't tell you a thing till you're here. I want to see you. You go and put your hat on. Well, whatever you do put on, then."

He ran upstairs two at a time, and whistled his way through a bath, a shave, and a change of linen. He downstairs just in time to see Clare purposefully making her way towards a dark man, a total stranger, at the far end of the dining room. He touched her on the shoulder.

"Goodness!" she said. "It's you! I thought *he* was. Now he looks too horrid for words. Ugh! Let's sit in that window out of the way. Now, tell me everything."

He did so, eating a large breakfast meanwhile. Clare hardly moved until the story ended, so absorbing did she find it. Then, fishing meticulously for tiny pieces of milkskin in her cold coffee, she asked, "What about Gray? He's puzzling. I don't see what he hoped to get out of it."

"Oh, well, he's obviously a white slaver. I expect the Yard'll confirm that when they get his picture and prints. I sent them off first thing. It's so characteristic, you see, the fake film job, the forged papers, the fact that he didn't seduce her. Business before pleasure, you know. He had to keep her in a trusting frame of mind. The line was, Once Aboard the Peruvian Barque..."

"And she'd take her medicine. Your ghastly Shakespearean puns! The awful thing is, I like them too. I say, how heavenly about Andrew!"

"Yes. Do you realize the old gypsy actually foretold that meeting yesterday morning? It's all in my notebook."

He passed it across.

"A single loss, a double find. One for you and one or another. Andrew for me, Ivy for Gladys, in fact. It's as plain as a pikestaff."

"Oh, I hope not. It leaves out the baby. Let me look at that gypsy interview again. No, it says a single loss, a double find. I'm sure it means Andrew and the baby. That little slut Ivy doesn't count. I say, give me a piece of paper and a pencil. I've had an idea. Suppose we write down all the possible meanings of the things she said? Like we would if she was an oracle."

"Coming round to the Sibyl at last, are you? All right. You do it. I'm off duty, for a few minutes more, anyhow." He leaned back and watched her, with at least as much attention as she was giving to her task. She finished a second page, and pushed the notebook over.

He read it. "You've really got something here, I think. But what does it add up to? I don't think the gypsies took her, not now. I think it was Syd."

"Well? This doesn't necessarily contradict that view."

"N-no. Pretty vague, isn't it? We'll just have to let it simmer. Perhaps the Yard has pulled in Syd by now. Meanwhile, I'd better go on with the routine stuff."

"What's that? Can I help?"

"No!" he said sharply. "It's not for you."

"Oh, dear! You're going to dig up that coffin."

"Yes, I am. I want to be sure. But I don't know if it can be managed at once."

"Shall I wait here while you ring up the station?"

"Yes, do. Then we'll know the program." They left the dining room together.

To their great surprise, Sergeant Plummer was sitting on a bench in the lobby.

"Why, Plummer! What are you doing here? You're supposed to be off duty."

"I've had a good meal, sir. I didn't feel like going to sleep, somehow, and they said you'd be carrying straight on. So I came to see if I could help. 'Course, I can't do much, I know. But there's always driving, and that." He gazed up with his sad spaniel look.

"I don't know what I'd have done without you last night," said Richard warmly. "You got those girls soothed down in record time. But are you really feeling all right?"

"Oh, yes, sir. I'm often up all night when Mrs. Plummer's having one of her turns. I'm as strong as a horse if I gets my meals regular. I'm sorry I haven't brought the car, sir, but there was nowhere near here to park 'er so I thought it wouldn't 'ardly be worth while."

"That's all right. We may not need it yet. I'll ring up the station first, and then we'll decide what to do."

He went off to telephone, and soon came back.

"They can't get anything ready for the exhumation till late this afternoon. The doctor won't be free till then. It's rather a pity, really, because Saturday evening in a village is just the worst time in the week for trying to be unobtrusive. Still, it can't be helped."

Clare could hardly conceal her delight.

"Does that mean you're free till this evening?"

"Good lord, no! There's other work to be done. I think we might go round to Dr. Field's house, don't you, Plummer? Not that he's likely to have been kidnapped. Still, it's odd his having disappeared too, and in such a quiet law-abiding place as this. We might pick something up; anyhow, it's worth trying."

"I'd better not come, had I?" asked Clare a little sadly.

"Better not, perhaps. I'm so sorry, darling…" He caught Plummer's mildly speculative eye.

"Plummer," he said stiffly, "perhaps you would be interested to hear that Miss Liddicote and I have just become engaged."

"No!" he exclaimed without the least shadow of surprise. "Well, I never! Who'd have thought it? Well, I'm sure I wish you both all the best." He beamed from ear to ear.

"Thank you. But perhaps it would be better not to say anything at the station yet, till the case is over."

Plummer looked immensely discreet.

"That's all right, sir. I won't say nothing. Don't you worry."

"Good. Thank you. Well, now," said Richard, hastily dismissing the subject, for Plummer was evidently bulging with further propitious remarks, and he did not trust his gravity, "look. That being so, be a good chap and wait for us outside, will you?"

Plummer withdrew, his little feet twinkling under his vast circumference, and his little eyes twinkling above it.

"Darling, I must stop dawdling. Can you possibly be here for lunch? I'll order it now, and if I don't get in by one, start having it, and I'll ring up when I can. Will you be all right till then?"

"I've been doing without you for twenty-two years now. But don't try me too far, will you?"

Richard rejoined Plummer and they walked together towards Merton Street, Plummer's feet going very fast to keep up with his superior's long strides. That they did not allude further to the engagement was due partly to Plummer's natural delicacy and partly to Richard's natural reserve, but their silence was big with a new bond, and they felt full of good will towards each other. Just outside the house, however, Plummer broke silence.

"About the young lady that works for Dr. Field, sir."

"The young…Oh, yes, the maid. Well?"

"They was saying at the station that she's a bit wanting, like. They couldn't get much sense out of her."

"Oh, lord! Why? Did he get her out of an asylum something?"

"I don't know, sir. But it might be as well to go easy with her, like, if you don't mind me saying so. I had a sister like that. Very easy put out, they are."

Richard could have bitten out his tongue.

"Thank you. I'll try to remember. Is this the house?"

He rang the bell and the door was opened by a young woman. Or was she a woman? She had the figure and clothes of an adult, but the expression and eyes of a child. Richard smiled at her and she returned his smile with the candid welcome of an eight-year-old.

"May we come in for a minute? We'd like to talk to you."

A shade of worry crossed her clear forehead. "Dr. Field says, 'Don't talk to strangers.' "

"We're not strangers. It's all right, we've come to help you find him. Will you show me your lovely clean kitchen?"

She smiled again and took his hand. "I'll show you," she said eagerly in her clear slow voice. "I'll show you my nice kitchen. And I'll give you a biscuit, too." Again the shade of worry. "Does Dr. Field say I can?"

"He won't mind, duck," said Plummer comfortably. "I expect there's plenty in the tin, isn't there? Which way is it?"

"This way, this way. Now, sit down and I'll get you some lovely elevenses."

But she's sweet, thought Richard. I imagined that idiots were uncanny, but this one is innocent and friendly, like a very nice little girl.

"There!" she said, serving them. "Is it nice?"

"Lovely, but won't you have some, too?"

"Does Dr. Field say I can?" she looked hopefully at Plummer,

"He won't mind," said Plummer. "Why, doesn't he give you biscuits generally?"

"Not always. Not like Matron," she replied sadly. "Matron gave me one every evening, because I was a good girl."

"Well, I'm sure you've been good today," said Richard. "What have you been doing?"

"Cleaned the dining room, cleaned the hall, cleaned the stairs, cleaned the study, did the bedrooms, did the bath," she recited enthusiastically, and then her face fell. "Didn't get the breakfast. Dr. Field didn't ring for his breakfast."

"Didn't he? I wonder why that was?"

"Didn't ring for breakfast yesterday either. Didn't ring for dinner, didn't ring for tea. I think he's gone away."

She laid a hand on Plummer's arm. He was evidently her favorite.

"Make him come back! Make him come back! I'm frightened. Make him come and take care of me!"

"Why, where's he gone?"

" 'Gone to London,' he said. 'I won't want any supper, but I'll be back for breakfast. You go to bed.' But he didn't be back for breakfast. Oh, dear!" The smooth childish face crumpled.

"There, be a brave girl, don't cry," said Richard. "We'll make him come back, don't worry!"

"But, oh, dear! He'll be cross with me. The stove's gone out. He'll be cross with me."

"Well, you can light it before he comes."

"No, I can't light stoves," she said sadly. "Dr. Field says, 'Don't touch it, leave it to me.' "

"There, my duck," said Plummer. "Don't you worry. I'll light your stove for you. You just pop out and get me some wood and paper, and I'll have it going in two twos."

She smiled again with that extraordinary candor and went out of the back door. Plummer opened the stove and began to rake out the ashes. Richard fell into a muse, but a smothered exclamation from Plummer brought him to his feet.

"Look, sir," breathed Plummer hoarsely. "Bones!"

"You're right," said Richard. "And, look! Surely that's a bit of wool. Don't touch a thing! Get me some newspaper!"

With infinite care and delicacy, Richard began to separate the bones, charred wool, and ash, laying them on separate pieces of newspaper. The maid had returned and stood waiting with her hands full of firewood, showing neither curiosity nor perturbation, but only a serene expectancy.

"Ask her for a sieve," whispered Richard.

"You got a sieve, my duck?" said Plummer aloud. "You show me. Well, isn't that a lovely one! Can I borrow it? I'll wash it up afterwards just like new."

He passed it down, and Richard sifted the ash methodically. He made three parcels, bone, wool ash, and ordinary ash. It was a task he did not relish.

"Why do you look so funny?" the girl asked him. "Are you frightened?"

"Just a bit giddy from stooping down," he said. He stood up and dusted his knees. "What's your name?"

"Edna."

"Well, Edna, you stay and help Mr. Plummer here. I'm going to look at your lovely clean house."

She assented, though not without a shade of worry, but Plummer found an occupation for her, and she was soon happy and absorbed again. Richard made his escape into the hall. He was looking for the study. The first door he opened led into the dining room, the next into a lavatory. The third was the study, opposite the front door. There was a large desk, stacked with orderly piles of typescript and sociological textbooks. Richard tried the drawers. He pulled out the top middle drawer first, and leafed through the papers inside it.

Right at the bottom he found a small thin notebook—so far the only document he had found that was not typewritten, which was perhaps his reason for looking at it first. It was a journal, and it began in March. He saw that there was an entry for every day, sometimes short but oftener covering a whole page.

"No, here's a gap. Quite a long one too. May the seventeenth to the twenty-first. Why's that? And the next entry looks extremely odd. *Attacked by E. Lost use of right thumb temply. Prob. moved too quick.* "Who was E.? Edna?"

He looked back to May 17. The entry was short but baffling: *Pong. Pyg. 5.15.*

Richard returned to the entry for the twenty-first.

C. seeing bandages & hearing of bite—bite?—indulged in some cheap sneers after Hall, at my expense, no doubt, chiefly in Latin. 'Did my patients often bite?' &c. Explained I was not a psych. & had no patients. That silenced him.

"The 'C.' stands for Costard, I think. But *Pong. Pyg.* What on earth does that mean?"

He read on, skimming through notes of meetings until the tone became more personal.

The I.Q. 67 from Sunniways certainly a comfort. Bowels functioning more normally since cooked veg. available, & study fire a treat. Chilblains still painful. Think have induced satisf. transfer-

ence, no sexual complications likely as I specified some emotional retardation as necessary in present case, when writing to Matron.. Cooks well if encouraged. MEM. Use of endearments produces v. satisf results. Find out which have been previously used.

Richard snorted. I.Q. 67, indeed! Kind hearts were more than coronets, and simple faith than bloody norms. Himself, he preferred to call the girl Edna. He read on:

M. to tea, v. talkative & actressy. Lipstick, &c. Seems to have lost former ideals. Full of social & literary ambitions. I now feel I wasted time on help given while at school. But seemed serious then. Did not ask abt. speaking, but instead tried to recall her to duty. Spoke strongly of economic importance of getting good degree. Seemed impressed. Asked me to see her in Shakespeare play, June 17th. Wd. send free ticket. May go, tho' waste of time, but cd. perh. see producer & ask abt. lessons in pub. speaking.

Richard came to another gap in the dates. The next entry struck him as most pathetic:

Broke bifocals. Cd. not see to find spare pair, but E. has at last located them after 2 days' search. Work held up meantime & eyes v. sore. MEM. Keep in Drawer 1.

Richard recalled his mind to business. He was really looking for an account of the experimental scheme which, as Costard had told him, had been voted down as a result of John Link's speech. But there was still no mention of it. Another curious entry caught his eye, irresistibly:

Learned today at Best. Gdns. that Pong. Pyg. F. preg. Event expected in abt. 3 wks. Intend keeping under close observation with view to seeing how far mat. instinct & possessiveness can be reduced by pre- & ante-natal conditioning. Starting in today. Keeper unhelpful, sentimental & sloppy, lacking in Sci. Spirit. MEM. Arrange to go during lunch hour & after closing time (5.30). Will mean changing own mealtimes, & acidosis will prob. recur, but have never spared myself in Cause of Sci. & do not intend to commence now.

"I do wonder what Pong. Pyg. is," Richard said to himself. "Still, it's obviously nothing to do with me. Ah! Here's an account of the affair in Congregation! Right at the end of the book. It doesn't amount to much." In fact, it merely ran:

MEM. Draft notices on Experimental Psych. material to send to forward-looking members of Con. rather than...

And there the diary ended on the last page, in the middle of a sentence. Just when it might have been some use; in fact, just before the week of the quarrel (if there was one) with Link. Richard felt that he was entitled to presume a second volume from the incompleteness of the first. He began to hunt for another notebook in the desk. But the sound of a key in the front door stopped him. He had just time to slip the little notebook back under the papers and shut the drawer before the front door opened and a man came in, saw him through the open study door, and called to him sharply.

"What are you doing there? Eh? What are you doing?" He had red hair turning gray, half concealed by a bandage round his head. The big bones of his sallow face stood out cadaverously. Richard could not see the expression of the pale eyes through the immensely thick bifocal glasses, and could only guess at illness or nervous strain by the pallor and the twitch that every few seconds pulled the mouth awry. He did not immediately answer, and the man hurried into the room with a jerky shambling gait, striking his shoulder on the doorpost as he did so. He came up very close to Richard and stared at him myopically, repeating, "Eh? Eh?"

"Are you Dr. Field?" asked Richard, giving question for question.

"Of course I am. And what are you doing at my desk, may I ask?"

"Perhaps this will explain it," said Richard, handing over his official card. He had often used this gambit, and occasionally the faces of those who suddenly thus realized that he was a detective-inspector from Scotland Yard had betrayed guilt or fear. This time Richard could observe nothing. Dr. Field was already pale, and his face, not naturally expressive, was masked further by the distortion of its recurrent twitches.

"Well?" he said in his jerky way. "What do you want?" He was gripping the back of a chair and the big knuckles were white on his red hands.

"It's you I want," said Richard, and paused watchfully. Dr. Field did not move. "You were reported missing by your college, and they sent me along to look into it." The hands relaxed and the red came flowing back over the knuckles.

"I was just going to look on your desk to see if I could find any addresses."

"Found any?" He still stood leaning on the chair-back.

"No. I'd only just arrived when you came in. I believe you were expected on Thursday night, weren't you? And it's Saturday now. One of your colleagues told us yesterday that King's College, London, had rung up, as you hadn't delivered your lecture there. And you missed an examiners' meeting yesterday. So everyone was getting a bit worried about you."

"Yes," said the doctor grudgingly. "Yes, I suppose you were within your rights. But here I am. So you can stop fussing now."

"Are you sure you're all right, sir?" asked Richard, with somewhat overemphatic courtesy.

"Obviously not. Can't you see my bandage?"

"Have you had an accident?"

"Obviously. I'm not the sort of fool who gets concussion on purpose."

"Would you mind giving me a short account, sir, for our records?"

"I suppose you're entitled to it. A fool in a car knocked me down when I was crossing Gower Street. When I came to, I found myself in a public ward in University College Hospital, yesterday morning. I stayed there till this morning, and then I felt better, and left. I traveled down here by train. That do you?"

"Thank you. That's perfectly clear. If you don't mind my saying so, you still look very ill. Shouldn't you have stayed in hospital another day or so?"

The pale face flushed suddenly.

"That's quite enough, quite enough. I can't take my orders from nurses and policemen. It's my business, not yours. I've got a great deal to see to here, a great deal. I won't be interfered with."

The skin was white and taut again on the big knuckles. Just then Edna came in through the open door behind him, ran forward, and touched his hand.

"You've come back! You've come back! Oh, I *am* glad." But then she fell back a pace. "What's the matter? Why do you look so funny? Edna's not a naughty girl, is she?"

An extraordinary change came over Field. The lines smoothed out of his face and suddenly he radiated kindness and reassurance.

"Edna's a good girl, a good girl," he said very slowly and distinctly. "I'm not going away any more. I'm going to stay here and take care of you. I've been ill in London."

"Poor head!" she said sympathetically. "Better now?"

"Yes, better now. But I want my lunch. Will you get it?"

Richard was watching in astonishment. Field handled the girl perfectly, and she was evidently devoted to him and overjoyed at his return.

"I'll get it," she said, with a little jump. "Oh, yes I'll be quick. What will you have?"

"Cold meat off the joint, and tomatoes. And you can open a tin of peaches."

"Oh, lovely! Can I have peaches, too? Are the nice gentlemen coming to lunch with you?"

"No, they can't stay. Run along, now, and tell me when it's ready." He turned to Richard, all sign of former agitation gone, with impersonal hierophantic benevolence.

"Was the girl emotionally upset by my absence? How was she when you arrived?"

"Well, she seemed a bit lost and frightened, like a child alone in a house," began Richard.

"Yes, she's a deficient, of course. About 67 I.Q., but well trained. She works quite efficiently under proper supervision. That class of mind ought to be more generally used for domestic work. Would be, no doubt, under a more rational system. I got her out of a home to prove my theory. Of course, it works out perfectly. Euthanasia would be a pure waste of useful material."

"I thought she was most likable," said Richard trying to conceal his indignation.

"Yes, most of them are capable of some degree of socialization, given proper treatment."

"My sergeant was wonderful with her."

"Your sergeant? What? Where is he?" Field stumbled jerkily towards the door. "Why wasn't I told?"

"Oh, he's quite happy. He's in the kitchen, I think, I'll just go and pick him up. Don't bother to see us out, you want to sit down, I'm sure."

But Field had already opened the kitchen door. Richard looked over his shoulder in some alarm. Plummer was doing something to the stove. The parcels of ashes were nowhere to be seen.

"What are you doing there?" said Field in his other, sharper voice. "Eh?"

"Just doing the stove for Edna, sir. She couldn't seem to get it going, like."

"Why, what was the trouble? Eh?"

"Just wanted raking out, sir. It's all right now."

"Well, here's Dr. Field back, Plummer," said Richard, "so we needn't stay any longer. Got everything?" He made a questioning grimace over Field's shoulder.

"Yes, everything," said Plummer stolidly, and followed him out.

"Goodbye," Edna crooned in a singsong. "Thank you for coming.

Come again soon! Come again soon!"

They were hardly through the front door before Field slammed it behind them and Plummer turned to Richard eagerly, his pond-like features mantling with excitement.

"Sh! Wait, Plummer! Wait till we're round the corner. We're probably being watched," said Richard in an urgent whisper, and they plodded on with conscious and almost intolerable slowness until they had turned the corner into Merton Street.

"Now! For God's sake, Plummer, where are those bones?"

"Here, sir," replied Plummer, patting himself on the belly.

"*What*? Heavens, you haven't swallowed them?"

"Bless you, no, I should hope not! No, they're inside me tunic. Though I must say," he added more soberly, "I never thought I'd go walking round Oxford carrying 'uman bones next me skin. Fair gives you the creeps, don't it? But it seemed the only thing to do. I heard him and you in the study, see."

"My dear Plummer," said Richard earnestly, "you're a wonder. I shall recommend you for promotion."

"Oh, no, don't do that, sir, thank you all the same. I get muddled enough as it is. I'm only an ordinary old chap, see, though it's very kind, I'm sure. But could we take them out now?"

"Hold on just a minute. We can't do it in the street. I know! We'll go on and see that Dr. Shawyer I met in Hall last night; it isn't far to go. I'm sure he can be trusted, and he's a doctor, which may be useful. And Plummer," he added, patting his shoulder, "it's not as bad as you think. It probably isn't human bones in those parcels at all. I expect it's just rabbits, or something. You know they use them for experiments."

Plummer looked relieved, but Richard, although he had come away without revealing his suspicions, had done so through policy rather than conviction that all was well. He had seen those bones. And he knew that rabbits never have finger joints.

CHAPTER FIFTEEN

THEY ARRIVED at the college lodge in a few minutes, though none too soon for Plummer, as he walked delicately and uneasily with his charnel burden intimately carried, like a circus elephant with a performing lioness on its hack

"Dr. Shawyer?" said the porter in answer to Richard's question. "Yes, sir, he's in. I've just seen him going across to his rooms. Do you know where they are? Second quad, staircase five, first floor, right."

They hurried across and up the stairs, and knocked on the half-open door. A cheerful voice called them in. Shawyer was standing with his back to the fireplace, a glass of sherry in his hand, looking extremely young and healthy.

"Hullo," he exclaimed in surprise, recognizing Richard at once and then seeing Plummer's uniform, "I remember you. You're the bobby that was dining with us last night. Don't tell me you've come back to have me up this morning! Which of my sins have found me out? Was it the torso in the trunk, or the black market egg?"

"Don't worry," said Richard, with a half smile. "You're not a victim this time. I hope you'll be an ally, though. I want your help. Could you sport your oak before I tell you about it? It's something rather serious and private."

Adjusting his expression to the gravity of Richard's words, but hardly able to conceal his cheerful curiosity, the young doctor went over and shut his heavy outer door, that last bastion of privacy in our progressively intrusive world. The most intimate friend still hesitates before the barrier of a sported oak, and Shawyer's had probably never been sported before in all his two years' tenancy.

"There," he said, returning to the fireplace. 'No one can get at us now. Do tell me what all this is about. I'm absolutely consumed with curiosity."

Richard nodded to his sergeant.

"All right, Plummer. You can show him now." Plummer began to unbutton his tunic.

"Hi!" cried Shawyer in alarm—medical etiquette alarms even the bravest of doctors. "Hi! You're making a mistake, I think. Do yourself up at once, please! I'm not a practicing doctor, and I don't know a measle from a mump. I can't examine you. You must go to your G.P."

"That's all right," said Richard, "we don't want you to examine him. Put them on the table, Plummer."

Plummer laid three small newspaper parcels on the table and began to button up his tunic crooked, with an air of heroic outrage. Richard undid the largest and knobbiest parcel, and spread out the charred bones to view, while Shawyer stared in bewilderment.

"We brought these along to you," said Richard. "Sergeant Plummer here had to hide them in his tunic so as to get them away safely, and he badly wanted to unload. So we came to you. I hope you don't mind. You were the nearest port of refuge. Also, I'd very much like to hear your opinion on them, though I know it's unconventional. It would take all of twenty-four hours to get them examined by our own people in London, and the case won't stand any delay."

"But, good God! They look like human bones. Where did you find them?"

"In a stove. Don't ask me whose, because I mustn't say. Just tell me, if you can, what the bones are. But perhaps I ought not to ask you."

"On the contrary, I'm delighted. This is really seeing life."

"I think it's probably seeing murder," said Richard, "or, at any rate, the results of it. But perhaps you'll be able to tell us that."

The natural brick-red of Shawyer's face deepened

"Sorry," he said in confusion. "I didn't mean that, exactly. I mean, of course I'd like to help you, anyone would. But I can't help being rather interested, anyone would be. Let's have a look."

He took a pair of forceps from a case on the desk, and began to shift and examine the fragments with great delicacy, talking rather absently as he did so.

"Of course you realize that I'm not at all the right chap to ask about bones. I'm no anatomist. In fact, I failed my anatomy paper in the exams and had to take it again. Pathology is my line. I'm afraid I haven't looked at an anatomy book for years. So don't believe a word I say, will you? All the same…Good heavens, this is very odd!"

He gazed at the bones with increasing perplexity, rubbed his nose.

"You know, I wish you'd taken these to old Tarns. He could really be some good to you. Greatest bone man in Europe, and knows the whole thing from A to Z. He's a dear old chap, too. I'm sure you'd get on with him. This doesn't look to me like a job for a nonspecialist."

"Why?" asked Richard.

"Well, it's all so damned odd. How many bodies did you reckon that you had here?"

"One, if that." Richard fidgeted as he watched the delicate forceps lifting and shifting. "Why?"

"Oh, lord!" A flood of light burst upon Shawyer's mind and he looked very serious indeed. "Don't tell me that you think that this is John Link's baby?"

"I can't tell you anything," said Richard, mastering his impatience. "I know it's abominable to barge in like this and ask your help, and then refuse to talk. But we have our professional etiquette too. You must just kick me out if you feel—quite justifiably—that you can't help me on those terms."

"Don't be silly. Of course I want to help. But it's all so damned odd, I can't understand it at all." He bent over the table again. "You say you only expected one body?"

"Yes. Why?"

"Well, don't believe anything I say, because anatomy, as I told you, is my weak point. But as far as I can see, you can't possibly make one body out of these bones. They're incompatible. Some are much too big, and some are much too small. How old was John's—how old would the victim have been ?'

"Two months."

"A girl, you say?"

"Yes."

Shawyer swore violently and savagely, presumably at the murderer, apologized, and then, collecting himself, beckoned Richard over to the table.

"Come and look, and I'll try to show you what I mean. You see this and this. That's a femur. Well, they're all right—I mean they'd fit a girl child of two months. And so would this." He pointed to something like a piece of eggshell. "That's a bit of cranium. But just take a look at these. They must belong to a much bigger baby—say, eight months old. Look how long they are. That's a tibia. But then, here are some vertebrae. They're quite small again, just what you'd expect in J—in quite a young baby. And yet, look at this jawbone. I think it's a jawbone, but it's so charred, one can't be sure. It's much too large for the head suggested by the curve of the cranium. D'you see the difficulty?"

"I think so. The suggestion is that there were two bodies?"

"That's it. Doesn't that fit the facts?"

"I don't know. It doesn't fit my theories or any of the facts I know."

"Well, as I said, I'm no expert. And of course the bones are in such a charred state, which is a pity, because we could have been more definite about age if we could have established the degree of ossification. One might still do it by taking a section—at least, an expert might."

"What's degree of ossification?"

"How hard the bones had got. But, as I say, it looks to me like two different sets. Wait a minute, I'll arrange them in their natural order and you'll see how disproportionate they are." He roughly arranged them in the shape of a human body. It was very small, and there were many gaps.

"Can't we find some duplicates?" asked Richard. "Surely if you could get two of the same bone, that would be a better proof that there were two bodies."

"I suppose it would," replied Shawyer despondently. "But I can't seem to see any. The shape is so hard to be sure of when they're charred and broken up like this. And, anyhow, I'm not at all good at this branch of medicine, even under laboratory conditions. I wish you'd let me take them along to old Tarns. He's the only man who'd be any use in this kind of a job, and I know him quite well. Would you mind?"

"Mind! I should be enormously grateful. He's much better, and much nearer, than any expert I could get hold of. And the matter is very urgent and important. Could you possibly ring him up now?"

"Nothing easier. Of course. Sit down and have some sherry."

"No, thank you. Oh, by the way, does your telephone go through the lodge?"

"Yes. Oh, I see!" He laughed as he saw the point of the question. "Don't worry, the porter won't understand our jargon. And, anyhow, he's discretion itself. They have to listen, you know, or they can't tell when the line's free."

But there was no need for either concealment or discretion. Professor Tarns was out and was not expected home until four o'clock that afternoon.

"Do you know where I could get hold of him?" Shawyer asked, "Gone for a walk, has he? Where did he go, do you know? Oh, yes, of course, I remember, it's the famous Saturday walk. Well, I'll come round at four, if, I may...Yes, it's Robin Shawyer. Will you tell him it's very urgent?"

He rung up the receiver and turned round.

"I'd forgotten. He always goes off for a long country walk on Saturday. He takes his lunch and stays out for hours. Amazing at his age, isn't it? One can't possibly get in touch with him until he comes back. But he always comes back when he says he will, so I'm sure to see him at four. He's a good chap. That'll be all right, won't it?"

"That's very good of you indeed, and I'm most grateful. I must try to get the ash analyzed too. I think it may be burnt clothes, or hair, or something. It doesn't look quite like ordinary stove ash, does it?"

"I can see to that too, if you like. I know lots of chemists, and I imagine it's quite a quick and easy job if you know what you're looking for. And you'd get your results sooner if the analysis is done in Oxford. Shall I take them along to the labs?"

"I say, could you really?" said Richard gratefully. "I can't tell you what a help it would be. But are you sure you can spare the time?"

"Saturday afternoon? Of course. It won't take long, and anyhow, it's so interesting and it makes me so bloody angry."

"I know. When shall I come and collect the results?"

"Oh, don't come here. I'll ring you up from Tarns' house. You'll hear quicker that way. Where shall I ring up?"

"The police station, if you don't mind. Hullo, Plummer, are you all right?"

Plummer had been standing by the window with his face averted. As he turned round, Richard saw that he was a most unhealthy color, with every feature drooping.

"I'm all right, sir. It's just..." He cast an eloquent glance at the table and its gruesome burden. "*Two!*" he said in accents of horror. "It's a bit much."

"Here, have some sherry," said Shawyer. "A lot of medical students feel like that to start with. It's nothing to be ashamed of."

Plummer looked at Richard with wistful inquiry.

"That's all right, Plummer. It doesn't count as drinking on duty if it's doctor's orders."

Plummer took the large glass that Shawyer offered him, and drained it at a single gulp as if it were beer. He choked slightly, and his eyes bulged. Then he felt the warm prickling sensation in his stomach, and brightened somewhat. But the sight of the table, though its contents did not present a particularly horrifying aspect, seemed still to be too much for him, and he resumed his position by the window.

"I'd better take him away," said Richard in a low voice. "I suppose this is the first anatomical job he's ever seen at close quarters, poor old chap. Well," he continued, a bit louder, "we'll be going now. I'm so grateful to you for all your help. You'll ring me up soon after four, then?"

"Right. And as for the help, as you call it, I'm only too glad. You may think it's a bit callous of me, which it really isn't, because I don't think any punishment is too bad for people who murder children, but I can't help finding all this very interesting, you know."

"You wouldn't be human if you didn't. I found it interesting myself, at first. Now, it's just my job. But I promise that I'll tell you the whole story once it's over—that is, if I ever know it myself. Goodbye."

"Goodbye, sir," said Plummer, sidling across the room with a crab-like motion to avoid the view of the table. "And thank you, I'm sure."

Once out, he took a large brown handkerchief out of his pocket and mopped his brow.

"My word," he said, "that fair gave me the creeps. Just like the Sunday papers, isn't it? Fancy me having two dead babies next me skin. Well, least said, soonest mended. That's a nice young gentleman, sir, isn't he? Though he was a bit lively when he was up. I remember 'im sitting on the roof of a taxi with a pot and a paintbrush, driving very slow, and painting all the street lights red. Singin' 'ymns in the station afterwards, too…But there! What are we going to do now, sir?"

"Come over here and talk quietly," said Richard, drawing him into the angle of a great stone wall. "You never know who might be listening. I think that even this doubtful report on the bones means that we shall have to watch Field. He must be mixed up with Syd Turner somehow. Also, I found a diary in his study that intrigued me rather—or at least, the first volume of one, that ran on in a way that made me absolutely sure there must be a second volume somewhere, starting this month. I'd like to get a look at it. But I don't think I'd be justified in arresting him, and if possible, I'd rather he didn't know I'm watching him. Then his behavior'll be more informative. I hope he doesn't know we found those bones."

"I'm sure Edna didn't take it in, sir. But suppose 'e's gone off already?" Plummer's eyes were round with anxiety. "We've been in there quite a time."

"We can soon find that out. Where's the nearest telephone box?"

"Up past the corner, sir."

"Come on, then, we'll see what can be done."

They went quickly to the telephone box, and waited in a frenzy of impatience while a middle-aged woman, leaning on the shelf with air of blissful relaxation, conducted conversation, fumbled for extra pennies, buttoned up a great many clothes, and at last emerged.

"You coming too, Plummer?" said Richard, not shutting the door. "Oh, no, quite, I see your point." The point occurred a little below the belt. "All right, you wait outside. I won't be a minute."

He found and dialed Dr. Field's number. It rang for a few moments and then an impatient and unmistakable voice answered him.

"Will you give me the Orders Department?" said Richard in an assumed voice. "Oh, isn't that Grimly Twining?…I'm sorry, it must be a…"

The receiver was slammed down.

"Well, that's all right," he said, rejoining his sergeant. "He's at home, and by the sound of him, disturbed at his lunch."

He glanced at his watch.

"A quarter past twelve. You go off and have some lunch, Plummer. Have it somewhere in the town, and be back here at one o'clock, will you? I'll watch the house till then. If I'm gone when you get back, that will mean that he's gone out and I've followed him. If so, I'll try to drop a note for you in the street near the house. It's a quiet street and there's quite a chance that it won't be disturbed. Just walk past the end of the street slowly when you arrive, and I'll come down and show you where to stand, if I'm here. If not, walk slowly up the street and see if I've left anything. If I haven't, wait for me."

"All right, sir. Walk past the bottom of the street slow, wait, come up it if you don't come, look for a message. I won't be long, sir. There's a place in the market where they 'ave beautiful sheep's hearts and thick gravy, and they don't keep you waiting long. I must say a sheep's heart would go down lovely." He smiled a little in anticipation and bustled away.

"Well, he's recovered his appetite, anyway," thought Richard, "in spite of the bones. I hope he'll find a beautiful sheep's heart or should I say, the beautiful heart of a sheep? What an extraordinary mixture the man is! So resourceful in some ways and so childish in others."

Richard settled himself behind another of those buttresses so conveniently disposed about the ancient city, where he had an oblique view of the house but could conceal himself at need. Nothing happened for a while. Then the dining-room window opened, and Edna was seen shaking out a tablecloth.

"Lunch is over, anyway. I'd better get farther back. He may look out of the window."

He waited some time longer. A party entered the street from the High. There was a light flurry of feet and high soft voices. It was Mrs. Luke with her two children. Unwilling to be found in hiding, Richard left his corner and passed quickly down the street ahead of them. Once round the corner, he turned to greet them, but Pippa forestalled him.

"Look, Mummy," she said. "It's my nice man."

"So it is, darling," said Mrs. Luke in placid agreement, while Richard felt absurdly flattered. "What brings you here? Are you going to see John and Perpetua?"

"Not just now," he replied evasively. "I'm waiting for someone to join me here. How are you getting on without your nanny?"

"Well, it ought to be dreadful, but we're getting on beautifully, only

I'm afraid that sounds too ungrateful. She's coming back tomorrow. We can be so dirty, you see, when she isn't there to keep us up to the mark." All three were as fresh as flowers. "And Daddy's going to give us lunch in college, so that's all right, and we've just been seeing the monkeys, because they close on Saturday afternoons. How are you getting on?"

"Not too well," said Richard. "I won't develop the subject *à cause des petits*. But that isn't a report to be passed on."

"Of course not, poor darling," she replied, startling him slightly. "She's being wonderful, really," she added, and Richard relinquished the endearment without grudging to Perpetua Link. "Well, we mustn't keep Daddy waiting, must we, my honey-buns? I do hope you'll come and see us properly when all this is over. I mean, really properly."

She floated away, leaving him to think it out.

He returned to a place of vantage farther up Kybald Street and soon heard other footsteps. He looked out cautiously and saw Field going down the street. He must have left his house stealthily, for Richard had not heard the door being shut behind him. He waited until Field turned the corner and then started quietly to pursue him. At the corner he stopped again. Field was making for the High round the bend of Merton Street. A tortuous way to come to it, as if he were avoiding the populous streets as long as he could.

Once he was round the bend, Richard followed with long silent steps. He watched him turn into the High to the right, towards the river, and then once more pursued. But when he reached the corner, he was unpleasantly surprised to see Field waiting just behind it. He must have been watching to see if he was followed. The pale intelligent eyes recognized him, he was sure, but were quickly averted, and Field dived into Magdalen College and began to walk round its large and beautiful grounds. Richard watched him as far as a long circular path, with no exits, known as Addison's Walk, and then waited for him to emerge.

In twenty minutes he did so, walking with short jerky steps, but this time Richard was well hidden. Field passed him and left the college. Richard followed at a safe distance, but once more luck was against him. Field had been caught by a fellow don in the street just outside and was being engaged in conversation, apparently against his will. There was another encounter, Richard thought, another recognition. At any rate, Field, his conversation over, seemed to have given up the plan of going wherever he had been going—Richard surmised that he was not the man for solitary walks—and made for home. You could hear his front door bang right from the end of the street. And Plummer, alas, was standing in full view at the corner, gazing towards the house and quivering with an alertness that could be perceived from a great distance. One felt that he was merely waiting for the word of permission to bound off and retrieve his quarry like a well-trained gun-dog.

Field could hardly be ignorant that he was being watched. Nevertheless, Richard still felt that the watch should continue, and that no advantage was to be gained by a premature arrest. He therefore instructed Plummer to keep out of sight and follow Field if he should come out of the house again.

"Mind you don't lose him if he does," he added. "It would be better for him to see you than for you to lose him by dropping too far behind. I don't think he'll go far. My feeling is that he is trying to go somewhere at the river end of the High, but to get there unobserved. He could easily have taken a bus out of the town when he went out just now, if he'd merely been wanting to get away out of reach. There was plenty of time before I got round the corner. What I should like to do is to find out where he's going—he probably wants to destroy some evidence— and catch up with him just as he gets there. Of course, he may not make another attempt. He looks desperately ill."

"That's all right, sir. I won't let him get away. You wouldn't 'ardly credit it to look at me now, but when I was a nipper I was the best in the 'ole street at that game where you follows somebody. You know the game I mean?"

"Yes," said Richard, smiling. "We used to call it Red Indians. I suppose all children play it, don't they? Well, I hope your early training will stand you in good stead. Had a good meal?"

"Ah," said Plummer with deep satisfaction. "Lovely. But not so good as my old woman's. Which is wonderful, really, considering 'er legs."

"Well, I'll go and have a spot of something now, and see how Miss Liddicote is getting on. I'll try not to be too long."

"Don't you worry, sir. You take your time. It seems a shame for the poor young lady, don't it? I expect she was looking forward to this weekend."

Richard smiled radiantly. It had not occurred to him that Clare, too, had been looking forward to this weekend, though he had himself been almost bursting with excitement for days beforehand.

"Never mind. The harder we work on this now, the more chance we've got of finishing it up quickly. Though I must say it gets more and more confusing and looks less and less like having a happy ending."

He took his leave of Plummer and ran all the way to the Mitre.

Clare was sitting at a table for two by the window in the dining room. She was eager for news of the case.

"I'll just order first, shall I?" he said, with a meaning glance at the waiter. "Something cold, I think, don't you? What'll you drink?"

"You choose," said Clare. "I don't know about wine. If they're sweet, people mostly say you ought not to like them, and if they're sour, I mean dry, they shrivel your mouth up inside and give you a tummy-ache. I like claret when it tastes like Parrish's Chemical Food, and port when it tastes like Syrup of Figs."

"Stop, stop!" said Richard weakly. " 'The very sound is like a knell.' And any *port* at luncheon on a summer day…"

He ordered a Médoc, explaining that it would be a good grounding for her, and that he would reserve the great wines for a later stage in her education.

"Lovely!" She sighed with pleasure. "I do feel so heavenly and worldly, if you see what I mean. Now tell me how you've been getting on."

He told her. The story of how Plummer had got away the bones drew an involuntary laugh, but at the end of the whispered account she looked very grave indeed.

"I suppose you're really sure that those were little Perdita's bones in the stove? And yet I don't believe you are."

"No, I'm not. How did you guess? For one thing, I don't believe anyone but an expert can really give a workable opinion. The bones were in such a bad state. And for another, if there really are two skeletons, it looks much worse, I know, two murders, you'd say. But I find them unconvincing, somehow. Real life is more economical than that. It's like the bad novelist in Wodehouse who was writing a thriller about a mysterious Chinaman with two twisted ears. Two babies' skeletons somehow sounds, as Plummer would say, a bit much."

She laughed. "Yes, and then if Field did it, what about the motive?"

"Yes, what indeed? Field's a fanatical, ornery sort of man, I grant you, but he's intelligent, and you only had to see him with that Edna to realize that he's an extraordinarily competent psychologist. Why would he go kidnapping babies and burning them in his stove? He's surely too intelligent to do a murder unless he can at least pretend to himself that he's going to get some advantage out of it or escape some danger. He earns a good salary, and he has pretty Spartan tastes, so it doesn't look as if ransom were the motive. What else is there?"

"Didn't John Link defeat one of Field's pet pieces of University legislation?"

"Yes, but if it hadn't been John it would have been somebody else. Surely Field's clever enough to realize that. He must know the strength of the opposing party."

"You'd think so, certainly. Still, if those really are human bones you found in his stove, you must take him seriously. Could he have been an accessory?"

"Whose accessory? Syd's, or the gypsy's, or the Mysterious Foreign Intruder's? He doesn't seem to fit in there, does he? I do wish I'd managed to see the rest of that diary! Oh, lord! It's ten to two. I must go and ring up the station and see if they've got any news. Will you order us some coffee, darling?"

He was away at the telephone some time, and came back in a state of fury and agitation, with his eyebrows drawn into a thick black line across his forehead. He flung himself into his chair.

"Well! They've got Syd."

"Have they? And did he do it?"

Richard lit a cigarette and began to smoke in quick angry puffs.

"Who can tell? He says he knows something about the kidnapping, but he won't talk unless they promise to drop all the other charges."

"What other charges? Ivy?"

"Yes, they broke him down on that by stating my hypothesis as a known fact. It was right, of course. And the blackmailing letter to the Links was proved up to the hilt. He can't deny either of those things. But when they asked about the kidnapping, he held out on them. He's a cool customer. He says yes, he knows something, but he won't tell them what he knows unless they drop the other charges. So there's a grand moral conflict raging at the Yard. Justice is justice, the guilty must be punished—all that stuff. I expect Parker's at the bottom of it; you know his high moral tone. They're going to have another conference about it this afternoon. Meanwhile, the baby is probably dying and my case is at a standstill. So what?"

He stubbed out his unfinished cigarette violently.

"So let's go to *The Winter's Tale* in Durham Garden. I've got tickets. You won't hear about the bones till four and you haven't got to be at Mayfield till the evening."

"Oh, dear! I should like to. It'd do me a lot of good, too. I'm so angry, I can't think at all. But we're watching Field's house, futile though it probably is. I can't leave Plummer to do that while I go off for the afternoon."

"Talk of angels," said Clare. "Look, there's Plummer himself, as large as life and going twice as fast."

"Where? Quick!"

She pointed out of the window. Plummer was just passing out of sight, trotting along with his little feet twinkling, and pointing like a gun-dog with his rudimentary nose, which he held almost as far forward as his stomach.

"He must be following Field. Quick! I must go."

"I'm coming too," cried Clare, and darted to follow him. The luncheon had been booked to Richard's hotel account, so there was nothing but the slow-moving public to delay them. They dodged in and out between the people, like football players or low-flying bats, and presently caught up with Plummer about halfway down the Turl.

"There 'e is, sir!" panted Plummer. "Came out into the 'Igh Street, started down towards the river, saw me, changed 'is mind, and came up 'ere."

The shambling red-haired figure, a bandage still round its forehead, was indeed striding jerkily ahead just in front of them.

"I wonder where he's going this time," said Richard. "Well, we shall see if we don't lose him."

Field crossed the Broad and to their surprise joined a queue outside Durham.

'Good heavens! I believe he's going to *The Winter's Tale*," said Clare. "Surely that's very out of character."

"It's very clever," said Richard thoughtfully. "A crowd is the best place to hide and the easiest place to get out of. I don't know how he's got a ticket. But if we hadn't got tickets too—as thanks to you we have—we couldn't have got in without an awful fuss, which we don't want, and he could have secured some measure of freedom, some chance to get away. Even as it is, he'll need a lot of watching. It's a big scattered crowd. Plummer, just go and make sure from the porter that this is the only way out."

"That's right, sir," said Plummer, after doing his errand. "All the other gates is shut in the afternoons. The porter says I can stay in the lodge and watch, sir, if you want me to. 'E's a friend of mine. Him and me uses the same house."

"Goes, I mean go, to the same pub," whispered Richard, seeing Clare's perplexed look. "Yes," he went on to Plummer. "I think that's a very good idea. You stay here, and we'll go in with Field to the play, and keep an eye on him, as luckily we have tickets. You have got the tickets, haven't you, darling? I hope our seats won't be too far from his. Perhaps we'd better join the queue."

Shepherding Clare, and, not looking at Field—for the great art of not being seen is to take no notice of a possible observer—Richard took his place at the end of a long and slow-moving queue.

"There he is," whispered Clare. "About fifteen away from us. Goodness, he does look ill. Well, aren't we lucky to be getting our play after all?"

"If we do get it," he replied. "I must say, I hope we shall. Shakespeare is just what I need at the moment to clear my mind and get it working properly. Have you noticed that about Shakespeare? If you are half thinking and can't get your thoughts clear to yourself, you just read some Shakespeare and sooner or later he says exactly what you mean."

"I know," said Clare, nodding wisely. "Like the Bible and the Common Law. That's why they're all so dangerous."

CHAPTER SIXTEEN

THE QUEUE, which stretched into the college right across the quadrangle to the garden entrance, a gate in the far right-hand corner, now began to move. Richard's height made it easy for him to keep his man in sight, but also made him embarrassingly conspicuous. He stooped down his head and went on talking to Clare.

"Is it going to be a good performance?" he asked. "I'm sure you must know all about it, going to so many parties and being hand-in-glove with the English school."

"I'm not hand-in-glove with the English school any more, darling. They gave me a second at the end of last year."

"But aren't you doing a B.Litt., or something?"

"Good heavens, no! Illiteracy is one thing. B-literacy is another, and far worse."

"I am sure, dear lady," said Richard, momentarily becoming Canon Chasuble, "that you do not deserve so neologistic a phrase. But that being so, why are you still at Oxford?"

"I'm afraid I'm just having a nice time and reading things I've always wanted to read. It's such heaven to have the freedom of the

place without being chivvied about. In fact, I'm becoming almost liter-
ate. But you were asking me about the play. Darling, it's going to be too
significant for words."

"Too significant for whose words? Shakespeare's?"

She laughed. "Well, that remains to be seen. Egon Toszt's producing it and he's going to have a quadruple interpretation."

"What on earth is that?" asked Richard. Then, looking up the queue:
"Oh, dear! Field's getting in. Give me my ticket, quick. Meet you in
your seat."

He walked boldly up to the head of the queue and forced his way
through the garden gate not far behind his quarry, whispering the magic
word "Police," but causing considerable though subdued indignation
behind him. Stepping behind a tree, he watched Field to his seat, and
then looked about him and took stock of his field of operations.

Durham Garden is laid out more simply and formally than any other
garden in Oxford. It is a great square lawn, walled on the three sides
that jut out from the college and fenced with an iron paling on the western side, where it adjoins the garden quad. Richard saw a man come
out of one of the staircases in this quadrangle, try the gate in the iron
paling, and find it locked. The western side, then, was secure. The
northern side was continuously walled, with a long herbaceous border
along its entire length, while the wall running along the eastern side was
broken halfway along by a huge wrought-iron grille set into it. Two
great crouching black yew trees flanked it, one to each side, and this
pattern of grille and trees was to form the background for the play. A
painted cloth hung behind the grille, substituting a Sicilian landscape for
the normal view of citizens bicycling down Parks Road outside. A good
background, formal yet pastoral, grand enough for the palace scenes
yet natural enough for the shepherds, and the yew trees made excellent
stage wings.

It was the south side of the garden alone, on the right-hand side of
the audience, which might afford opportunity for escape or concealment. In the southwestern corner was the gate by which they had come
in, and quite near it, in the southern side, was another gate leading into
a little rose garden, which, Richard vaguely remembered, in turn led
into the front quad near the lodge. The rose garden, however, though
open, was defended ground at present, since the players were using it
as a retiring room. This side of the garden was the only place where
there were trees encroaching on the grass. First there was a sparse line
of yews, and behind it, nearer to the edge, a lime avenue. Behind this

again, stood three hives of bees, busily making their famous lime-honey, and Richard was amused to see how careful the actors were to give them a wide berth. There were terrible stories of what the bees had done to Durham toughs who had been disrespectful to them. No Dean had ever inspired such awe.

On the whole, Richard was pleased with his ground. He had had worse places to watch than this enclosed square, with its sparsely planted trees and its two guarded entrances; and so far, he had never lost his man. Moving with bent head where the crowd was thickest, he bought a program from a somewhat unmathematical young man, found himself sixpence to the good on the transaction, pointed this out, found himself sixpence to the bad, refrained from pointing it out, and climbed unobtrusively to his seat, which was in the very middle of the audience in a tier raised about five feet from the ground. In the no-man's land below prowled displaced children and college cats. Clare was already installed.

"Do you see him?" she said. "Bang in front, at the right-hand end of the row."

"I know," said Richard disgustedly. "What luck! He has an easy getaway, and we have to push past all these people, if he decides not to stay out the show. And I can't tell them to stop him at the door. He may be a perfectly harmless character."

"Never mind," said Clare. "Perhaps he is, in which case I expect he'll stay and let us see the play. I hope so. And we're very well hidden here. He can't possibly spot us from the front row. Why, even the actors can't see us unless we sit up like anything!"

This, and its converse, was unfortunately true, as is so often the case in improvised theaters.

"Now, tell me," he said, "what's all this about a quadruple interpretation? What on earth does it mean?"

"Well, you know the play. Leontes of Sicily groundlessly suspects his wife Hermione of unfaithfulness with—"

"Yes, of course I know it. I do read Shakespeare, poor bobby though I am. And, anyhow," he added with a certain loss of dignity, "I did it for School Cert."

"Sorry, sorry, sorry. In that case the interpretation will be as clear as day to you. Well, Leontes is—let me think. Theological interpretation first. Leontes is interpreted as Adam."

"Adam who?"

"Just Adam. Adam and Eve, you know."

"But why?"

"Oh, they always start with Adam."

"Very sound idea, really. I mean, don't we all? But why Leontes specially?"

"Well, partly he's the origin of Perdita—she's the unfallen Eve, of course. And partly because he talks about the spider in the cup. That's like the Serpent in the Apple, you see."

"What, in Eden? But the serpent wasn't in the apple."

"No, in a sense it wasn't, darling. But we mustn't press poetic parallels too closely. That's one of the rules. Well, next we come to the mystical interpretation. According to that, he's Judas Iscariot."

"Good lord! How do they make that out?"

"Leontes himself suggests it quite early on. Though as he expresses a hope in the same sentence that his best blood may be turned to an infected jelly, perhaps he didn't mean it so seriously as the producer thinks."

"Oh, Clare, how fantastic!" said Richard laughingly. "Is there any more of it?"

"Goodness, yes. It's quadruple, you see. There's the historical interpretation, too, where Leontes represents English Protestantism."

"Lord, why?"

"You'll see," she said evasively, "if you know any history. They're saying now that Shakespeare was a crypto-Catholic. And so it follows that Hermione is Mary Queen of Scots, by way of a delicate compliment to her son James I."

"But that throws an entirely new light on Leontes' jealousy, doesn't it? I mean, if one's wife were Mary Queen of Scots any suspicions would be justified. Look at Bothwell."

"My dear!" said Clare in a mock-scandalized voice. "You talk as if Leontes were a real person."

"Well, he is, in the play. Not so real as Autblycus, but still—"

"But that's frightful heresy, talking about Shakespeare characters as if they were people. They may sometimes seem to be, but that's just a by-product of genius. The poet had far greater things in mind. Besides," said Clare, laughing in spite of herself, "Hermione isn't only Mary Queen of Scots. She's Shakespeare's Muse, too."

"I say! This is coming it very strong. Why?"

"It's all part of the personal interpretation. That's the fourth, you know, where Leontes is Shakespeare himself."

"You don't say!"

"No, of course I don't, but they do. It's one of those things you

have to say. You see, Shakespeare in his period of disillusion makes an
idol of his poetry. But the idol comes to life and bursts into glory, and so
Shakespeare is saved."

"H'm. And how are they going to get all this across?"

"I can't imagine, but I'm sure Egon Toszt will be very ingenious.
We'll soon see, in the intervals of watching Field." She opened her
program and began to study the cast. Richard meanwhile was watching a heavy girl in Elizabethan dress who had run across from the rose
garden to speak to Dr. Field. She was smiling and animated, though her
smile faded slightly during their conversation. Presently she made a
slight gesture of farewell, and, picking up her skirts, ran back to her
fellow actors.

"Look, Richard!" said Clare, pointing to her program. "*Lady-in-
Waiting—Marjory Field.* Is she a relation, or just a coincidence?"

"Relation. Not approved of. I remember now. She came into the
diary. She sent Field his ticket. Look, that must be her talking to him
now. Poor thing! She looks as if she found it rather discouraging, doesn't
she?"

"Heavens! What a lump! Poor thing! I hope he hasn't put her off
too much. Do you know any other people in the cast?"

He looked over the program. "Deborah Dingham, of course. I've
often seen her in London. She must be a very ripe age by now."

"Must she? What a pity! She's playing Hermione. She's the only
professional unless you count Leontes. He's still an undergraduate but
he was practically born on the stage, as you see by his name. He'll be
good. But I don't know about the others."

"Upon mine honor," murmured Richard half to himself, "the best
actors in the world, either for theological, historical, mystical, personal,
mystical-historical, theological-personal, theological-historical-mystical-
personal, scene indivisible or poem unlimited. Seneca cannot be too
heavy…"

"Hush! They're beginning."

He stifled his irreverent laughter and sat up. A very small string
orchestra was playing in a very distant potting shed. One could hear a
phrase from time to time. A shaky but enthusiastic burst of trumpeting
sounded from behind one of the yew trees, and a second or two later
the two splendidly dressed trumpeters on the stage lifted their instru-
ments to their lips with a guilty start, and puffed out their cheeks. But
the Noises Off had already downed tools. Now a vivid silken company
tripped, strode, or shuffled on to the greensward while the two courtiers

exchanged the preliminary high courtesies of the first scene.

"Look, that's Leontes," whispered Clare, as a man in a vermilion wig and beard walked on with more assurance than his fellows. "The true Judas color, you see."

"And I suppose that's Hermione," Richard whispered back, "the stout lady with three chins. You can't paint them out by daylight, can you? Why does she have such an arrant canary-colored wig?"

"Oh, that's to show she's a Muse. Muses always have yellow hair. Robert Graves says so. Haven't you read *The White Goddess*?"

"And who's the boy?" he asked, as an angular child swaggered on as Mamillius.

"Oh, that's Piers Pirley. It always is, every year. I can't think how they keep him so small."

"Feed him gin, I expect."

"Nothing more probable. Only I expect he orders it for himself. He's a very progressive child, I believe—calls his grandparents by their Christian names, and so on."

"Darling, we're barracking," said Richard. "We must behave."

"I know. Suppose everyone did it."

But quite apart from the proprieties, it was now impossible not to listen, for Deborah Dingham, past mistress of her art (and also of the Duke of Blankshire), was holding the stage as Hermione, and her voice had that authentic tragic rasp which plucks the guts like cello strings, so that every word and gesture found its mark, although (presumably to indicate Mary Queen of Scots) she spoke with a slight French accent. Leontes, though he looked like her son (he was in fact her great-nephew), supported her adequately, and Polixenes, though inaudible, stood fairly still and looked extremely handsome. Richard sighed with pleasure, and Clare perched on the edge of her chair, straining to see. Hermione walked apart with Polixenes under the limes, and Leontes watched them, choking with jealousy and speaking his mad, broken lines to his son. As he talked, he picked an apple from one of the yew trees, having some difficulty with the string. Richard and Clare exchanged a glance.

"Adam!" they whispered triumphantly.

Richard was watching Field with half an eye, but he gave no trouble at all. He was slumped in his chair and appeared to be asleep. The old spell began to work on the audience, who sat very still. A few furtively wept (of whom Richard was one) when Hermione swept out to her captivity in a glory of sorrowful indignation, while Antigonus, a slender swanlike youth in a gray wig, was left to impart whatever right-thinking sentiments he could through his woolly gray beard. Paulina, his wife, also gray-haired, but with a tiny waist and dimples that no makeup could disguise, added her fresh little voice in the prison scene which followed; and later, before Leontes, with the baby in her arms, piped her poetry of bitter maturity and fighting worldly wisdom. The anomalies were unimportant, for the verse was well spoken and did its own work. Leontes, moreover, was acting with real fire and skill and by the end of Act II, when the newborn child was carried away by Antigonus to be exposed in "some remote and desert place, quite out of our dominions," the audience was filled with awe and pity. But at this moment, of course, the act ended and there was a ten-minute interval for triviality to reassert itself. Some of the spectators left their chairs and began to walk about the garden, but Field did not move, so Richard and Clare kept their seats. She saw the tears in his eyes, and was silent for a little while. Then, having as she thought given him time to recover himself, she spoke.

"I always think the supreme moment in that act is Antigonus's prayer to 'some powerful spirit' to teach the kites and ravens to feed Perdita, don't you? You know—'wolves and bears have done like offices of pity.' There's something incredibly moving in that realistic view of nature, so violent and cruel, and yet absolutely nothing to Man, when he gets going. Like the storm in *Lear*."

"Yes," said Richard, in an unnaturally bright and objective voice. "I wonder if that's what made Shakespeare think of the Bear, a favorite character of mine. Perhaps his first idea was to let Perdita be brought up by it."

"The Natural-Historical interpretation, in fact?" said Clare, following his lead. "And talking of natural history, that book you bought yesterday is a perfect mine. There's quite a lot in there about babies being suckled by wolves. It really happens, you know."

"Like Romulus and Remus?" Richard was interested and spoke in a more natural voice.

"Well, yes, I suppose so. Or Mowgli. But I meant actual historical examples. Mothers really have left unwanted babies in the jungle in India, and wolves really have found them and brought them up. There are authentic records. But they usually die after about two years."

"I'm rather surprised that they last as long as that. Is the wolves' milk all right for them?"

"Apparently, yes. Perfectly digestible. It's when they get on to nothing but raw meat that they succumb, poor poppets. After all, it's a discouraging substitute for rusks. And they get very wolfish in character—bite as soon as look at you."

"Like the chap in Virgil who was suckled by Hyrcanian tigers," said Richard reflectively. "If our baby had to be adopted by an animal, I'd rather it were something more human. A nice, kind sheepdog, say..."

"Or a chimpanzee. According to this book, they're frightfully human and absolutely sweet to their babies."

She broke off with a start, for Richard had made a strangled noise and buried his face in his hands. He sat rigid in an agony of thought, lost to his surroundings. Clare watched him, till he raised his head and looked at her with a painful intensity.

"Oh, Clare! Don't you see? Chimpanzees! *The tibia's too long, the femur's too short, the jaw's too big for the skull.* Clare, I believe we've got it!"

He sprang to his feet and looked eagerly over towards Field's seat. But Field was not in his seat. He was in the crowd under the trees, and he was very near the edge, near the exit.

"God! He's getting away! Look!"

Richard pointed a wild denunciatory finger, and just at that moment, whether by chance or telepathy, Field turned and saw himself pointed at. He broke into a shambling run. Richard, yelling "Stop that man! Police!" began to trample across the people sitting in his row. Clare followed him, apologizing.

The fugitive psychologist, cutting across a procession of guards and courtiers who were marching up the lime avenue with careful dignity, cantered past the beehives, making for the rose garden. But there he checked for a moment, as if struck by an idea. Then he turned back and pushed them over before taking to his heels again. One, two, three, the hives toppled to the ground, and clouds of angry bees poured out of them. Some streamed after Field in a long dark phalanx, while others more and more unceasingly fanned out towards the audience. Confusion spread and people ran hither and thither; the bees still exuded in their myriads from the fallen hives, and the air was thick with their murmurous menace.

Richard pulled his jacket over his head, narrowed his eyes, and plunged into the cloud of bees. He was stung several times, but not as much as he expected, before he reached the rose garden. There he found his quarry out of sight and the garden deserted, all the players having fled save the Bear, who stood, a huge nightmare figure with white fangs and claws and crimson chops, completely enclosed in his papier-mâché shell, and cried in hollow and sepulchral tones from the depths of his disguise:

"I say, you chaps, what's all this? Do let me out! Something's stung me."

Richard passed the Bear, losing a few dozen bees to that unfortunate character, and came out through the other end of the rose garden, arriving on the side of the quadrangle next to the street and on the same side as the lodge.

Plummer had been standing in the lodge with his rudimentary nose dutifully pressed against the windowpane, watching the garden gate in the far right-hand corner of the quadrangle with devoted attention. But the gate from which Field, and later Richard, emerged, so far from being on the opposite side of the quadrangle, was on the same side as Plummer and screened from his view by projecting buildings. Field, therefore, came on unobserved till he passed the amazed sergeant almost under the window. Plummer uttered a kind of hoarse squeak, spun round and blundered out of the lodge, bumping against counters and boxes, but he was too late. Field was away into the street; not only into the street but into a taxi; not only into a taxi but into the last taxi in the rank. The driver was in his seat. Field waved a piece of paper money at him and he drove away up the Turl immediately.

Plummer stood still and scratched his head. His superior came past him like a whirlwind.

"The Bestiarick Gardens! Come there quick, and get help!" he cried and made off down Holywell, running strongly.

"Hi, George!" cried Plummer to the porter, who had come out to see what was happening. "Ring up the p'lice. Tell 'em to come to the Bestiarick Gardens, quick!"

"Right, Sam," said the porter, and went to his telephone. Plummer looked desperately round for a means of conveyance, for he knew that he could never run there in time. The cars, parked in the road, were sure to be locked, and there was no taxi. Suddenly his eye lit upon an electric invalid chair standing outside the vicarage next to the college. He stepped into it with a look of relief, switched it on, grasped the steering-wheel, and began to move. The chair bumped down the curb into the road and Plummer accelerated to top speed. He shot over the crossroads against the traffic lights and went buzzing down Holywell at what seemed to him an awful speed, lurching from side to side in his attempts to steer the single wheel in front, purple in the face, bursting buttons and blowing through his mustache.

Clare, emerging a few minutes after Richard, for she had not braved the bees but gone round the other way, also found no transport in the Broad and therefore began to run down Holywell, as Richard had done, towards the High and the river. But after a hundred yards her light steps grew slower and she had a stitch in her side. She stopped running. Just then, a delivery van slowed up beside her.

" 'Op in, miss, if you're in a hurry. Where d'you want to go?"

The Bestiarick Gardens were shut for the weekend, and when Richard reached the great gate, he found it locked. He thought he could hear the sound of hurrying feet somewhere inside. He ran his eyes quickly over the gate and wall and, deciding that it would be too slow and difficult to climb them, he pulled his revolver out of his pocket and shot twice into the heavy lock. It was badly bent and cracked by the shot, but it held firm so he took the gate in his powerful hands and shook and wrenched it with all his strength, till at last the iron buckled and he burst his way in.

The gardens were green and peaceful, dappled with the shade of their exotic trees, calm in the stateliness of their straight walks. A peacock spread his tail against a dark bay tree, golden carp flashed in a pool, petals drifted down like summer snowflakes from a flowering tree. Hardly a leaf moved in the tranced sunny afternoon air. Richard paused and listened. Then he began to run again, shattering the silence, scaring the peacock, for he had heard a clamor from the ape house the other side of the garden, outside the wall. Another iron gate led to it, and this, too, was locked, though the lock was less massive than the other. He spent two more shots from his gun in forcing it, and so won his way onto the lawn by the river where the new ape house stood in all the freshness of its architectural atrocity. The gorilla, in its outdoor cage, was alternately shaking the bars and drumming on its chest as it roared and gnashed is teeth in some recent and unexplained alarm.

The door of the house was shut and would not yield to Richard's shoulder in spite of his weight. He had only two more shots in his gun. He fired once and the door held. He fired again—his last shot—and it gave and he stood peering into the rank-smelling darkness.

All the apes seemed to be disturbed, for a great sound of roaring, gibbering, chattering, rattling, and screaming poured from the cages in a babel of insane inarticulate rage and fear. Richard shuddered and plunged into the yammering malodorous gloom.

At first he was blinded, coming from the sunshine outside, but gradually his eyes adjusted themselves and he could see into the various cages, the groups of chimpanzees and the old solitary orangutan next but one to the end, sitting in a corner with his hands over his ears. He looked for a light switch, but there was none, since the lights were worked from an office, so he ran in half-darkness and unarmed to the last cage of all, where there was no visible occupant and from which no sound came. He tried the door, and it yielded at a touch. He went up into the empty cage. At the back of was a blank, square hole, the door of the apes' sleeping place He took his little electric torch from his pocket, and stooping by the hole, he shone its thin feeble beam into the inner chamber. The light fell upon the inexpressive eyes of a large female orangutan which crouched in the far corner over some small thing cradled in its arms. Then, traveling past her, it lit up the prostrate body of Dr. Field, huddled in an ungainly heap, with blood flowing from his head on to the foul straw and muck of the floor.

CHAPTER SEVENTEEN

INTO THE dark den he went, by the thin light of the torch. He had to stoop, for the ceiling was hardly higher than his own shoulders. His first and simplest duty was to rescue Field from further injury, but he could not use the torch, since he needed both hands to move him. So he switched it off and took the man under the arms in the darkness, and began to drag him to the cage and the light. He could hear the ape stirring in its corner, but it kept its distance and did not attack him. He got his man safely out of the den, and laid him in the far side of the cage, alive though unconscious. Richard could do no more for him as yet, for another life, he felt sure, was at stake, and perhaps a more precious one, so back he went again through the square hole into the dark chamber. The thick-set beast was still squatting motionless and watchful on a low platform in the blackest corner.

Using his torch again, he went close up to it, trying to see what was in its arms. It showed its teeth at him, and struck out with the long nails of its clawlike left hand, while it hugged its burden closer with its right arm, turning it away from the man with a possessive, protective gesture. But as it turned, an alien cry sounded from the depths of its hairy armpits and bosom—the thin piercing cry of a young child, unmistakably human although so inarticulate—and Richard knew that his reasoning had been right and that he had come to the end of his quest.

Immediately he grasped the hairy arm, but it tightened over the child and the ape snapped at his hand. The crying broke off in a strangled little choke, and he paused in agonized irresolution. What ought he to do? If he wrestled with the ape, the child might be crushed in the struggle; indeed it might already be injured or dead as a result of his first impetuous action. Should he go for help? But help, he knew, was on its way. Plummer and Clare were seeing to that. And it still might be more dangerous to leave the child alone now with its monstrous foster-mother. Had he not read somewhere that animals would eat their young in moments of danger? He bitterly regretted having emptied his revolver. One bullet would have solved everything. He decided to stay and watch, but it was torture to him not to act; a fight would be far better than this impotent anxiety. Was the child still alive? He had heard no sound since the little choking cry. He switched off the torch and stood stooping in the darkness, weighed down by loneliness and indecision and by the nightmare quality of his vigil. He had been standing so for what seemed an eternity, when a blessed sound from the world of every day came to his straining ears—Plummer's slow broad voice calling him.

"Inspector Ringwood! Where are you? Where are you, sir? It's me, Plummer. Are you all right, sir?"

"Here!" cried Richard, risking a shout. The ape muttered threateningly at the sound of his voice, and he froze into silence again.

The dim light of the opening was obscured and Plummer came in, saying, "What about Dr. Field?" But Richard checked him.

"Quiet," he whispered, and shone his torch on the ape. "Don't frighten it." He did not dare say more, and hoped that Plummer would see the baby and understand.

But Plummer either misunderstood or disregarded his instructions; he was entirely fascinated by the animal. No animal had ever feared him in all his life and it did not occur to him that the ape would fear him now. He went straight over to it by the light of Richard's torch, hardly needing to stoop, and made that half-pitying, half-amused sound so often elicited from an English crowd by the sight of an animal for which it has a fellow-feeling.

"Aow!" said Plummer, on a long-drawn descending note, with a world of protective affection in his voice. "Why, it's just a dear old monkey. I won't frighten you. You're not frightened of me, eh? What you been doing, eh, duck? What's the matter with you? There's a poor old monk, then!"

The ape peered up at him with its sad wrinkled face. Sitting there, it looked like a very dirty, very broad old woman. He put out a plump hand, entirely without fear, and stroked the coarse scanty hair on its great head. It flinched, but bore the caress. Plummer continued to stroke it, and went on with his soothing monologue, while Richard stood paralyzed by apprehensive indecision, not daring to move or speak lest the ape should attack the sergeant or crush the baby.

"Blessed if you ain't the image of my old auntie!" said Plummer, with loving admiration. "There's a poor old girl, then. You feeling lonely, eh? Didn't you like Saturday afternoons, eh? Nobody to feed the poor old monk, eh? Never mind, I got something for you. Here you are, duck! Cheer up."

He fumbled in his pockets and brought out a crumpled packet of chocolate and, breaking off a piece, held it out in his palm. The animal snatched it timidly with its left hand and crammed it into its pouch. Then it looked up hopefully, waiting for more. The torch was beginning to fail and its light no longer reached across from where Richard stood.

"What you got there, eh? A little baby monkey? Aow!" Again that note of compassionate amusement. "Come on now, let's have a look. I won't 'urt you, eh? What you got there? Come on, let's 'ave a dekko and then I'll give you another bit of choc. There's a good girl. Come on, then!"

He bent closer and closer, stroking its head but he could not see the baby, for it was burrowed deep into the thick fur, and besides the light was bad, showing outlines but not details. Then suddenly, losing the nipple, it wailed again, an unmistakably human cry. Plummer had been a father too often not to recognize the sound, and he suddenly realized why he had been brought to this unexpected goal.

"Gawd!" he said—almost a prayer. "Help!" he added—an injunction—and seized its arms without a moment's hesitation, forcing them away from its body to release the child. The ape turned savagely and buried its teeth in his upper arm. He groaned, but held on. Richard, with a kind of joy in action at last, after his wretched passivity, sprang forward to help him. He got one hand under the jowl and pushed its head back. Then, getting a purchase with his knee against its body, he pulled fiercely with his other hand at the hairy right arm that held the baby. It was immensely strong, but he and Plummer at last loosened the grip a little and the baby began to slide out. Plummer caught it away before it fell.

"Take it out!" said Richard between his teeth. "Get the keeper."

Plummer hurried, away, the blood soaking his sleeve, with the baby in the crook of his arm. It began to cry again, missing the warmth and the milk, and the ape sprang after its foster-child just as Plummer reached the entrance of the den. Richard grabbed it by an arm and a handful of fur and hauled it back. Angry and terrified, it turned and attacked him, clinging round his legs with its strong prehensile feet, enfolding his body and arms with its long powerful arms, biting savagely at his belly and sides with great yellow teeth like chisels. Hampered by the low roof, which cramped him and gave him no advantage of his height, Richard kept his feet with difficulty and struggled vainly to throw the creature off. The hairy limbs seemed to be everywhere at once and to cling all about his body, while the sharp teeth tore and worried at his clothing and were already piercing to the flesh beneath. He got a hand free, and once more seized it by the hair of its head, forcing the snapping jaws away from him. He stood swaying, his legs and left arm imprisoned in a Laocoon coil, and felt the hair beginning to tear away from its straining head while it howled with pain and fury.

At last it got its head free, leaving him with a scanty handful of hair. Then it changed its tactics, and, leaving the ground, began to climb up his body as if he were a tree, digging its long nails into him with every new hold of its hands and feet. It came swarming up with appalling speed, and now its muzzle was close to his face and it was making for his head and throat. He could see its eyes glitter, and the stench of its breath sickened him, as it closed against his whole body from thigh to shoulder, its crushing arms wrapped round his arms and back, its legs wound round his hips and thighs, and its horrible hot womanish bosom pressed like a succuba against his chest. He twisted and turned desperately to avoid the snapping teeth, and strained to free his arms, but the long hairy limbs held him like fetters. So he flung himself hard to the ground on top of his enemy. It was not a long enough fall to knock the creature senseless, but he did at least manage to profit by its surprise and work one arm free. He grasped it by the throat, squeezing its windpipe; its grip loosened a little, and he struggled to his knees, and, holding it at arm's length, began to work his way painfully towards the cage, while its hands clawed at his face and neck.

The baby's cry was heard again, from a great way off, and the ape, with a convulsive wriggle, broke free and swung itself off towards the light, using its long arms like crutches. Richard hurled himself after it. The cage door was open and the beast made straight for it. It was almost through when Richard caught it by the foot and began to drag it back. It struggled powerfully, but Richard put forth all his strength and at length managed to slam the cage door. The spring lock clicked, and Richard saw in a hasty glance that he had shut himself in, for the cage could only be opened from the outside. Nevertheless, it was without real regret that he turned to face the creature again, for the battle was in his blood now, and his one desire was to win; indeed, he had forgotten why he was fighting. His enemy crouched, with its long arms swinging, a couple of yards away from him. It was making a great clamor of rage and distress. Richard had heard very much the same sounds from drunken criminals in street fights, but this vituperation was worse, for it was uncannily wordless and yet uncannily human. Hatred and fear, moreover, were written on its face as on the face of a man. Only its eyes were the unfathomable eyes of a beast, and this proved to be Richard's undoing, for it looked so human that he instinctively adopted human tactics of fighting with it. He watched its eyes, as a boxer or a fencer watches the eyes of his opponent, for the eyes will give warning of a move a split second before the move is made. But the eyes of an ape are not to be read like the eyes of a man, so Richard was taken by surprise when it attacked him for the third time, springing upwards at his face and shoulders.

This time at least the light and his size were in his favor, and he could move and think more quickly than his adversary. Although he did not have time to dodge the springing beast, he was able to grasp it by the arms and thrust it away before it got to close quarters with him. So holding it away from him, though it snapped at his wrists, he whirled it round and thrust it against the bars which divided its cage from the next one. Pinning it with one knee against its horribly feminine chest, he slid down his hands to its wrists. Then, holding each wrist, he forced its arms wide apart, stretched his fingers and succeeded in grasping a bar behind either wrist, and so held wrist and bar together. This gave him a means of holding it pinned, provided his hands arms would bear the strain. And so he pinned it, spread-eagled to the side of the cage, and stood the full length of his arms away. It lashed out with its feet, clawing at his legs and ripping his trousers, but he held it fast, not caring for lesser wounds so long as he was out of range of its teeth. He felt he had won, for he believed that he could hold it thus for five minutes, and surely help would have come by then. Aching and in danger as he was, he was filled with the joy of victory.

But then he raised his eyes and looked through into the other cage, where the old male orangutan was kept. It was no longer sitting in its corner, but standing on the other side of the bars quite close to him, roused by the cries of its mate. It stood watching for a while; but at last, after a particularly frenzied struggle on the part of the female, it suddenly leaned forward and bit Richard's hand to the bone. He lost his grip, and the female got free and closed with him instantly. Over its shoulder as it came he saw the door of the end of the house open to the sunlight, and he heard Clare's voice calling his name. Then the ape bit into his neck just above the collarbone. He felt the warm blood trickle over his chest, lost his footing, fell heavily backwards, and lay unconscious where he fell.

It was less than five minutes ago that Plummer, with the baby in his arms, had rushed out for help. He met Clare halfway across the main garden. She took the child from him and they ran off in different directions, shouting for the keeper. Plummer found him and explained confusedly. The keeper ran for a gun and caught up with the other two at the cage, where the ape was crouching motionless over the prostrate bodies. The keeper, with angry words and upraised hand, drove it back into its den, and then crossing the cage after it, released a steel shutter from above, which fell across the opening with a clang and shut the animal in.

Then they looked at the victims. Plummer pronounced that the inspector wasn't so bad but that Dr. Field looked awful. It would be better not to move them till help came from the police station. They had not long to wait. An inspector and a constable soon arrived in a car and they telephoned at once for an ambulance. Meanwhile Richard and Field were carried out of the cage and laid on the grass outside the ape house. Presently two ambulance men came into sight. They had left their vehicle outside the main gates, but brought a stretcher across the space of the garden. Field, as the more serious case, was taken first. They had loaded him on to the stretcher and were carrying him off when the policemen, who were going to go with him, were distracted. Richard was returning to consciousness and trying to speak. They all bent over him eagerly, Clare nearest.

"Oh...Hullo, darling!" His utterance was weak and confused. "Where...oh, good! You've got the baby." Then he began to remember. "Where's that ape?"

"Shut up, sir, quite safe," said Plummer. "Don't you worry."

Richard raised himself on one elbow, and his voice took on the rasp of command.

"Listen! We've got the baby. Clare, will you take it back? But I've no proof Field did it. There is a proof, the second volume of Field's diary. I saw the first volume in his desk this morning. The second volume must be found at once. It'll be in his house somewhere, if he hasn't got it on him. Get it at once, d'you hear? It's vital."

His voice grew fainter and he spoke with increasing agitation.

"There must be a second volume, there must be…And I say, look after that maid—don't leave her alone."

Then speech failed him and he fell back and fainted.

Plummer did his best to explain, but he had never been a lucid expositor and the pain of his bleeding arm did not help matters. Precious time was wasted in talk, and the ambulance men had returned all the way across the garden with a second stretcher before the Oxford policemen felt themselves in a position to act. Finally, they decided that one of them should accompany Field to hospital, where he could be more safely searched, while the other began to go through the house in Kybald Street. Clare meanwhile was to take the child back to its parents. They set off across the gardens in a body, following Richard's stretcher, and were about to part outside the gate when a cry from the ambulance men stopped them. "He's gone!"

It was true. Field had disappeared.

It looked as if he must have been removed by some accomplice, considering how ill he was, though one of the ambulance men did mention that he had seemed stiff to carry, not limp like an unconscious man. But how had he been got away so quickly, so in the nick of time? Plummer suddenly gave a hoarse cry.

"Look! The taxi! The one he came down in. There it is, just turning up into Long Wall."

"Come on!" shouted the Oxford inspector, jumping into the police car. "You, Badger, and Plummer. We'll follow it. You, take the inspector up to hospital, don't wait."

"I'll be up there as soon as I've taken the baby back," said Clare to the ambulance men, and went her way.

The taxi proved unexpectedly difficult to catch. It showed a wonderful turn of speed, and its driver knew all the side roads and dodged out through the suburbs to the north of the city, leading them a fine dance. They could not see inside it from behind, though now and then a pair of eyes peeped out of the back window. The behavior of the taxi left them in no doubt that it was in flight from them, and they hung on grimly round every twist and turn though they did not catch it up. Presently, coming out into more open country, they reached an important crossroads with a roundabout in the middle, a low grassy mound with a glass sentry box upon it, where a man in uniform stood watching the traffic. The taxi went round it on the left. But it did not take the road to north, east or west as they expected. It simply circled the roundabout at high speed, round and round while the man in the sentry box spun round and round like a mechanical toy watching it. Seven times it made the circle, with the police car in hot pursuit, and seven times the bewildered man spun in concert. Then it shot off along the eastern arm for some two hundred yards and pulled up suddenly under the sign of a roadside pub. As the police car drew up beside it, two tall young men clambered out, leaving it empty. The fairer of the two said, with a disarming smile:

"Sorry we couldn't give you more of a run. Trouble was, we got thirsty, didn't we, Francis? Better luck next time."

The inspector at last found his voice.

"You—you—you again! You're—"

"Bevan. Just, though I hate to say it, like the cabinet minister."

Clare, as she stood before the Links' front door with the baby in her arms, was feeling, despite her own weariness and her anxiety for Richard, the pleasurable sensation of one who comes with good news—of a comforter, a welcome visitor, a kind of vicarious savior. She rang the bell with a certain lifting of the heart, conscious that the Richard-Clare combine had indeed brought home the bacon; her face glowed and she was suffused with good will.

It was John Link who opened the door. He gave one look at Clare and the baby, and then shouted, in a curiously shrill and broken voice:

"Pettie! Here! Quick!"

His wife came out, her small dark face strained with apprehension. Then she, too, saw the baby in Clare's arms, and Clare's radiant smile, and she came quickly down the steps and almost snatched the baby from her without a word, parting the covering, gazing at her child as if she could not believe her own eyes. It was to her husband that she spoke.

"It's Perdita! We've got her back! Oh, John, I do hope she's all right. How dirty she is! And where are clothes?"

"She hadn't any when we found her," said Clare, "so I wrapped her up in my jacket. Richard—"

"Couldn't you find a woolly? I do hope she won't have caught cold." She continued to peer at the baby, who now, thoroughly roused and smelling its mother's milk, began to cry and to weave about with its head, searching for the breast.

"She's hungry," said Perpetua to Clare, not looking at her. "I must feed her at once—do you mind?—and get her clean and properly wrapped up. My husband will deal with any formalities. Will that be all right?"

"Of course," said Clare, feeling deflated. "Can I be of any help to you?"

"Oh, no! No, thank you. I always do everything for her myself." She clasped the baby tighter to her, with a defensive look, and went up the stairs, calling over her shoulder, "John! Ring up the doctor at once, will you?"

Clare and the somewhat embarrassed father were left facing each other on the doorstep.

"Is there anything I ought to do?" he asked with a lame formality. "Anything to sign, or anything?"

"I don't think so," said Clare. "If there is, it's no business of mine. The police will see to it. They asked me to say that they're sending a doctor along at once to look at the baby."

"Oh, I think we'll get our own doctor, thank you very much all the same," he replied. "We have a child specialist for her. G.P.s are so seldom competent pediatricians. I'll ring him up at once."

He turned to go, and then hesitated again as Clare still stood there.

"Don't you want to hear how we found her?" asked Clare, feeling that even if he took her for granted as a functionary, he might at least have a normal curiosity about the pattern of events.

"Well, yes, of course," he said, with a constrained smile. "Another time we should be most interested, naturally. But perhaps not just now, if you don't mind. She's safe, that's the main thing. Do forgive me for not asking you in at present. I'm sure you'll understand. We shall look forward to seeing you later. Excuse me, I really must go and ring up the doctor. Goodbye, and thank you so much. Please thank Richard too."

Leaving the door open, he disappeared into the back of the house, from whence he could be heard telephoning.

"Well!" thought Clare bitterly. "Of all the—! I suppose they think people like Richard are simply laid on out of the rates and taxes, like dustmen. And, oh, dear, blast them, they've got my jacket. Shall I ring and ask for it? No, I'm damned if I will. It's quite unwearable now, anyway, and I must get back to Richard."

She turned angrily and began to walk up Merton Street. It was then, and only then, that she saw Dr. Field. He was half-lying, half-sitting on the pavement, halfway down the street, propped against the wall of a house. By his side, let into the pavement, was a barred grating of the sort that leads to a cellar window. But one could not see what was beneath this grating, for it had been blocked by a board fixed immediately under its bars. The cellar was perhaps disused, and the board may have been put there to stop rubbish getting through into the hole below. Nevertheless, Field seemed to be trying to do something to the grating. His back was turned, and Clare crept up behind him unobserved. Field, she saw, held a small thin notebook in his hand and was trying to push it through the bars of the grating, clumsily, blindly, feeling for another place each time the notebook was impeded by the board and could be pushed down no farther. As he groped and poked, he talked to himself in a toneless voice like a sleepwalker.

"They won't think of looking here. These gratings are disgrace. I always said so. Tripping people up and harboring rubbish. I'd like to pull the whole street down. Unhygienic and inconvenient. I can't see. Did I take off my bifocals? I can't remember. There's something the matter with these bars. I can't feel the chinks, I wish I could see. But it's too far off. Better not stoop, Field. You'd never get up again. You know that. Patience and accuracy, patience and accuracy, that's what sees the experiment through."

He tried again—the fourth attempt since Clare had been watching him—to push the notebook between the blocked bars. This time it bent, and slid under them horizontally, till it lay flat under the bars on the board below them. But Field evidently thought it had dropped right down. He sighed with relief, and dragged himself painfully away from the grating and into the gutter. He could not see Clare standing, motionless, hardly six feet away. His sore, shortsighted eyes were even dimmer than they had been before; yet there was something like triumph in his look. He began to declaim, like a man reading aloud.

"Dr. Field is always conscious of acting in the best interests of the human race. Dr. Field...Dr. Field..." He faltered, and spoke in a fainter, more natural voice. "You'll never get up, Field."

She was not in time., to catch him as he collapsed. Blood was oozing, out of his ears and he was breathing with a dreadful sound of strife and pain. Clare knocked at the nearest house for help to move him to a safer position and to get an ambulance. Then, waiting beside him, she drew out the little notebook from under the bars. It was the second volume of the diary.

CHAPTER EIGHTEEN

THE PASSAGES of the diary eventually incorporated into Richard's official report ran as follows:

Learned today at Best. Gdns. that Pong. Pyg. F. preg. (*Pongo Pygmaeus is one of the two scientific names for the orangutan. The other, Simia Satyricus, probably repelled Dr. Field on account of its lacking classical associations. The symbol F. means female.*) Event expected in abt. 3 wks. Intend keeping under close observation with view to seeing how far mat. instinct & possessiveness can be reduced by pre- & antenatal conditioning.

Starting in today. Keeper unhelpful, sentimental & sloppy, lacking in Sci. Spirit. MEM. Arrange to go during luncheon & after closing time (5.30). Will mean changing own mealtimes & acidosis will prob. recur but have never spared myself in Cause of Sci. & do not intend to commence now.

May 2nd. Visited Pang. Pyg. F. in lunch-hour with ¼ lb. grapes (1/ 4). MEM. 1 . Keep note of expenses. Is quite active & intelligent specimen but diff. to follow thought-stream therefore diff. to condition. Tried it with small toy monkey (10/6) but does not seem to anticipate own maternity. Yet is capable of crude symbolism, e.g. interested in picture books. MEM. 2, Get lifelike picture of young Pong. Pyg. See MEM. 1. Responds moderately to endearments. Must try to fix up daily visits.

May 3rd. Pong. Pyg. 1 P.M. Nothing to report. (*A similar visit is reported every day from now onwards.*)

May 6th. Pong. Pyg. has taken violent dislike to my glasses. A problem, as if removed I cannot observe so accurately. Dislikes a prolonged stare in any case. MEM. 1. Find out from keeper if poss. why. Painful incident in past w. spectacled man? Dislike due to association? Transference shaping up quite satisfactorily otherwise. Shows pleasure when I arrive. MEM. 2. Grapes 11½d.

May 12th. Shall in future refer to Pong. Pyg. F. as Emmeline, that being its silly name, as may have to record later experiments on other Pong. Pygs. Still dislikes my glasses, and keeper unhelpful—cannot or will not throw light on any poss. reason in past life history. Shall have to remove them during visits. Inconvenient, but can just see her if I keep sufficiently close. MEM. Tell Edna to spray my suit with D.D.T. Fear parasites. Keeper however denies presence of. Emmeline shows no interest in picture of young pong. pyg., and appears unaware of own pregnancy, despite noticeable development of lactatory organs. MEM. Perh. this is just as well. Cd. not conditioning reduce unnecessary excitement in human female? Birth cd. then be regarded as short isolated incident, and early redirection of child to crèche would be accepted without tension, thus improving economic output and civic spirit of female. Write this up tomorrow for Drawer 3.

May 13th. Emmeline still nervous when am in close proximity, even without glasses. Poss. due to my movements wh. are I confess apt to be clumsy and nervous due to lack of proper early training. Perh. not too late now? Ought to try eurhythmics. But risk of sneers if it got about, damaging not only to self but to Cause of Science. Might ask M. about possibilities. Have heard eurhythmy produces amazing results.

A blank, followed by Field's account of his injury and Costard's remarks in Hall.

May 22nd. Emm. distinctly noncooperative. Am trying her with simple constructive toys (lent by special school) but so far she will only take apart completed structure. Shall try to build up other interests before birth to get parallelism with my plan for human mothers (see *Planned Society,* ch. IV), in order to minimize tension due to subsequent separation. Wish her interests cd. be widened. At present she seems to care for nothing but food and endearments. Latter waste much valuable time but am sure they are essential part of treatment. (Cf. my domestic arrangements—a real parallelism with Edna here.) Find the physical contact trying, esp. having hair searched for nonexistent fleas, but keeper says it is expected by all pong. pygs. and a mark of confidence and intimacy.

June 2nd. Emm. has safely produced young Pong Pyg. F. They advise against—i.e. are determined to prevent—my visiting her for at least 5 days. Shall then visit daily for 1 week in order to regain her confidence in new circs. Might then attempt to separate her from young for about 5 minutes daily, gradually extending period, meanwhile reawakening her prenatal interests. Am rather glad to have bit of breathing time, as University is to vote on my proposal for Experimental Material this week, and tho' I do not anticipate trouble must make sure sufficient numbers of progressives attend to vote. Am having notices cyclostyled & am circulating widely. Think this more aboveboard, also less time-wasting, than personal canvassing wh. is no doubt going on among reactionaries, whose methods I consider cowardly & underhand. *They flatter the ego of others in order to prop up their own.*

MEM. Copy this useful phrase for Drawer 4.

June 4th. Voluntary experiments before Con. today. Outvoted. Owe this to J.L. Thought he was progressive as had seemed sincerely interested in my experiments in B.G. Realize now he was just showing off his south-country manners—smile in face, stab in back. Will be difficult to undo effects of his smarmy rhetoric. But will GET EVEN. Must take lessons in pub. speaking. But where? Do not want to risk more cheap sneers, and it might get about. Might ask Marjory, who is wasting her time and scholarship in amateur play-acting. MEM. Ask her to tea.

June 5th. Still feel v. discouraged after yesterday. Experiments on the higher anthropoids not without value, but difficulties of communication v. great. Undergraduates wd. have been quicker & more cooperative. Had even hoped J.L. might volunteer himself but has evidently been two-faced all along & merely making a show of Sci. Spirit wh. he is really devoid of. My acidosis v. bad again and fear my depression has affected Edna as her cooking has deteriorated. MUST NOT GIVE WAY. This is only first setback, & Oxford is known to be ceiling of selfish individualistic viewpoint. Am looking forward to Bangor next wk., as feel in great need of support from like-minded, forward-looking people. Colleagues here good in own fields but narrow in outlook, and their policy is too influenced by personal factors.

Provost told me yesterday that he "sympathized with my disappointment." Told him straight out that what the Cause of Sci. needed was hard work, not soft soap. That silenced him. MEM. Rather neat. Copy for Drawer 4. Shall not go into Hall. Flatulence too bad & colleagues either insincere or openly hostile.

June 9th, Visit to Emmeline. Is v. shy & inclined to bite. MEM. Wear gloves tomorrow. Shall have a job to carry out my program & must proceed v. cautiously. Keeper is if anything even more unhelpful than before, & seems to positively encourage Emm.'s obsessive interest in young. Has put her in end cage & railed it off against visitors. This may invalidate experiment as outside interests essential. She growls when stroked. Alarming but must persevere. She keeps to dark inner chamber.

June 12th. Managed to lure Emm. into outer cage today by means of banana. Much more convenient to me & real advance psychologically. I do not feel v. happy in inner chamber—too dark, and light can only be turned on at main & impracticable. Need all light I can get, as diff. to see without glasses. She let me stroke her but withheld young.

June 15th. Have obtained bottle of Teething Syrup (1/9) which shall try on young Pong. Pyg. tomorrow. MEM. Copy out formula.

June 16th. Teething syrup, offered on finger, great success. Young Pong. Pyg. appeared to fancy it. Mother meanwhile busy w. banana. (MEM. Bananas not to be entered on expense account, as strictly reserved for children, but feel it is justifiable to obtain them in circs.) Emm. seemed pleased at young Pong. Pyg.'s gurgles etc. over syrup. Hope she will allow me to hold it soon. Keeper will not allow me to introduce male Pong. Pyg. (the father) into cage. A pity as results might be good. But if there were trouble, shd. not fancy facing two angry, Pong. Pygs. so perh. just as well from personal angle, which I must however try to eradicate. Sci. Spirit. shd. cast out fear. cf. Darwin, Galileo etc. Also must AND WILL prove Link & Co. wrong.

June 17th. 9 A.M. Solemnly record my firm resolution to temporarily remove young Pong. Pyg. from mother TODAY.

12 noon. College meeting 10 this morning. J.L. acted deceitfully. Pretended to be on my side but abstained from voting. Clear type of regressive, unable to make up mind therefore a time-saver. Shd. be removed from present responsible position. My duty to point this out in right quarters. But how?

2 P.M. Long session with Emm. Syrup, bananas, toys etc. Seemed amenable and interested but I was unfortunately in state of personal tension (due I know to factors in early life but ought to have sublimated them by now) and suffered from nervous hiccups, acidosis etc. Had to give up, but will obtain pineapple and make another attempt after closing time this evng. Am suffering from irrational emotions of guilt and distress despite informed self-analysis. Wish I had been in position to afford Bumpf analysis offered in 1922, as he cd. have helped me deal w. this recurrent phenomenon. But WILL succeed tonight. My last chance as I lecture at King's Coll. London this evng. & have to start for Bangor Sat. aft., & have not completed writing up paper for latter. EXCELSIOR.

(The following long entry is in a very shaky hand.)

7.30 P.M. (in train). Do not know how I can go on with this account. But must externalize, otherwise am in danger of developing psychosis. May have done so already. Objection—suppose this diary found by someone? V. unlikely, in any case acted for best on long view, wd. stand by my action if forced to do so by circs. MEM. Keep in Drawer 1 locked, or (better) find hiding place. Should I not write my account till home again? But better to do while details clear. Also will relieve tension & leave mind clear to lecture tonight. Must keep account objective. Glad carriage is empty, tho' 1st class really against my principles.

A blank of two lines follows. Then, in a firmer hand:

FINAL STAGE OF EXPERIMENT TO ASCERTAIN DEGREE OF MATER-
NAL ATTACHMENT IN PONG. PYG. F.

At 5 P.M. on June 17th Dr. Victor Field visited Pong. Pyg. F. Emmeline
with view of removing young for first time for a short period. He in-
tended to lengthen this period day by day to facilitate weaning and
complete removal at earliest poss. date. He had subjected her to 1
month's prenatal conditioning & had resumed treatment on June 9th,
parturition having taken place on June 1st. Dr. Field had broken down
emotional resistance and encouraged external interests. The young animal had been conditioned to expect & enjoy a preparation known as
Blogg's Gripe-Water, a compound of sugar, dill and ol. menth. There
was therefore hope that it cd. be removed in contented condition.

At 5 P.M. Emm. was becoming drowsy, as the Pong. Pyg. like other
primates sleeps for 12 hours due to tropical 12-hour night. Dr. Field
tempted her into cage by means of a banana, leaving cage door ajar and
placing himself directly in front of it. He then offered Emm. a small
pineapple, a fruit requiring use of both hands due to prickly outer integu-
ment. Both hands were used, & young pong. pyg. clung to fur. Dr. F.
rapidly detached young pong pyg. from mother and withdrew from cage,
slamming door. Mother evinced excitement and distress, shook bars,
etc. Young p.p. also emitted cries prob. indicating discomfort. Dr. F.
attempted to soothe it with gripe-water in order to leave mother in state
of non-anxiety. But was wearing gloves, g.w. could not be offered on
fingertip. Gave it from bottle. An excessive quantity was taken & young
p.p. choked violently & shortly after died, prob. due to asphyxiation.

Other inmates of ape house now v. noisy. Dr. Field, unwilling to
attract attention in these difficult circumstances, which some might have
found overwhelming, withdrew immediately from the gardens, first con-
cealing cadaver of young pong. pyg. under adjacent bush. He realized
immediately that it was vital to conceal this death, in interests of Sci., as
otherwise liberty for future experiments would be endangered. But for
this, he would have accepted consequences of accident fearlessly.

On way home, however, a solution suggested itself, while passing
pram containing newborn human infant in empty street. Dr. F. decided
to secretly transfer this infant to pong. pyg. as substitute till newborn
p.p. cd. be secured and substituted. Reasons for this step:

1. Immediate discovery of accident wd. be avoided.

2. Unprecedented opportunity was given for entirely new experimental work to establish essential common psych. features of Man and

Higher Anthropoids. Query: could even train anthropoids for crèche work in Planned Society, perh. even use as wet nurses. MEM. Ask progressive biologist if milk always suitable.

3. Infant in question was child of parents who were reactionary & had already hampered important experimental work, and therefore

(a) Was unlikely to grow up useful citizen. Possible death not much loss.

(b) By using it Dr. Field justly punished the obstructionism of its father.

4. The infant was healthy and extremely apelike in appearance.

Dr. Field therefore transferred infant to Bestiarick Gdns. under his jacket. (No one in Gdns). He undressed and rubbed it all over with cadaver of young pong. pyg. to give it approximately similar odor, & gave it gripe-water on finger to soothe cries. Offered it to mother and was severely bitten in process, but infant clung to fur, found breast, began to feed. Emm. appeared appeased and withdrew to chamber nuzzling it. Dr. Field left the ape house, picking up cadaver and clothes, both of which he destroyed at home. He then left Oxford to carry out his important duties in London, and will report on the further progress of his experiment on his return.

N.B. Dr. Field has no feelings of guilt or distress. If he had, he wd. discount them as irrational & unworthy of a true scientist, as he is conscious of acting always in the best interests of the human race despite all obstructionism.

EPILOGUE

SUNDAY morning sunshine was streaming on to Richard's bed next day as he lay in the Boreal Nursing Home, an institution in the northern suburbs to which he had been taken the previous evening, the hospital being full up. He had seen the diary before he went to sleep. His friend, Andrew Thorne, had by then arrived from Liverpool to hear of the triumph. Now, with his case completed and Clare and Andrew sitting beside him, Richard's cup of pleasure was full.

"I still don't see how you solved it, though," said Clare. "I know the diary proves it up to the hilt, but I don't see how you got that far. After all, you knew what had happened before the diary was actually found, didn't you?"

"The gypsy told us the whole thing, really, as your analysis shows.

Look, Andrew! How's that for a first attempt in detection?"

He pointed to a page in his notebook covered in Clare's delicate italic.

"There's danger there...stowed away...away from the white breast to the dark...the stink...she lacks her own...What is lost will be found...a single loss, a double find...one for you and one for another...No man keeps it from you...It will be the same if you find it today or tomorrow or the day after.

"Two possible meanings," Clare's note continued. "There is danger (for the child) there, stowed away from the (its mother's) white breast to the dark (of the grave). She (the bereaved gypsy) lacks her own? The stink (of the dead)! A single loss (Perdita) a double find (two bodies). Out of man's keeping, etc.

(2) There's danger there, snatched away from the white breast (of its mother) to the dark breast of somebody else? A gypsy? She (Perdita) lacks her own (mother)? The stink, the stink (unexplained). A single loss, a double find (will be made by R. Ringwood—i.e. his friend Andrew and the baby. So cheer up!) Out of man's keeping (but in keeping of *woman*—i.e. foster-mother who will be trustworthy for at least three days. Is this a hint for a large bribe and a surreptitious return? Anyhow, look for dark foster-mothers, possibly smelly ones)."

"Well, there you are," said Richard, with far greater pride than he had yet shown. "Clare gave me the idea of a foster-mother. Your coming back so appositely made me take all the prophecy stuff more seriously."

"Still," said Clare, "there must be a lot of foster-mothers with a dark breast and—possibly—a nasty smell."

"None with such a nasty smell as that blasted ape Emmeline," said Richard, feelingly.

"Ugh!" said Clare, with a shudder. "Still, I don't see what got you within smelling distance of her in the first place."

"Well, I was in the Bestiarick Gardens on Friday," said Richard. "And there I heard—though I didn't really take it in at the time—that the female orangutan Emmeline—"

"Pong. Pyg." Andrew chuckled.

"All right, Pong. Pyg. had just had a baby. And the keeper said she was sulky and put it down to her being interfered with by these University scientists. I didn't think it had anything to do with the case. I just remembered it in that silly way one does remember odd details of casual conversation."

"So then?" said Andrew, leaning forward in his favorite attitude with his hands on his knees.

"So then the next morning Plummer—may his shadow never grow less—found that set of bones in Field's stove."

"That set?" said Clare. "But I thought there were two sets? I thought the sizes were incompatible?"

"Work it out, darling. Two long arms, two short legs, one small skull, one large jawbone—"

"Oh!" cried Clare. "Of course! The baby orangutan! Like it said in Field's diary."

"Yes, and like it said in Professor Tarns' letter to me, which they sent up this morning. He was quite positive, which so great a man hardly ever is."

"Then when did you see the whole thing? When did you solve it completely?"

"Well, at lunchtime yesterday I had that sort of odd uncomfortable feeling one gets sometimes—you know what I mean?—that all the pieces were there if I could only fit them together. But they didn't really come together till I'd stopped worrying about them and began worrying about the tragedy in the first act of the play. The moment I'd begun to feel that nothing mattered except saving Hermione. Bang! They jumped together by themselves. Mental clearness produced by dramatic catharsis, in fact. A valuable treatment for detectives. And Clare as usual spoke the operative word."

"What was that?" asked Andrew with interest.

"Chimpanzees"

"How did you get to that from Shakespeare?"

"By way of Perdita—*Perdita*, you see! Wasn't that fantastic? 'Bears and wolves have done / Like offices of pity.' Well, perhaps it was partly Clare and partly Shakespeare. The one couldn't, in any case, effectively exist without the other."

"Don't talk like a Charles Williams character," said Clare crisply. "Show some literary tact! Is this a time for metaphysics?"

"Judging from the noises off, it's time for me to talk to the local bobbies. They were coming up for an explanation about now—and surely no other feet could sound so like hydraulic hammers? Come back when they're gone, won't you?"

But they were so deep in conversation in the garden that Richard had to come to his window and shout before they realized that he was alone again. Clare exclaimed and rushed into the house. Andrew followed at a calmer pace.

"Richard! Get back into bed at once! How dare you get up?" she cried. "Andrew's been telling me all about your past."

"I bet he hasn't told you anything about himself, what's been happening to him all this time. Oh, well, we shall get it out of him in a month or so, I expect. Here he is. Well, you'll be pleased to hear that the locals don't think one of their own men could have done better. Aren't I proud and happy!"

"Was it the fat pink man again? Did he have any news? Has Field confessed?"

"No, nor likely to," he replied gravely. "He's dying, the doctors say, though, as usual, they're moving heaven and earth to keep him alive. It seems he got concussed twice on the same spot. He was in a pretty poor state of health already, and he's not all that young. Still, we've got all the confession we need in the diary."

"I suppose he was mad, not bad, wasn't he?" asked Clare.

"Difficult to say. He got like that as a result of the way people treated him. A society gets the criminals it deserves."

This gnomic remark brought the conversation to a standstill. Then Richard continued:

"Well, anyhow, Scotland Yard won't have to decide whether to buy Syd's evidence by dropping the charges. By the way, the Mysterious Foreign Intruder has shown up. He's a pathetic, innocent little refugee, and frightened out of his wits. He was looking for somebody who had digs in Merton Street. And he noticed Syd hiding behind a buttress. Described him quite accurately. I suppose Syd was watching the house to make quite sure Gladys didn't go home too early. Anyway, he must have seen Field take the baby. That's how he could write the letter. But of course he didn't know where Field had taken her to."

"Oh!" said Clare indignantly. "How dishonest of him!" She could not understand why Richard and Andrew both roared with laughter. So loud was their mirth, and so deep her bewilderment, that no one heard the tap on the door. Sergeant Plummer seemed to be in their midst by magic, beaming all over his large face.

"Well, sir," he said shyly. "You do look better, and no mistake. I hope it's all right me coming in?"

"No one I wanted to see more," said Richard, "though I doubt if you ought to be walking about yet. Sit down. How are you?"

"Oo, I'm all right!" said Plummer, easing himself into a small fireside chair. "It was nothing, reely. It's scabbing over a treat, and there's no matter to speak of, only round the edges. It just shows, don't it? People always say monkey bites are poisonous, but don't you believe it. It just depends how they're kept. It's their teeth, see. And how are you, sir?"

"I'm fine," said Richard. "In fact, I'm going to get up in a minute. Have you heard the news?"

"Yes, I have, sir. I met them on my way and they stopped the car and told me and then gave me a lift up. And *she's* all right, sir. I went to inquire. I knew you'd want to know." He looked up for a pat on the head. "She's a bit mopy, off her food. But they think they'll pull her round."

"But they said she was all right yesterday," said Clare. "At least Mrs. Luke did, and I'm sure she ought to know. She's a trained nurse."

"Not about monks, she don't," said Plummer stolidly. "Why, she didn't get a look at her."

Clare was all at sea, and looked at Richard for enlightenment,

"Darling, it isn't the baby he's talking about! It's Emmeline! You know, Pong. Pyg. Female."

"That's right, miss," said Plummer encouragingly. "She's doing fine. The keeper was up all night with her, and I saw him this morning. He's ever such a nice chap. He's going to let me into the cage with him later on, to make it up, like."

They gazed at him in stupefied incredulity. But he continued without self-consciousness:

"Oo, and I'll tell you another thing, sir. I met That Gladys. And she says Mrs. Luke's going to keep That Edna on to work for her."

"Oh, good!" said Richard delightedly. "Now that really is something positive. I'm frightfully glad."

There was another knock at the door.

"Come in!" said Richard.

The door was opened cautiously and the leonine and hoary head of Costard appeared, followed—an anticlimax—by the rest of him. He bore a dusty bottle and moved with extreme care, like a father with a newborn child.

"Good morning, my dear fellow! I am sorry to hear of your accident. I hope," he added to the company at large, without embarrassment, "I hope I don't intrude?" He looked round genially for a chair. There were only three in the room, and all were thrust towards him instantly.

"Mr. Costard," said Richard delighted. "How extremely kind of you to come! May I introduce Miss Clare Liddicote, my future wife, Mr. Andrew Thorne, Sergeant Plummer."

"Won't you sit down, sir?" said Andrew, with cheerful deference. "I've got to go and get myself somewhere to sleep tonight, if Dicky's getting up. I've been using his room at the Mitre."

"Thank you," said Costard, subsiding massively. "It would indeed be a relief. My legs are not what they were. I have ventured to bring you some port," he continued, addressing Richard, "and I did not like to risk the vibration of mechanical transport."

"My dear sir!" exclaimed Richard, touched to the heart. "You haven't walked with it all the way here?"

"This vintage," said Costard, with a twinkle, "*quorum sacra fero ingenti percussus amore*, will tolerate some variation of temperature, but, like its devotees, it does not take kindly to the Machine Age. It should be drinkable by this evening, dear man."

Clare smiled at Costard bewitchingly.

"Now he'll have to stay in bed," she said. "Richard, you can't leave this place till tomorrow with such a reason to stay. I'm sure it won't stand another move. We're all very grateful, Mr. Costard. He's such a naughty invalid."

Costard, who was not impervious to female charm despite his bachelor habits, treated her to one of his famous smiles.

"Delightful to find one of the sterner sex putting first things first!"

"But I don't really know anything about wine."

"That is immaterial. You have learned, dear lady, to be happy in your own way. You have also learned to let others be happy in theirs. No wise man can learn more; my late colleague Field had learned neither."

THE END

If you enjoyed *The Missing Link* ask your bookseller for the second Inspector Ringwood mystery, *The Cretan Counterfeit* (0-915230-73-9, $14.95) to be published by The Rue Morgue Press in November 2004.

The Rue Morgue Press specializes in reprinting traditional mysteries from the 1930s and 1940s. To receive our catalogs or to suggest titles telephone toll free 800-699-6214 or go to our webpage: www.ruemorguepress.com. As of October 2004, The Rue Morgue Press has more than 50 books in print.

Some of our Anglo-Irish titles include:

Joanna Cannan. This English writer's books are among our most popular titles. Modern reviewers have compared them favorably with the best books of the Golden Age of detective fiction. "Worthy of being discussed in the same breath with an Agatha Christie or a Josephine Tey."—Sally Fellows, *Mystery News.* Set in the late 1930s in a village that was a fictionalized version of Oxfordshire, both titles feature young Scotland Yard inspector Guy Northeast. *They Rang Up the Police* (0-915230-27-5, $14.00) and *Death at The Dog* (0-915230-23-2, $14.00).

Glyn Carr. The 15 books featuring Shakespearean actor Abercrombie "Filthy" Lewker are set on peaks scattered around the globe, although the author returned again and again to his favorite climbs in Wales, where his first mystery, published in 1951, *Death on Milestone Buttress* (0-915230-29-1, $14.00), is set.

Joan Coggin. Meet Lady Lupin Lorrimer Hastings, the young, lovely, scatterbrained and kindhearted daughter of an earl, now the newlywed wife of the vicar of St. Marks Parish in Glanville, Sussex. You might not understand her logic but she always gets her man. *Who Killed the Curate?* (0-915230-44-5, $14.00), *The Mystery at Orchard House* (0-915230-54-2, $14.95), *Penelope Passes or Why Did She Die?* (0-915230-61-5, $14.95), and *Dancing with Death* (0-915230-62-3, $14.95).

Sheila Pim. *Ellery Queen's Mystery Magazine* said of these wonderful Irish village mysteries that Pim "depicts with style and humor everyday life." *Booklist* said they were in "the best tradition of Agatha Christie." Beekeeper Edward Gildea uses his knowledge of bees and plants to good use in *A Hive of Suspects* (0-915230-38-0, $14.00). *Creeping Venom* (0-915230-42-9, $14.00) blends politics, gardening and religion into a deadly mixture. *A Brush with Death* (0-915230-49-6, $14.00) grafts a clever art scam onto the stem of a gardening mystery.

Sarsfield, Maureen. These two mysteries featuring Inspector Lane Parry of Scotland Yard are among our most popular books. Both are set in Sussex. *Murder at Shots Hall* (0-915230-55-8, $14.95) features Flikka Ashley, a thirtyish sculptor with a past she would prefer remain hidden. It was originally published as *Green December Fills the Graveyard* in 1945. Parry is back in Sussex, trapped by a blizzard at a country hotel where a war hero has been pushed out of a window to his death, in *Murder at Beechlands* (0-915230-56-9, $14.95). First published in 1948.

Some of our other recent titles include:

Stuart Palmer. *The Puzzle of the Blue Banderilla* (0-915230-70-4, $14.95). Schoolteacher Hildegarde Withers (Anthony Boucher's favorite female sleuth of the Golden Age) heads down to Mexico City when Inspector Oscar Piper finds himself in over his head. First published in 1937. Picked in *The Reader's Guide to the American Novel of Detection* (1993) as one of the 100 best American detective novels of all time.

Lucy Cores. Her books both feature one of the more independent female sleuths of the 1940s. Toni Ney is the exercise director at a very posh Manhattan beauty spa when the "French Lana Turner" is murdered in *Painted for the Kill* (0-915230-66-6, $14.95) "Miles better than most of today's product."—Jon L. Breen, *The Weekly Standard*. She's a newly minted ballet reviewer when murder cuts short the return of a Russian dancer to the stage in *Corpse de Ballet* (0-915230-67-4, $14.95). "This brilliant novel…presents a vivid portrait of the backstage workings of a dance company…eye-catching cover illustration…must read mystery."—*I Love a Mystery*.

John Mersereau. *Murder Loves Company* (0-915239-69-0, $14.95. Young Berkeley professor James Yeats Biddle finds love and murder while looking into a murder at the 1939 San Francisco World's Fair. First published in 1940. "A classic of its genre…characters are well-rounded and alive…Some of us were lucky to have lived in those times. Those who were born too late can relive some of that happiness as they read this light-hearted adventure tale."—*Nob Hill Gazette*. "The cover is stunning, and this book is highly recommended."—*Deadly Pleasures*.

Frances Crane. *The Turquoise Shop* (0-915230-71-2, $14.95). Mona Brandon's artist husband disappeared several months ago. Had he just grown tired of his domineering, artsy wife or was it his body lying out there in the desert, rendered unrecognizable by turkey vultures? And was it just a coincidence that a handsome private detective from San Francisco just happened to pick that time to show up in Santa Maria to pursue an art career? Young Jean Holly, owner of The Turquoise Shop, hasn't much use for Mona, who uses her wealth to dominate this small New Mexico community. Mona isn't very popular with much of the local Mexican population, especially after she sent one of their own—a beautiful teenager—to prison. When murder strikes a second time, this time at Mona's enormous adobe mansion at the edge of town, suspicion falls not only on her but on several of the artists and writers she had encouraged to move to Santa Maria. Mona is loosely based on Mabel Dodge Luhan, a wealthy Easterner who came to Taos in 1918 and turned the town into a mecca for the arts, luring D.H. Lawrence, Georgia O'Keeffe, Robinson Jeffers, Ansel Adams, and many others there.